The Black Feather

A Novel

by

Olivia Claire High

Fireside Publications
Oxford, Florida 34484
www.firesidepubs.com

Printed in the United States of America

Copyright © 2015 by Olivia Claire High
ISBN: 978-1-935517-34-4

For additional copies of this book, please visit:
www.firesidepubs.com or
www.Amazon.com or
Contact the author at:
Joeclaire2424@comcast.net

Dedication

To my husband, Joe,

With all my love,

Always!

Acknowledgment

Many Thanks to my friend and fellow author,

Sherry Long,

who never lets me give up.

One

Two months is all the time it took for Suzanne Conway's life to unravel. Her fiancé jilted her for her cousin, her mother left for some fancy resort with a guy she met a week ago at a gym, and her father ran off to parts unknown with a great deal of money that didn't belong to him. She felt like the Titanic with all the rats deserting leaving her to sink or swim, which wasn't the most helpful analogy considering she was currently standing on an upper deck of a large cruise ship.

A tropical breeze, scented with the sea blew softly against her bare arms making her shiver despite its warmth. The coldness came from within. She hadn't felt warm for weeks. She wanted to shake off the chill, embrace the future, but she didn't know how. Not when the past continued to plague her like an aching tooth.

Early morning light highlighted her delicate features, emphasizing her paleness. Her hands gripped the wooden railing while she stared at the indigo ocean below. She watched as the ship's hull sliced through the waves splitting the water into a wide vee, edged with bubbling white foam.

How would it feel to descend into the cobalt depths sinking down until darkness blocked out everything else? Probably like a deep sleep on an endless winter night until the cold and the pressure crushed the life out of you. The depressing thought made her shiver again.

"I wouldn't if I were you. It's a long way down."

Suzanne spun around, startled by the deep masculine voice and almost bumped into a tall powerfully built man. Her short stature made her lean her head back to see his face.

"What did you say?"

"I said it's a long way down. In case you're thinking of jumping, that is."

"Whatever gave you the idea I'd do something so drastic?"

"You look kind of sad." He shrugged wide shoulders, straining the material of his sweat dampened tee shirt stretched across an impressively broad chest. "I'm a good listener if you need to talk."

"I appreciate your concern, but I'm fine."

"I hope so. This is the second day of a week-long cruise. It'd be a shame to waste it worrying about something." He held out his hand. "My name's Thad Novak if you change your mind about that talk."

Long fingers engulfed her much smaller hand. Suzanne felt a pleasant jolt reminding her of the nice little buzz she usually got after a couple glasses of wine.

"I'm Suzanne Conway. I thought I'd be the only one up here this early."

"I like to run at a pretty fast clip. Early is better when I don't have people getting in my way."

"I bet," she said, thinking he looked like a guy who needed a lot of room. "Well, I'd better get back to my cabin before my roommate wakes up, sees that I'm gone, and calls out the Coast Guard."

"Surely he'd come looking for you first."

"He is a she, and she's the type to panic first and ask questions later."

"Then you mustn't let me keep you. Remember what I said about enjoying yourself."

"I'll keep that in mind. Thanks for the advice."

He nodded.

"My pleasure."

Suzanne leaned back in a lounger trying to read the book in her hand without much success. The noisy distraction from swimmers in the nearby pool coupled with various conversations going on around her made it difficult to concentrate. Her friend and roommate, Heather Martin shifted restlessly on her own lounger and slid her sunglasses down her nose.

"Oh wow. Major hot man alert at 3:00 climbing out of the pool. Check him out, Suzie."

Suzanne peeked over the rim of her book and felt her heart do a little jump at the sight of Thad in his black swim trunks. Hot man, indeed!

"I already have. His name is Thad Novak. We met this morning up on deck."

Heather's head jerked toward her.

"And you didn't tell me? What kind of a friend are you?"

"One who's reminding you that you're a married woman."

"Hey, I promised not to touch when I took my wedding vows, but there wasn't anything about not looking. I'm not the only one ogling him in case you haven't noticed. It appears every female between eight and eighty are getting an eyeful. Who can blame them? Just look at those linebacker shoulders and six pack abs. The guy's one big mass of lean man flesh. I sure wouldn't mind smearing sunscreen over those hard rippling muscles or running my fingers through all that gorgeous chestnut hair. "

"Did anyone ever tell you that drooling is a very unattractive sight in an adult?"

"Are you going to lie there and tell me you didn't salivate when you first saw him?"

"I had other things on my mind at the time."

"Oh, I'm sorry, Suzie." She squeezed her arm. "I didn't mean to sound so insensitive."

"I know." A long, frustrated sigh escaped her. "I need to work on crawling out of my pity pit. Thad advised me to try and forget about my troubles and enjoy the cruise. I've decided he's right."

"He said that? And you're on first name basis? Just how long did you two talk to each other?"

"Not long. I guess he saw that I was looking kind of down and offered to let me vent."

"Ya' gotta give the guy points for a unique pickup approach line."

3

"He wasn't trying to pick up on me, Heather. He was just trying to be nice."

"I like my version better. Oh. Oh!" She squeezed Susanne's arm again. "It looks like he's coming over here. Please nudge me if my slobbering becomes too noticeable."

Thad stopped in front of them and smiled.

"Hello, again, Suzanne. I thought that was you."

Suzanne nodded.

"Hi. Thad Novak, meet Heather Martin."

"The roommate, I assume. It's nice to meet you."

"That would be me; nice to meet you, too."

He turned back to Suzanne. "I'm glad you decided to come out and enjoy the sunshine."

"Well, like you said, it'd be a shame to waste the rest of the cruise being in a blue funk. I'd ask you to join us, but as you can see there aren't any empty loungers nearby."

"That's okay. I prefer spending time in the pool." He looked at Heather. "Take care of your friend."

"That's the plan."

He started to walk away and stopped.

"I don't want to intrude," he said, "but would you ladies like to join me for lunch? I'm on my own. I'd enjoy the company."

"We'd love to," Heather rushed to answer before Suzanne could say anything.

"Great. Which do you prefer, hamburgers on deck, the buffet, or the dining room?"

"Oh, I think the dining room sounds nice, don't you, Suzie?"

Suzanne shrugged.

"Food is food. Whatever you choose is okay with me."

"The dining room it is, then. I'll meet you at the entrance, say, 12:30."

"Perfect,"

Heather flashed him another big smile.

"Thanks for the invite."

He grinned in return, gave a two finger wave, and ambled back toward the pool.

"Jeez, Suzie. You might have tried to sound a little more enthusiastic."

"I think you took care of that for both of us."

"Well, why not. He sure is yummy looking. I wouldn't mind having him for dessert."

Suzanne snorted out a laugh.

"You're incorrigible. Are you going to embarrass me by flirting?"

"Nope. Waste of time. I could see you're the one he was interested in."

"Stop trying to read something into his invitation. He's probably just lonely."

"I disagree. You don't see it because your radar is off. There's definitely a spark there."

"Well please don't go trying to fan it on my account because I've sworn off men."

Suzanne may have sworn off men, but she wasn't dead. She had to admit Thad looked way too handsome dressed in a pair of expertly tailored tan slacks and a long sleeved white collarless shirt, as he stood outside the dining room. He could easily make any woman's blood pressure shoot off the charts, including hers if her racing pulse was any indication.

"Where's your friend?" he smiled, glancing over her shoulder.

"She claims she has a stomachache. But I think it's her not so subtle way of trying to see that we lunch alone, which is silly when we'll probably be seated at a table with half a dozen other people."

Thad took her by the elbow and led her into the large dining room.

"Then we mustn't disappoint her," he said and promptly told the maître d' they preferred a table for two.

"You didn't have to do this," Suzanne said once they were settled with menus in their hands.

"Would you be more comfortable sitting with other people?"

5

"Not necessarily, but you may be. I haven't been my usual chatty self lately."

"My offer to listen still stands if you've changed your mind about sharing."

Suzanne set her menu aside.

"Let's just get it out of the way, then. My fiancé left me for my cousin, and my divorced parents each took off with people young enough to be their kids. End of tale."

He winced.

"Ouch! For what it's worth, I think your fiancé is a fool."

"Ex," she reminded him. "For all you know he may not be. You don't know me all that well."

"True, but I'm hoping you'll let me change that. Were you surprised by your parents?"

"Not really. But the fact that my dad left with a lot of money that didn't belong to him came as a real shocker." She wrinkled her nose. "I can't believe I told you that. Talk about airing my family's dirty laundry. Sorry."

His dark eyes, with the ridiculously long lashes that Suzanne thought no male had a right to, opened very wide.

"Your father stole money?"

"That's what the police said when they contacted me to see if I knew where he'd gone. He's had his hand in the cookie jar at his job for quite a long time according to their investigation."

"And here I am telling you to forget about your problems. Forgive me."

"No need to apologize. I'm not responsible for what my parents do. Heaven knows they've pulled some really embarrassing dillies over the years. But this is the first time one of them has gotten mixed up in something so serious. It's not like my dad. I suspect his latest paramour helped convince him to forget caution and go for the big E, as in embezzlement."

Thad's brows lifted.

"She must be quite a woman."

"I wouldn't know. I've never met her."

"Do you have any idea where he might be?"

6

"Not a clue; and neither does my mother. But I wouldn't expect her to since she's in La La Land most of the time, and especially right now with her latest conquest."

"You must have had an interesting childhood."

"That's a nice way to put it."

A bittersweet laugh escaped her.

"But even the circus gets to be too much after a while."

"Do you have other family besides your man-stealing cousin? Siblings? Grandparents?"

"She's not really my cousin. Her mother lived with my dad during one of his longer relationships. We thought it'd be fun to say we were related. I'm an only child. I never knew either set of grandparents. They cut ties with my parents long before I came along and their snub ended up extending to me."

"Too bad they included you in their ban. That rejection must have been rough on you growing up."

"They didn't want me, so why should I want them? Besides, I've always had my Nanadoo."

Thad frowned.

"What's a Nanadoo?"

She smiled.

"She's a *who*, not a *what*. Nanadoo is my childhood name for my godmother. She's a wild, eccentric old lady. She's been married more times than anyone can keep track of and done more things than any ten people. But I love her to bits, and I've never been in doubt of her love for me."

"She sounds wonderful. I'm glad you have her."

"So am I. Now I think it's time we change the subject. I've gone on about my family long enough, and believe me, they are not my favorite subject at the moment."

"Then we won't talk about them. Why don't we spend the rest of the cruise getting to know each other better and exploring the ports together?"

"What about Heather? I wouldn't feel right deserting her."

"No desertion necessary. She can join us. What do you say?"

"I'll think about it."

7

She picked up her menu again.

"What looks good?"

"You do," he said making the menu tremble ever so slightly in Suzanne's hands.

Heather pumped her fist in the air when Suzanne told her about Thad's suggestion.

"Yes! See, I told you he was angling to get closer."

"He probably feels sorry for me. I told him about James and my parents. Oh, he invited you, too."

"Well that's not happening. There's no way I'm going to be a third wheel. This is exactly what I hoped would happen to you when I suggested the cruise. You may never get another chance to enjoy the company of such a hunk like Thad. Go. Have fun. Goodness knows you deserve it."

"I don't want to leave you on your own. What would Aaron say?"

"My husband would agree. He told me he hoped this trip would help you find your smile again."

"Did he? That's very sweet of him, but I'm still not going to abandon you, Heather."

"You're not abandoning me. I want you to go."

Suzanne shook her head making Heather sigh.

"I forget how stubborn you can be sometimes. Okay, how about a compromise? I'll do a few things with you if you promise to spend some time doing stuff with Thad."

"What kind of stuff did you have in mind?" Suzanne asked suspiciously.

"I'll leave that up to him."

"When I said I would try to enjoy myself, I didn't mean with a man I've just met."

"You said yourself you wanted to crawl out of your pity pit. Why not take the hand he's offering? You could do worse. Give him a chance, Suzie. You have to get over James sometime."

Lying in bed that night, Suzanne admitted being around Thad wasn't exactly a hardship. She discovered behind his handsome face and mouthwatering body, he was also an intelligent and a genuinely nice man. She found him even more interesting when he told her he taught architecture in a small community college, since she was a teacher herself.

She thought his childhood sounded wonderful as he explained how he grew up on a small farm with three younger siblings. When he told her his parents just celebrated their thirty-fifth wedding anniversary, Suzanne couldn't help envying the fact that he came from such a stable family.

They spent the day together at the first port, Roatan; the largest of Honduras' Bay Islands. Heather tagged along, but found plenty of excuses to leave Suzanne and Thad alone. The ship was scheduled to be in Belize City, Belize all day tomorrow. Thad invited them to meet some friends who lived there.

Suzanne was having a much better time than she expected, thanks to Thad and Heather. When thoughts of her parents popped inside her head she forced them away. She did the same thing with unwanted images of her ex-fiancé and her so-called cousin.

She wondered if Thad might be the guy who could help her get over feeling depressed. Suzanne felt tempted to give him the opportunity to help her become interested again, despite what she'd told Heather about swearing off men. She needed to do something to boost her self-esteem. Lots of people had shipboard romances. It would only be for a few days. Then he'd go his way and she would go hers.

How could anything possibly go wrong by having an affair with a guy as nice as Thad Novak? She lay there mulling over the idea until her restlessness made it impossible to sleep. She heard Heather's soft snoring and decided a few turns around the deck might make her sleepy. She slipped into her sweats and sneakers before letting herself out of the cabin.

Suzanne had just completed a couple of laps when a dark figure dressed all in black complete with a hooded sweatshirt hiding his face sprang from the shadows and grabbed her by the arm.

She gasped, and tried to pull away.

He thrust something into her hand before relaxing his grip.

"You've been warned," a heavily accented male voice whispered harshly; then he released her, and was gone.

Suzanne ran to the nearest door, jerked it open, and rushed inside, breathing a sigh of relief when he didn't follow. Her heart was pounding so hard it took her a moment to realize something tickled the palm of her hand. She looked and saw she was clutching a black feather. She shivered and dropped it, watching as it drifted to the carpeted floor while she wiped her hand down the side of her pants.

Warned about what? Had she imagined the cryptic message? What was with the feather? If this was part of the ship's entertainment, she wasn't amused.

Two

Suzanne climbed into her bed thankful that Heather didn't stir. She wasn't in the mood for a lecture on how dangerous it was to go out walking the deck alone at night. She'd rather concentrate on the day ahead of her instead of some creepy guy passing out bird feathers. Thinking about the strange encounter and spooky message sent icy fingers dancing down her spine making her huddle beneath the blankets.

Suzanne took a last spin in front of the mirror, picked up her purse, and headed out to meet Thad.

"No nanny today?" he asked, as they left the ship.

"She bailed. I know your friends were expecting both of us. I'm sorry."

"No problem." He glanced at her white linen slacks and peach silk blouse with its pattern of lime green leaves. "You look nice. That color looks good with your red hair."

"Thank you." She eyed his navy shorts and pale blue polo shirt. "You look nice, too. You didn't say if you were going to get a cab or rent a car, but either way I want to pay my share."

"Actually, my friends are going to pick us up. I told them we'd meet them across the street." He took hold of her hand and laced their fingers together.

"Ready?"

His touch made her skin tingle with a pleasant warmth. She'd been doing her best to act composed around him. But in reality he only had to smile and her blood flared up. Her fiancé's rejection had doused those flames, but being around Thad was rekindling the fire. Apparently her body was letting

11

her know that she was ready for some sizzling sex with this hot man. The thought of that made her blush.

"Um, I think so."

"Don't look so worried. You'll like my friends. I know they're going to like you."

"How can you be so sure?"

"They trust my judgment. So should you," he added after a brief hesitation.

Suzanne wondered for a moment if she heard a hidden meaning behind his words, only to have it vanish when he squeezed her hand and smiled. She intended to give him more than trust if things continued on the way they were going. The thought of that sent a little thrill zinging through her body.

"Okay, I'm all yours."

"Not yet, but one can always hope."

She felt her heart skip a beat and quickly changed the subject.

"What kind of car do they drive?"

"They have two vehicles. They'll be in a white Mercedes. The other one is a Jeep they use for off road excursions. Ah, here they come," Thad said pointing, as the luxury car slid to a stop at the curb.

They climbed in, and he introduced Suzanne to a thin dark haired woman.

"Maya Lincoln, meet fellow shipmate, Suzanne Conway."

"It's nice to meet you, Suzanne. Welcome to Belize."

"Thank you. I appreciate you inviting me to your home."

"My husband and I are looking forward to having you."

"Where's Linc?" Thad asked, as Maya eased back into the flow of traffic.

"Something's come up with the job. He'll fill you in when we get to the house."

Suzanne thought the woman's voice sounded strained, but she couldn't be sure because they'd just met. She also had the distinct impression of some kind of undercurrent going on between Maya and Thad. First her feeling that he was hiding something from her, and now this. Suzanne pressed her lips together, annoyed that her brain was making her behave like some third rate seer.

"Maya's husband is a freelance photographer. He's been asked to design several brochures for the tourist board here. He runs into snags sometimes."

Suzanne realized she hadn't imagined Maya's anxiety. At least Thad's explanation provided a plausible reason for the woman's tension. It didn't take a psychic to know the last thing Maya needed right now was having to entertain a stranger.

"It sounds like company will only complicate things. I don't want to impose. Please just drop me off in town. I can do some shopping and get a cab back to the ship."

"Oh I wouldn't think of it. I didn't mean to put you off. We love having visitors, really."

Thad kept the conversation going while Maya drove. They arrived in a neighborhood filled with beautiful beach houses. She pulled into a driveway and barely shut off the engine when a man came out to meet them. Tall and rangy, he offered his hand along with a warm smile.

"I'm Jacob Lincoln, Linc to everyone," he greeted Suzanne shaking her hand before grabbing Thad in a bear hug. "I'm happy to meet you, though I wonder why you'd want to hang out with this big oaf."

Suzanne's body relaxed, as she returned his smile.

"I guess it must be his gentlemanly manners."

"Thad, a gentlemen? Are we talking about the same guy?" he said, as they entered the house.

"Tell your husband to stop trying to sabotage the image I have going," Thad retaliated, while giving Maya a belated hug.

Suzanne laughed at their good humored teasing. Maya excused herself, but returned minutes later carrying a tray with four glasses of mineral water. Linc offered one to Suzanne before handing another to Thad. He took a glass for himself and smiled at Suzanne.

"Mind if I steal Thad for a minute? I'd like to show him something I'm working on in my office."

"Oh, I think I can live without him for that long."

13

Thad clutched his chest in mock pain causing the others to laugh before the men entered a room just off the living room. Suzanne asked Maya if they could go outside when she caught a glimpse of the view through the sliding glass door.

"Your skin's so fair. Don't you mind the sun?"

"I'm okay as long as I take it in small doses. I can actually get a tan if I'm careful."

They stepped outside. The sun sent bright amber rays flickering over the surface of the water in splashes of molten gold. Suzanne watched the surf nudging its way lazily back and forth against the shore while Maya fixed her eyes on the water further out where a large yacht sailed into sight.

"This is a wonderful setting and your home is lovely."

"We're just renting. Linc's work keeps us on the go too much to buy a place of our own."

"I bet you've seen some pretty fantastic sights in your travels. How long have you lived here?"

"Just a few weeks."

She tore her eyes away from the yacht and looked at Suzanne. "How are you enjoying the cruise?"

"Very much. Have you ever taken one?"

"Only on private yachts."

"Speaking of yachts, do you know the people on the one out there now?"

"Can't say that I do. What do you think of Thad?"

Suzanne smiled.

"He's an easy man to like."

"Easy on the eyes, too."

"You won't get an argument from me there. Have you known him long?"

"Linc and I met him in college. We try to get together whenever we can, but it's difficult because we move around so much."

"I thought you seemed very close."

"I'd trust him with my life."

Maya's eyes darted to the boat and back to Suzanne.

"So can you."

14

"I live a pretty dull life, so I doubt if I'd ever have to. But I'll keep that in mind in case I ever have anyone chasing me with a chainsaw," she joked, but Maya didn't return her smile.

"Just remember what I said."

"Do you sunbathe out here?" Suzanne asked, wanting to change the direction of their conversation.

"No, why?"

Suzanne pointed to the water.

"I thought that might be why that man on the yacht has a pair of binoculars aimed our way. That's what I'd call being a peeping Tom in the extreme."

Maya's eyes narrowed at the boat.

"I hate having people staring – makes me feel like I'm on display. Let's go inside, shall we?"

She slid open the door before Suzanne could answer.

"Why do you think they would be watching you?"

"The house is for sale. Maybe they're interested in buying it," Maya said maneuvering them into the living room where she knocked on the door to Linc's office.

He opened it immediately.

"Everything okay?"

She shook her head and pointed over her shoulder. "We've got company."

Linc hurried across the room, followed closely by Thad. They grabbed binoculars and looked toward the water. Thad set his binoculars aside after a few seconds and gave Linc a barely perceptible nod.

"Why don't you and Suzanne go for a spin, Thad? Take the Jeep in case you run across a jungle trail you can't resist."

"Sounds like a good idea."

Linc tossed him a set of keys while Maya handed Suzanne a scarf. "You'll need this. The Jeep's open, and the wind will tie your hair in knots."

"But we just got here."

Suzanne frowned at Thad. "I thought you wanted to visit."

"I do, but Linc just received an unexpected phone call. He and Maya have to meet a man in town."

Linc nodded.

"I apologize for this, Suzanne, but I've been trying to meet with this guy for days."

Thad hustled her through a door that opened into the garage where the Jeep stood waiting. He lifted her into the passenger seat.

"Tie that scarf on real tight. We don't want it to blow off."

"How fast are you planning on driving?" she asked, donning the scarf and knotting it under her chin.

"Depends on the road. Did you bring your dark glasses?"

"Yes."

"Better put those on as well."

She rummaged in her purse.

"I feel like I'm putting on a disguise, so I can travel incognito." Suzanne chuckled at her little joke, but no one laughed in return.

Thad clicked both their seatbelts in place, turned the ignition key, and let the engine roar to life.

"I'll be in touch," he yelled to Linc and Maya seconds before the Jeep sped out of the garage.

Suzanne gripped the edge of the seat.

"Where's the fire?"

"Are you afraid of a little speed?"

"No, but I do get nervous when the vehicle I'm in feels like it's about to break the sound barrier," she gasped, as the tires squealed around a corner.

"All part of the fun."

"What did you mean about being in touch? Aren't we going back to their house?"

"Depends on how much sightseeing we do. I may have to leave the Jeep at the dock."

She watched as he glanced in the rearview mirror.

"Why are you driving like a maniac? Oh God, watch out for that dog!" she yelled, pointing at the road in front of them.

"I see it."

"Slow down, can't you? I feel like I've been scooped up into the middle of a tornado."

"I'll slow down once we get to where we're going."

"Where is that?"

"I'll let you know when we get there."

Thad drove completely focused with every muscle on the alert. He whipped onto a side road causing several chickens to scatter out of the way. The birds reminded Suzanne of the feather from the ship and the man's warning. Could this be what he'd meant? She fought to keep her voice calm.

"I'd like to go back to the ship now if you don't mind."

"What, and miss your private tour of the island? Where's your sense of adventure?"

"I lost it a few miles back at that last pothole. You're lucky that's all I lost. My breakfast has already bounced up into my throat. If you want to go tearing around like some teenager, that's your business. But I don't want any part of it. Turn this vehicle around and take me back to the ship right now."

"I wonder if you realize how sexy you sound with that demanding attitude."

"I should warn you that this is definitely not a time where flattery is going to make me change my mind. You'll have to continue this craziness on your own. I want to go back. I mean it, Thad."

His fingers flexed on the wheel, and he shook his head.

"I'm afraid I can't do that," he said.

"Can't or won't?"

"What difference does it make? Either way, I won't be taking you back."

Her fingers gripped the edge of the seat as a disturbing thought filled her head with painful clarity.

"Wait a minute. Are you saying we're not going back to the ship? Ever?"

He gave her a quick, pitying look.

"I'm sorry, Suzanne," he said, his voice sounding truly apologetic. "I had hoped it wouldn't come to this."

"You hoped what wouldn't come to this? What's going on, Thad?"

The panic forming in her belly swiftly began to rise to her throat.

"What's wrong?"

"I know you're frightened. I promise I'm not going to hurt you, Suzanne."

"If you really mean that, you'll let me go to the ship, or let me out and I'll find my own way back." She grabbed for the tie on her scarf as a tuft of wind threatened to blow it away.

"Please, Thad," she pleaded when he didn't answer. "You really are scaring me now."

"I know; and I am sorry. Remember when I said you should trust my judgment?"

"Ye . . . yes," she stuttered in a shaky whisper while her fingers dug deeper into the seat.

"Well, now would be a good time to start."

Maya's words popped inside her head. Had she suspected something like this was going to happen?

"I don't understand why you're doing this. Please just tell..." She stopped, thinking of a way she might get Thad to turn back. "I have to call Heather. She's going to be frantic when I don't return."

She fumbled in her purse and dug out her cell phone.

Thad surprised her by reaching over and snatching it out of her hand. The Jeep jerked sideways while he jammed the phone into his shirt pocket.

"I'd rather you didn't make any calls right now. Linc and Maya will contact Heather."

"What about my stuff? My clothes? My jewelry?"

"They'll get everything."

"So their meeting in town was just a ruse to get me out of their house. Why?"

"Let's just say it's for your own protection."

Suzanne gritted her teeth.

"Can your friends also get me a refund for the days I'm going to be missing on the cruise? Or is that not part of your crazy scheme?"

"I'll reimburse you myself if that'll make you happy."

"What would really make me happy is to turn the clock back to the day we met, so I could run the other way."

"Aw, now you've hurt my feelings."

18

"What feelings? If you had any you'd turn this vehicle around and get me out of here."

Thad answered her by swerving the Jeep onto a much smaller road that wasn't really a road at all, but more of a muddy trail barely wide enough to accommodate them. They were in deep jungle now with no signs of civilization that Suzanne could see in the increasingly thick foliage.

He'd been forced to slow down and adjust to the terrain, although they were still going much too fast for her comfort. Large plants swept against the vehicle, and an occasional one slapped its way inside causing Suzanne to jerk away. Thad drove over vines crisscrossing their path, crushing the leaves beneath the wheels, while small rocks sprang up making pinging sounds against the underside of the Jeep.

The dense jungle greedily trapped the sun making the air hang heavy and hot around them. Suzanne could feel perspiration popping out on her body creating random splotches over the material of her blouse. Dampness soaked her hair beneath the scarf. She tore the offending strip of silk off of her head and tossed it defiantly to the floor. She glared at Thad ready to argue if he insisted she put it back on, but he merely raised his brows and continued driving.

"I have a feeling you lied about being a teacher, considering what's going on right now. Who are you really and why all this mystery?"

"I didn't lie. I do teach – well, on rare occasions, anyway."

"What's the course description? How to defy the law of gravity and make a Jeep fly? Obviously teaching isn't all you do. Why do I get the feeling you lead some kind of double life?"

"Must be your imagination, but it sounds intriguing."

Suzanne studied his profile. She didn't miss how he looked in the rearview mirror or how his eyes kept careful watch of their surroundings.

"Why do you keep looking around like that?"

"Just taking in the scenery."

"Don't give me that. You're worried we're being followed, aren't you?

"Whatever gave you that idea?"

She glared at him.

"I'm not blind. Does this have anything to do with the guy watching the house from that yacht? I think I have the right to know who we're running from since I'm being abducted."

"Who said anything about abduction?"

"I'm being taken on your version of Mr. Toad's Wild Ride against my will. This obviously isn't a leisurely sightseeing trip. I want to know why you aren't giving me straight answers."

"Maybe because you're not asking the questions I want to hear."

"There you go again dodging the issue. Listen up, Thad Novak. I'm hot. I'm thirsty. I'm scared and I've just had my vacation ruined, so you should know I'm in no mood for . . ."

Another Jeep came crashing out of the jungle at that moment causing Suzanne to let out a startled shriek. A small projectile whizzed by her head before it smashed into the windshield poking a neat hole in the glass. Thad ground out a curse and pressed down on the accelerator, as he glanced over his shoulder.

"Undo your seatbelt, and get down on the floor. Now!" he yelled when Suzanne hesitated.

"Please tell me that wasn't what I think it was. It almost gave me a new part in my hair."

"Get down unless you want that new hairdo," Thad growled, as another bullet ricocheted off the rearview mirror followed by a third shot that grazed his upper arm causing him to swerve the Jeep.

Suzanne clawed at her seatbelt while her heart pounded like a jackhammer. She scrambled to the floor a nanosecond before another bullet whistled over her head splintering a small branch. She watched in horror as blood began to seep through Thad's shirt, staining a spot bright red.

"Oh my God, they shot you!"

Thad shook his head.

"Just scraped me."

His expression became a mask of grim determination, as the Jeep careened crazily through the jungle cutting through the thick foliage like a huge machete. Thad crouched low over the steering wheel doing his best to dodge more bullets that continued to fly at them.

"You're bleeding. Let me see if I can use the scarf to try and stop it."

"No. I want you to stay down."

Suzanne fixed her eyes on his wound. She'd never seen anyone who'd been shot. If he continued to bleed would he lose so much blood he'd pass out? The thought of Thad being unconscious leaving her to face their assailants on her own made her shiver despite the warm air.

How much longer could they go on like this with bullets popping around them like firecrackers at a Chinese New Year's celebration? She didn't even want to think about what would happen if one hit the gas tank. Suzanne decided she couldn't stay down cringing like a coward while Thad risked his life, even if she did blame him for getting them into this jam.

She grabbed the scarf, determined to help. She eased herself up onto the seat keeping her body bent low, as she faced Thad. "Please at least let me shove this under your shirt."

"No. We'll be in the clear soon now."

"I'm happy to hear it. But in the meantime I want to try and plug up your leak."

"Forget about that, but you can drive as long as you insist on being up here."

"What!?"

"You heard me. I'm getting tired of being used as target practice. Grab the wheel while I do something about that. Lucky for us they're lousy shots."

Suzanne grappled with the wheel sending the Jeep wobbling over the trail like a malfunctioning pendulum. "Lousy? That's not exactly tomato juice on your shirt."

Her mouth gaped open when Thad reached beneath the driver's seat, pulled out a gun, twisted around, and took aim. The sound of it firing so close to her head made her ears ring.

"One down, one to go," he said with a steely calm Suzanne couldn't help envying.

"I think you just broke my eardrum, and I'm not sure how much longer I can control the Jeep at this speed," she yelled gripping the wheel so hard her knuckles ached.

"You're doing fine," Thad said, as more bullets flew back and forth.

"Great, because I'm . . . ow!" she yelled while struggling to retain control of the wheel.

White-hot pain ripped into her shoulder tearing a jagged line through the thin material of her blouse, burning the smooth flesh beneath. Suzanne stared, while blood crept over peach silk spreading across the fabric in a vivid red pattern.

"Suzanne!" Thad shouted her name. "Oh, Jesus!"

She shifted her eyes from her driving to his startled expression.

"I . . . I think I've been shot."

Shock, fear, and the sight of her own blood made the inside of her head spin with dizziness. She blinked a few times struggling to focus her eyes while dots danced across her vision. Red became a gray mist, Gray began to fade, growing darker, taking with it all the surrounding light.

Suzanne thought she heard Thad calling to her again, but she couldn't be sure. Her body felt heavy and her hands slid away from the steering wheel. She was falling, tumbling helplessly into empty space. The jungle swirled around her and the ground rushed up to meet her seconds before a sudden sharp pain burst inside her head.

Everything turned to black.

Silent and black.

Engulfed by deepening shadows, she closed her eyes and slid into the void.

Her last coherent thought was how the bullet hole and bloodstain had probably ruined her new blouse.

Three

"Come on Suzanne, open those pretty green eyes and let me know you hear me."

A man's voice penetrated her fogged brain. James? No, it sounded too deep to belong to her ex-fiancé. She struggled to answer, but couldn't get the words out. The voice persisted.

"Come on, sweetheart."

She was a child again. She'd fallen off her bike while visiting her father and bruised her shoulder. It hurt so much she couldn't help crying. He'd comforted her. Had she fallen again?

"Daddy?" she muttered.

"No, but I'll be your daddy if you'll open your eyes and talk to me."

It took a lot of effort, but Suzanne finally managed to drag her eyelids open. She groaned when she realized it was Thad leaning over her.

"Ugh, it's you."

"Oh good, you recognize me."

She turned her head, so she wouldn't have to look at him.

"Go away, and let me die in peace."

"You're not dying. How's the shoulder feel?"

"Like a huge gorilla took a bite out of it. He's also pounding on my head."

"I'm pretty sure there aren't any gorillas living around here."

"Oh shut up."

She looked at Thad again and touched her temple.

"I know why my shoulder hurts, but why do I have a bandage on my head?"

"You fell out of the Jeep and hit your head on an exposed tree root before I could grab you."

"Well, that was clumsy of me."

She looked around the room. "Where am I?"

"In a safe place."

"Kind of late for that, isn't it? Does this place have a location?"

"You're still in Belize – but in a different area than I'd originally intended, due to our reception committee."

"Why were those men shooting at us?

Thad pulled a chair over and sat down by the side of her bed. "It's about your father."

"Dad? Oh no. Did someone try to kill us because he stole their money?"

"It's a bit more complicated than that."

"How complicated are we talking here? How about enlightening me?"

"Let me ask you something first. Do you have any idea who your father worked for?"

"No. He never stayed with a job very long. All I know is he was keeping books for some guys."

"That would be the Montane brothers. You were right about him having his hand in the cookie jar. He's been siphoning money off the top for the last several months. He kept the amounts small enough so no one noticed. That all changed a couple of months ago when he took a much larger handful."

Suzanne wrinkled her nose. "No doubt for his latest female conquest."

"Her name is Muriel Montane. Her family's been involved with a myriad of criminal activities for many years. I can only assume your father apparently couldn't resist her feminine charms and decided to do something really big to impress her."

"Dad was working for crooks and fell for a family member? Way to go, Dad," she said with heavy sarcasm.

"He may not have known the full extent of the Montane's illegal operation when they hired him. They have a way of covering things, so they appear to be legitimate businessmen."

"But you think he's aware of it now?"

"Oh yeah."

24

"So what has my dad done besides steal their money and run off with this Muriel?"

"The Montanes have been slipping through the cracks for years because no one has been able to provide enough solid evidence to convict them, until your father came along. He contacted the Feds. He said he'd give them his information in exchange for protection. They agreed. We're not sure why he chose this particular method, but he said he put everything on a couple of phones. His plan was to mail one phone to your mother and one to you."

"Really? Well, I certainly hope you don't think I'm in cahoots with my father because I haven't received anything from him; and as far as I know my mother hasn't, either."

"That's because he hasn't mailed anything yet. It appears Muriel is just as infatuated with your dad as he is with her. Either that or she's using him to help her get away from her family. Her father's been keeping tabs on you and your mother hoping you'll lead him to your dad. That's why the people on that yacht were watching the house and we were chased. Someone was also on the cruise ship keeping an eye on you. They followed us to Linc and Maya's."

"I see. So I take it you were on that cruise to babysit me. Are you a cop or something?"

"Or something."

Suzanne rolled her eyes toward the ceiling.

"You're as secretive as a woman hiding her age."

"Well, I can't have you thinking that. I'm thirty-six."

"It's looks good on you. How is it you know how to handle a gun so well?"

"I was in the military."

"Good thing. Those men would have killed us if it hadn't been for your expertise. I assume it was the Montanes trying to get revenge."

"Revenge is like life's blood to them. They only wanted me dead, so they could kidnap you to lure your father out of hiding. I'm sure you getting shot wasn't part of their plan."

"So you had to kidnap me, to save me from being kidnapped. What a strange irony. I thought things were bad enough being chased. Obviously, I was wrong."

She shook her head, winced in pain, and closed her eyes.

"Do you want another pain pill?"

"What I want is to have my old life back. It wasn't exciting, but at least it didn't involve being shot."

"You'll get your life back. Until then just concentrate on getting well. I'll take care of the rest."

She opened one eye and looked at him.

"Do I have a choice?"

"Not really."

Suzanne felt well enough by the end of the week to go outside. She reclined on a lounger watching Thad as he lifted weights. Either his shoulder wasn't bothering him or he was too macho to admit it. His body gleamed with sweat. She'd kidded Heather about drooling over him, but Suzanne knew she was close to salivating every time his muscles bunched and relaxed between reps. She may be angry with him, but he still presented a treat to the eyes.

She supposed he needed the exercise to burn off some of the excess energy he seemed to have in abundance. He was relegated to lifting weights and running on the treadmill that stood in one corner of the patio, since coming to this isolated spot. The house was on the small side. The floor plan included a kitchen, living room, two bedrooms, and a bathroom all with a minimum of space.

They were sharing it with two burly young men, Louis and Kenny. Kenny turned out to be a pretty fair cook while Louis helped keep the place clean. But Suzanne had a feeling they were here so they could serve as extra bodyguards, and not to take care of domestic chores.

She had one of the bedrooms to herself, while the three men alternately took turns sharing the two single beds in the other bedroom and the couch in the living room. Whoever had stocked the house with food and other creature comforts obviously expected her, as a small cache of feminine toiletries and some clothing suitable to the climate had been left in her room.

Suzanne wondered if Maya had done the honors. Maybe the clothes belonged to her. Had she and Linc suspected Thad would end up bringing her to this house on that crazy Jeep ride, or had Thad contacted them later, as he'd promised?

She discovered only recently that Louis and Kenny were already here when she finally got up the nerve to question them. But that was about all they would say. The more she asked, the more they clammed up.

Thad finished working out and ambled over to the table standing between the two loungers. He poured himself a glass of water and quickly drained it. She watched while he lifted the pitcher and emptied it over his head before grabbing up a towel to wipe his face. Suzanne stared as the water dribbled down over his body in tantalizing streams, pooling in his navel and disappearing beneath the waistband of his dampened swim trunks.

He stretched out on the lounger next to her. Suzanne caught the scent of his sweat and almost moaned out loud when the sunlight played over his long, lean body kissing the smooth muscles with its warm rays. She wouldn't mind doing a little kissing there, too. Talk about driving her hormones crazy. The man should be made to carry a sign warning about the dangers of all that testosterone emanating from him.

Kenny appeared, breaking into her erotic thoughts. He set two plates down on the table.

"Lunch." Kenny was a man of few words.

He went back into the house and returned with a pitcher of iced tea and two glasses. Suzanne eyed the large avocado halves filled with crab salad. Four toast triangles covered in melted cheese lay neatly surrounding the main course. His meals were simple with few ingredients, but tasty.

"It looks delicious as always, Kenny. Thank you. I'm feeling much better now. I want to start helping you with the kitchen chores."

He shrugged his massive shoulders.

"Whatever."

"Thanks, buddy," Thad called, as his friend headed back inside.

Suzanne looked over at Thad. "I hope I didn't hurt his feelings. I wouldn't want him to get the impression I didn't like his cooking."

"Kenny's too easygoing to be offended."

"I bet he's not always so laidback. He and Louis are here to help you watch over me, aren't they? And please don't insult my intelligence by pretending otherwise. I'm not stupid, you know."

"I never said you were."

"Then level with me. Do they do this kind of thing for a living? Are you expecting more people to come and shoot at us?"

"They're on vacation. Now eat your lunch like a good little girl and let me do the worrying."

Her cheeks blushed a furious red.

"Stop treating me like a child. I am not a little girl. I may be short, but I'm a grown woman in case you haven't noticed."

Thad's eyes moved slowly over her soft curves amply exposed by the skimpy blue bikini she wore.

"Believe me, I've noticed."

Suzanne recovered to the point that she began to feel fidgety. How much longer would she be expected to stay cooped up here? Some women might think finding themselves trapped in a tropical setting with a stud like Thad would be akin to being in paradise. The problem was they were not here as lovers, and were both being very careful to give each other a wide berth.

She assumed Thad received updates on their situation from Linc even though he never gave her any information. It infuriated her that he wouldn't tell her anything. She felt like she was in prison, despite the fact that the house didn't have any bars.

Thad continued to evade her questions about how much longer she'd have to stay hidden. Her frustration level reached a peak one evening making her yell at him in the hopes he'd get mad enough to slip and reveal something. He merely arched a brow and told her to go to bed.

She'd stormed off to her room where she paced and plotted ways to punish him for his annoying reticence. Suzanne did realize he was being vigilant about her safety because he or one of the other men continued to check outside the house every night. But that didn't mean she had to like being the focus of their attention.

All the stealth and evasiveness finally frayed her last nerve making her think of ways she could get away. Maybe then she'd be able find some kind of road and hitch a ride back to civilization. But her three bodyguards never let her out of their sight, except when she was in the bathroom. Unfortunately, the window in there was too little even for her small stature to use as a means of escape.

She tried going on a hunger strike. Thad threatened to force feed her after the first day. She faked feeling ill and demanded to be taken to a doctor. He offered to bring one to her instead. It didn't take long to realize appealing to Kenny and Louis turned out to be a waste of time because they were completely loyal to Thad.

Suzanne stood at her bedroom window now, after another round of pleading with Thad. She stared at the night. Moonlight coated the green jungle turning it to silver, while pungent plant life filled the air sending a rich aroma drifting through the screened window. Mysterious sounds of nocturnal animals murmuring their strange chorus flowed through the house.

She went to bed, but ended up kicking off her sheet and getting up after only a few minutes. She slipped on a short robe over her nightshirt and eased her door open before tiptoeing into the living room. Thad instantly rolled to his feet, gun in hand, alert and ready to investigate what had disturbed him.

"What are you doing out of bed?" he demanded, startling her.

Suzanne tried to ignore how tantalizing he looked and how the sight of his bare chest made her pulse race. She was young and healthy and hadn't been with a man in a long time.

But now wasn't the time to be thinking about sex. She nailed him with a hostile glare.

"Relax warden, I'm not armed. I want a drink of water. Don't you ever sleep?"

"I was sleeping. You woke me up," he yawned and set his gun aside.

"I don't see how. I was quiet."

"I have very good hearing."

"So I've noticed. I wouldn't be surprised if you could hear a gnat pass wind."

"Cute. Now tell me why you're really up at this time of night."

"I can't sleep. If it gives you some kind of perverted satisfaction to hear me beg, then I will."

Thad leaned against the back of the sofa and crossed his arms over his chest.

"I do not enjoy hearing you beg, but go ahead, vent if it'll make you feel any better. You're entitled."

"You're darn right I am. I'm being punished for something that isn't my fault. I didn't steal anyone's money, and I didn't run off with a gangster's daughter. But I'm the one being made to pay. I want to go home. You know that. How many times do I have to keep saying it?"

He stood up and eased his arms down to his sides.

"Suzanne, I know how . . ."

"Don't you dare try to pacify me. I'm sick of it. I'm sick of you and I'm sick of this place."

"I was about to say you'll be going home, but if you'd rather not hear it, then I'll shut up."

She grabbed his arm when he started to turn away.

"I'm going home? When? You'd better not be lying, buster."

"I planned to tell you at breakfast. You'll be leaving here tomorrow."

"Finally!" She gripped her hands together and raised them up in a prayerful gesture.

"Thank you, Jesus. What time is our flight? I don't have much here in the way of clothes. Maybe you can let me buy

30

something before we get to the airport. Does my mom know I'm coming home? How about Heather? Did you tell them? I assume you've been in contact."

Thad held his hand up.

"Slow down a bit. Your mother and Heather haven't been informed. It's safer for all of us that way. I can't risk you shopping in public, so forget about that. Find something here to wear. It doesn't matter what you put on because we'll be going via a private jet late at night. But if changing your clothes is so important, you can do it on the plane. Your things from the cruise will be there. Arrangements have been made for us to go through security in a secluded area to minimize the fact that we're leaving."

"I'll get my stuff from the cruise? That's good news." She started to say something else, but stopped.

"Wait a minute. Did I hear you right? Are you going to be on that plane with me?"

"Of course I'm going with you. I thought you understood that."

"Okay, fine. I don't care if you want to continue this bodyguard gig for a few more hours as long as I get to go back to my place. But once I'm home, we end our cozy twosome."

He shook his head. "I'm afraid not."

"What!"

Her mouth gaped open.

"Do not tell me you're going to be staying with me in my house."

"Got it in one."

"No way, pal. My home is my turf, and I call the shots there."

"Not this time. Your father hasn't followed his original plan, so no one knows what he's going to do at this point. I'll be your shadow in case he tries to get in touch with you."

"I have to go back to school once my summer break is over. What are you going to do about that?" she challenged.

"We'll handle it when the time comes. Hopefully your father will come through, and I'll just be a bad memory by then."

"Which means in the meantime I'm stuck with you as my jailer."

"Houseguest sounds more pleasant, don't you think?"

She continued to scowl at him. "You don't want to know what I'm really thinking."

"This might be a lot easier for both of us if you'd try to accept the situation for what it is."

"What would be easier is if men like you and my father left me out of your schemes."

They arrived at Suzanne's house under the cover of darkness. Thad set their bags down on the front porch. He snatched the key out of Suzanne's hand as soon as she retrieved it from a nearby flowerpot.

"You hide your house key in a flowerpot?" He shook his head. "Incredible."

Suzanne stuck out her chin.

"It's my house. I can hide the key wherever I please." She held out her hand. "Now give it back."

"Not just yet. Tell me the layout of the floor plan before we go inside."

"I'm sure you already know exactly what everything is like, since you seem to know everything else about me."

"Let's just see if our information matches up."

She huffed out an impatient breath.

"The front door opens directly into the living room. The hallway to the left has two bedrooms divided by the bathroom. The kitchen and eating area are to the right."

"How many exit doors?"

"Two. This one and another one in the kitchen."

"Where does it lead to?"

"The backyard. It's also small and has a wooden fence with one gate that goes to a service alley."

"Do you have an alarm system?"

"I'm sure you know I don't; and before you start lecturing me, I've never felt the need for one."

"You should think about it. Your door lock would be child's play to any self-respecting burglar. Stay here while I check everything out and don't turn on the porch light."

Suzanne watched Thad disappear into the house. She stood, tapping her foot waiting for him to return. He came back after a few minutes, picked up their bags, and motioned for her to enter ahead of him. She walked into the living room and took a deep breath, comforted by the familiar surroundings. It felt so good to be home again she almost forgot that she wasn't going to have the house to herself.

"Where do you want me to put your things?" Thad asked, holding up her suitcase.

"I'll take it. I sleep in the second bedroom. Since I'm going to be stuck with you I have no choice but to offer you the other one. Try not to snore. The walls are thin."

"I rarely snore, and if I do you won't hear me."

Suzanne narrowed her eyes at him.

"Is that so? How do you know you aren't noisy if you're asleep?"

"I don't always sleep alone."

"Well, you will be while you're here. There's only one bathroom. Don't leave the toilet seat up, or wet towels on the floor. I'd say welcome, but because I don't want you here I won't waste my breath."

Thad surprised her by gripping her arm. He spun her around to face him when she would have walked away.

"Look. I don't want to be here anymore than you want me, but I have a job to do and I'm going to do it. I've about had it with your constant complaining. You whine more than any ten women. If this is how you acted with your ex-fiancé it's no wonder he left."

Her eyes flashed with fury before she flung the suitcase down and slapped him across one cheek.

"You macho swine! God, how I hate you!"

"I'll let you have that one because my comment was out of line. But don't ever try it again."

"Then keep your mouth shut, and your hands to yourself." She grabbed her bag and stomped away.

Thad heard a door slam. He rubbed a hand over the red mark on his cheek.

"Well, crap."

Suzanne dropped her suitcase as soon as she entered her bedroom. How had she ever considered Thad to be nice? She must have been blinded by faulty hormones. The man was an insufferable pig and to think she'd be forced to share her house with him made her hand itch to slap him on his other arrogant cheek, despite his warning.

She rubbed her eyes. It'd been a long day. Hopefully she'd be in a better mood after getting some sleep. Suzanne walked across the room thinking how wonderful it was going to feel being in her own bed again. She yanked back the bedspread and froze.

Thad said her door lock was child's play. Apparently he was right.

A bird's feather, as black as a raven's wing lay in stark contrast against the bright white of the pillowcase.

Four

Suzanne's first thought was to go running to Thad, but she made herself stop as soon as she reached for the doorknob. If she mentioned the feather she might never get him to leave her house. She took her time walking back to the bed and stood there with heart pounding staring at the feather. She'd dismissed the feather on the ship, but having this one in her home was too much of a coincidence to brush aside.

Now that she knew what her father had done to the Montanes she wondered if this could be a theatrical prop to scare her. Whatever the reason, it appeared to be doing a good job in that respect when just looking at the feather made her heart race and her palms sweat.

The feathers were a warning. First the one on the ship and she didn't have to remind herself what happened after that. Now this latest one. Did that mean something drastic was going to happen again?

God, she hoped not.

She pulled the pillowcase off, wrapped it around the offending feather, and stuffed it into a small wastebasket. Now what? She couldn't take it outside without Thad getting nosy. Her eyes strayed to the closet. She pulled open the door and shoved the basket inside. Hopefully in this case out of sight, out of mind would help to calm her nerves.

Suzanne wasn't surprised when she had trouble sleeping. She couldn't stop thinking about her missing father, the vengeful Montanes, and their black feathers. She'd probably be sitting here with a baseball bat in her hands worrying about someone breaking in if she'd been alone in the house. But she reminded herself Thad was here to protect her. She suddenly felt very glad about that and also swamped with guilt for the way she'd treated him.

The Black Feather
Olivia Claire High

It wasn't his fault she was in this predicament. He was only trying to keep her safe from whatever danger her irresponsible father had brought down on her. Thad had a job to do, as he reminded her, and all she'd done was criticize and find fault with him. The least she could do was try to be more cooperative and make the best of a bad situation as long as they had to cohabitate. Suzanne decided she would be as nice as she possibly could and treat him with the consideration she would have with any houseguest.

She closed her eyes determined to make peace with Thad and show him she could be a team player.

Suzanne waited until she heard him leave the bathroom in the morning before she shrugged into a robe and left her room. She would convince him that she really wasn't a sniveling crybaby. She followed the sound of his voice to the kitchen and found him pacing the floor while talking on his phone.

He ended the call as soon as she entered the room and shoved the phone into a pocket of his faded jeans. His dark tee shirt outlined every hard muscle as though the material had been painted on his body. He'd left his shoes and socks off. Suzanne stood there staring at him. God help her if she had to continue living under the same roof with him when even his bare feet looked sexy.

"I hope you don't mind, but I made coffee. Would you like some?"

"That'd be great. What better way to start the day?" she said trying to match his casual tone.

His eyes traveled over her thin robe that did little to disguise the delicate curves beneath.

"Oh, I can think of a few." He poured a mug and handed it to her. "We need to talk."

"Yes we do." Suzanne took a sip and held up her cup. "You make excellent coffee."

"Thank you." He leaned back against a counter. "Ladies first."

Suzanne cleared her throat. "A couple of things. First, I think I'll take your advice and have a security system installed. Do you happen to know how much they cost?"

"Depends, but don't worry, I'll have a friend do it for nothing."

"I appreciate that, but I would like to pay something."

Thad inclined his head. "We'll talk about it later. You said you had a couple of things to talk about."

"Yes. I owe you an apology. I've been acting like a spoiled brat. I'm not usually so difficult to get along with. I know you're trying to do your job and I appreciate that." She took another long swallow of her coffee before looking at him again. "I'm sorry I slapped you. James is a sore subject with me."

"Apology accepted. But you're not the only one at fault here. You've had it rough. I should have remembered that. It's a wonder you didn't try to cut my tongue out after that crack about your ex. I'm really sorry, Suzanne. That was uncalled for."

"That's okay."

"No it is not okay. I couldn't have been more insensitive. I guarantee it won't happen again."

She was about to ask him if he'd ever been dumped by a woman. But looking at his body, she decided it was highly unlikely. He probably was the one who did the dumping.

"Um, what did you want to talk to me about?"

"Ground rules. We stick together twenty-four/seven. I go where you go. That is not negotiable."

"What do I tell people if they ask me who you are?"

Thad moved away from the counter. He pulled a kitchen chair out, sat down, and began to tug on his socks and tennis shoes

"Give them enough truth to cover the lie. We met on the cruise. We hit it off and you invited me to follow you home."

"That ought to give the neighbors something to buzz about." Suzanne twisted her fingers around the tie of her robe. "I hope we can be friends, Thad. It will make things a lot easier, especially since you're going to be staying here. I had the opportunity aboard ship to see what a nice man you really are. I'd like to get to know that man better."

"You have it all wrong. I was acting. I am not a nice man. But that doesn't mean I won't still continue to play my role when we're around people. Let me remind you that you'll have to do your share if we're going to be convincing as a couple who are supposed to be attracted to each other."

His bluntness made her offer of friendship dissolve like ashes in her mouth. Pride demanded that she refuse to let him know how much his callousness hurt her fragile emotions. He expected her to be a team player without them sharing any team spirit.

"You certainly managed to fool me. Your performance was Academy award material."

"It's better this way."

"I'm beginning to think the only way is your way for everything."

Suzanne banged her cup down and ran from the room.

Thad swore under his breath. It seemed as though every time he tried to talk to Suzanne he ended up driving her away. That might not be such a bad thing considering his job was to protect her, not get personal. But that was easier said than done. He'd fought the personal part from the moment he first saw her standing at the railing on the ship. She looked so vulnerable and in need of comfort that he probably would have offered to help even if it hadn't been his assignment to get to know her.

His feelings for her came into sharp focus the day she'd been shot. Seeing the blood soaking into her blouse and then having her fall out of the Jeep almost made his heart stop. Having to spend the time holed up with her and watching while she sunbathed in that skimpy bikini left his body aching with need, leaving little doubt that he was physically attracted to her.

Picturing her sleeping in the next room while they were in the house in the jungle had been sheer torture. Now it looked as though things weren't going to get any easier. He'd hoped someone else would take over once the orders came to move Suzanne back here, but that wasn't going to happen.

He would have to ignore his feelings and pretend she was just another case. He felt like a hungry lion sent to guard a tender little lamb. Being with her these few minutes had him tied in knots. He stood up, dumped his cold coffee down the sink, and slammed out the door.

Thad finished checking the area outside just as Suzanne met him in the kitchen doorway.

"We're picking up Heather for brunch." She dangled a set of car keys in front of him. "Do you prefer to drive or will you trust me behind the wheel?"

Her chilly voice matched the frosty look in her eyes, but Thad knew he'd asked for it.

"Your town. Your car. You drive," he said, imitating her icy tone.

She gave him a mock salute.

"Yes, sir!"

Suzanne led the way outside to where her small sedan was parked.

"You'll have to excuse me because I'm still getting used to this cloak and dagger stuff. Do you need to check the car for bombs?"

"I already have."

"Of course you have. How silly of me to ask."

Thad clenched his jaw barely managing not to grind his teeth.

"Stop trying to make the situation more difficult than it already is. Carrying that chip on your shoulder isn't going to make things any easier for either of us."

"If I'm carrying a chip on my shoulder then you must be balancing a log on yours. I'm not the one who set the stage for this farce. You do your part and I'll do mine. But don't expect anything more from me," she informed him in that same cold voice before climbing into the car.

They were sitting outside on the patio of a trendy little café. Thad stayed quiet, his eyes constantly scanning the area while Suzanne brought Heather up on all her news since leaving the ship.

"You were shot? Oh my God. Are you sure you're all right? Does it still hurt?"

"It did, but I'm fine now. The bump on my head actually bothered me more."

"Thad's friends should have told me," Heather scolded.

"They didn't know about it at the time."

"Is this all because of your dad?"

Suzanne nodded. "I'm afraid so. Needless to say I'm pretty upset with him right now."

"I should think so. I don't suppose he thought how his running off with all that money would impact your life. I could throttle him when I think of the danger he's put you in."

"Get in line. You know my dad. Self-gratification comes first where he's concerned."

Heather scooted her chair closer to Thad. "You never know what to expect from her parents. They've always been kind of flighty."

"So I've heard."

Thad let the two women talk while he kept his attention focused on what was going on around them.

Heather put Suzanne in a much better mood. He was grateful for the small reprieve. Being around a female who acted like she had permanent PMS was enough to bring any man to his knees.

Suzanne left Heather at her house after lunch and they made promises to meet again soon.

"You probably noticed there isn't much food in the house," she said to Thad, as she backed out of the driveway. "I need to go to the grocery store. Is that going to be a problem?"

"Only one way to find out."

Suzanne concentrated on getting through traffic while Thad continued to stare around, including the rearview mirror.

"You'll have to tell me what you like to eat. Kenny fixed a lot of tropical dishes. I may not be able to duplicate that kind of cooking. I'm not sure what other kind of food you prefer."

40

"Anything is fine. You cook it, I'll eat it."

"Aren't you afraid I might try to poison you?"

"Nope. Too much trouble trying to get rid of my body," he said before turning his head to look over his shoulder. "Take the next right."

"That's not the way to the store."

"Just do it. Please."

Her head jerked toward him. "What's wrong? Are we being followed?"

"I'm not sure yet." He looked in the mirror again. "Turn left here."

Suzanne did as he asked while darting anxious glances at him in between watching her driving. They were getting into a residential area where the streets were narrower. She slowed down when she saw several children playing close to the curb up ahead.

"Is everything all right now?"

"Where does this street lead to?" Thad asked without answering her query.

"I don't know. I've never been this way before. What should I do?"

"Just concentrate on driving for now. Take a few more left and right turns indiscriminately and we'll see what happens. Stay on this street." He pulled his phone out and made a call. "We have a tail."

Suzanne gripped the wheel, as he gave their location and description of the car behind them.

"I can't believe this is happening to me here."

"You didn't think the bad guys would stop going after you just because you came home, did you?"

She thought of the black feather lying on her pillow. "Whoever said home sweet home was lying through their teeth."

Suzanne pulled into her driveway ten minutes later and leaned back in the seat, pale and breathing heavily. Her hand shook when she lifted several strands of hair away from her sweaty temples.

"I'm a trembling like a leaf. I may never want to drive again if this keeps up."

"You did fine. Let's get you into the house. You look like you could use a stiff drink."

"I feel like it."

"Try to hold back criticizing my poor manners, but I'll have to forego being the gentleman and ask you to stay behind me when we go inside."

"You want to use yourself as a human shield?" She waved toward the door. "Be my guest."

Once inside Thad grasped her elbow and steered her to a chair.

"Try to relax. I'll be right back."

He went into the kitchen, opened a cupboard, and took out a bottle of whiskey he'd discovered while searching for the coffee. He splashed a small amount into a glass, took it into the living room, and handed it to Suzanne.

"Thanks." She took a hefty swallow and coughed. "Yuk, I hate the taste of this stuff."

"Yeah? How is it I found the bottle in your cupboard?"

"My dad left it here on one of his rare visits." She took a smaller sip and set the glass aside. "Do you think that car was following us when we left the house?"

"Not that I could see, but it's possible. The Montanes are going to be watching your every move. Or they could have already known we were going to be at that café and took it from there."

"The only person who knew besides us was Heather."

"They may be watching her house."

"Is she in danger?" Suzanne sucked in a breath. "I couldn't bear having something happen to her or her husband because of their association with me and my wacky father."

Suzanne's phone rang before Thad had a chance to comment. He looked at the caller ID before handing her the phone.

"It's your mother. Just so you know, your calls are being monitored."

"As if my privacy hasn't been compromised enough," she said before taking the phone from him. "Mom? I'm glad you finally called. I've been worried after the way you took off on such short notice. Are you okay?"

Thad took the glass back to the kitchen. He would check later to hear the full conversation. He rinsed the glass out and leaned against the counter. He couldn't help feeling sympathy for Suzanne's dilemma, especially knowing how she was forced to deal with such selfish parents. It made a person think how some people should be banned from procreating.

But then Suzanne wouldn't have been born. He shook his head trying to remind himself again that he wasn't here to hit on her. The key was to keep his emotional distance while continuing to make sure she stayed safe. Losing his focus could end up being a deadly mistake.

For both of them.

Thad turned from the kitchen window when Suzanne entered the room.

"My mother's in Mexico soaking up some sun and fun. She says she hasn't heard from my dad. You probably already know all that, or you will soon enough since you bugged my phone. Lucky for her she's getting to extend her vacation."

"I told you I'd see to it that you'll get reimbursed for your cruise."

"Forget it. I don't care about that anymore. I'm just venting as usual. I also came in to tell you I'm sorry for falling apart when that car started following us."

"Don't be so hard on yourself. You got us here okay."

"I wish I could be as blasé about it as you seem to be. It gives me the creeps to know I'm being watched. Do you think I should tell Heather about this latest development?"

"No. She knows enough already. You said she has a tendency to panic."

"She does. Now that I think about it, there's no sense adding to a pot that's usually pretty much ready to boil over as it is."

"There you go."

Suzanne opened the refrigerator and shut it after staring inside for a few seconds. She faced Thad.

"I don't know why I'm looking in here. I let everything pretty much run out before my trip. We never made it to the store. I need to buy food. I also have several errands to run. How do you feel about going shopping?"

"About as excited as a visit to a proctologist."

His expression and dry tone gave Suzanne the first genuine laugh she'd had in far too long.

Five

They were arguing by the end of the week like a couple of people stuck in a bad marriage. To make matters worse, the sexual tension between them had risen to the point that the air practically crackled with the sparks they were sending off each other. The more they tried to ignore the magnetism, the more the attraction seemed to build. That pressure came very close to exploding early one morning when they literally ran into each other in the narrow hallway outside the bathroom.

Thad, fresh from the shower and clad in a towel slung low on his lean hips, eyed Suzanne in her short robe, as he grabbed her by the upper arms to steady her. She instinctively pressed her hands against his bare chest. Their eyes locked.

They stared at each other like a couple of hungry animals ready to pounce. No one would be able to mistake his body's obvious reaction to her nearness and the thin material of her robe did nothing to hide the fact that her breasts had responded to his touch. A vein beat a mad tempo at Thad's temple while Suzanne's pulse throbbed in the small hollow at the base of her throat. He rubbed his hands up and down her arms while her fingers flexed against his chest.

"I'm sorry. I thought I waited long enough for you to be back in your bedroom."

"You don't have to apologize. This is your house."

"I'm going to take my shower now."

His eyes gleamed, as though he was imagining her naked.

"I left you plenty of hot water."

"Thank you. I guess you'll be going back to your bedroom now."

Thad watched in fascination as Suzanne touched her lips with the tip of her tongue.

He groaned, and pulled her against him, covering her mouth with his. Suzanne's arms went around his neck as he deepened the kiss. He lifted his head several seconds later.

"I'm going back to my bedroom, but I won't be going alone," he growled in a hoarse voice before swinging her up into his arms to carry her down the hallway.

He laid her on the tangled bedding and came down beside her. His towel inched down his hips. Her robe slipped off one shoulder. Thad nipped the exposed area before letting his lips travel to kiss the tender flesh above one breast. He moved to her mouth and several seconds went by as their kisses became increasingly heated. Suzanne dug her fingers into his shoulders and moaned his name when he suddenly pulled away and jackknifed into a sitting position. She frowned and rose up on her elbows to stare at him.

"Why did you stop?"

"We can't do this, Suzanne."

She frowned at him.

"We both want to, and you know it."

"Because we want each other doesn't make it right. I'm here to protect you, not seduce you."

"It's not seducing if I'm cooperating. I want you to make love to me, Thad."

"The last few weeks have been very unsettling for you. You're not thinking straight."

"Yes I am, and I know that I want you."

He lifted a brow.

"I thought you said you hated me."

"Looks like you kind of grew on me."

He smiled before his expression turned serious again.

"Are you sure I'm not just someone you're using as a rebound to get over your fiancé?"

"Ex-fiancé! And if you think mentioning him is going to make me hate you all over again, it's not going to work. I really, really want you."

"I'm flattered, but I'm all wrong for you. You're the kind of woman who should have marriage and kids with a guy who'll be a real husband to you. Those things have never even been a blip on my radar. I'm doing you a favor by backing out before this gets too complicated for both of us."

Suzanne scrambled to her knees and put her arms around him when he started to stand up.

"Stop thinking so much about the future and go with the now. We're two consenting adults who happen to be attracted to each other. I'm not talking marriage here. I won't expect a commitment from you, Thad. When it's time for you to leave I'll let you go. I promise. No strings."

He pulled her arms away and rolled off the bed.

"I appreciate that. The problem is I may not be able to let you go."

"Wait, please." She grabbed him by the hand to stop him from leaving. "Can't we just talk?"

"Not with you dressed like that," he said pointing to her gaping robe.

She quickly yanked it closed.

"Is this better?"

"Not much. I still know what's underneath there."

"Come on, Thad. Give me a break. You just told me you may not be able to let me go, and now you want to walk away. That's like starting a sentence and leaving off the punctuation. Was that a tease?"

He shook his head.

"No, I'm just trying to be honest. I can't deny that I'm attracted to you, but I can control whether or not I act on those feelings. I told you I'm not the right kind of guy for you. You need someone in a nine-to-five job, who comes through the door Monday through Friday to have dinner with you. Someone who mows the lawn on Saturdays and sits in his recliner and watches Sunday football on television."

"I already had that. It didn't work out."

Thad ran a finger down her cheek.

"Because he didn't love you."

"Well, certainly not enough to stick around."

"That's just it, Suzanne. You deserve a guy who will stick around, and I'm not that man."

Thad stood outside the kitchen door drinking his coffee while he looked around the yard. Suzanne sat at the table watching him. She couldn't seem to make herself pull her eyes away. So many different emotions were swirling around inside of her she didn't know what to think. She felt a certain amount of embarrassment at his rejection and tried to appreciate the fact that he didn't want to hurt her. Her brain understood that, but her body struggled to accept his decision.

Could this be more than a sexual thing she was feeling for Thad, or was she falling in love with him? She and James had been together for two years, but he never made her feel the way she did when she was around Thad. She turned out not to be the woman James wanted. Could things be different with Thad?

Would she ever be what any man wanted? Was it so wrong to want to be loved? James made her believe she lacked something, even if she didn't know what that something was. Suzanne buried her face in her hands. Another new, complicated level had just been added to her life.

Suzanne looked up and stared at Thad again, and the emotion came pouring out of her. She really had fallen in love with him. It made her realize what she'd felt for James paled in comparison to this newfound feeling. Thad was right about her. She did plan to have a husband and kids with James. But now she wanted that and so much more with Thad. Never mind what she told him about not expecting a commitment.

She'd have to find a way to convince him they could make a relationship work. Her plan with James fizzled, but there wasn't any law that said she couldn't come up with a new plan. This time it was definitely going to include Thad if she had any say in the matter. No way was she going to let him disappear out of her life, whether he thought he was right for her or not

Of course, there wasn't a lot either of them could do as far as planning their future until all this craziness with her father ended. If only he'd go to the police she wouldn't have to keep worrying about the Montanes getting to him. It gave her the willies thinking about their black feathers. She'd emptied the wastebasket getting rid of the one in her closet. But throwing it away hadn't stopped her from remembering the two feathers she received so far were each followed by two scary situations.

Would there be a third? If so, what catastrophe did the Montanes have in store for her next? How many feathers did they give before they decided to get rid of a person? Would there be more car chases? Threats to her and her friends? Or, God help her, death to anyone who dared to help her? Her whole body clenched with fear at such a horrible thought.

Suzanne got up to rinse her coffee cup. She stood at the sink wishing she could stop thinking about the feathers and wondered if she'd made a mistake by not telling Thad about them. On the other hand, what good would it do other than give him one more thing to watch out for? He didn't need any dramatic symbols to tell him they were in danger. As much as she'd like to pretend his attraction to her was the only thing keeping him here, she knew better.

The phone rang at that moment breaking into her troubled thoughts. Suzanne saw Thad look at her, but he stayed outside. She checked the caller ID and lifted her brows in surprise at the name. She joined him outside a few minutes later.

"Problem?" he asked.

"No. That was my roommate from college. Her name is Cissy Bordly. She lives a couple hours away. She's married with a baby boy, so I don't see too much of her these days. But she's going to be in town this afternoon and wants to meet me for lunch. I accepted because she sounded so anxious to see me. Now I'm worried about being followed again or something happening to her. I don't want to put her in danger like I did Heather. Maybe I should call her back and cancel."

"Don't do that. I think the visit will do you good. We'll use the service alley gate and cut through your neighbor's yard. I'll call a cab after we walk a couple of blocks and have it pick us up there. No one will know we left the house and you won't have to worry about anyone tailing your friend."

"Okay. Just as long as no one goes after Cissy. Thank you for letting me go see her."

"I'm not here to control your life. I'm just trying to see that you stay alive long enough to live it."

"I realize that, but sometimes it's kind of hard to differentiate between the two."

Cissy, a short, slightly chubby blonde with a harried expression met them inside the dark paneled pub she'd chosen. The two women embraced. Her eyes widened in surprise when Suzanne introduced Thad as a friend from her cruise.

"We used to come here in our younger days," she explained to him. "I guess I'm feeling a little nostalgic. I hope you don't mind that I didn't choose someplace fancier, Suzanne."

"Of course not. I remember the sandwiches here are great." She turned to Thad. "Try the roast beef."

"I just might do that."

Thad and Suzanne ordered beer with their sandwiches while Cissy opted for water explaining she was nursing her baby. Suzanne couldn't help noticing that her friend only ate a few bites of her food. She asked Suzanne to accompany her to the restroom as soon as Suzanne finished eating. Cissy checked to make sure the two stalls were empty immediately after the door closed.

"Cissy, is everything all right? I don't mean to pry, but you seem a little jumpy."

"Your father called me this morning," she blurted out.

"What!"

"It's true. That's the real reason I asked you to meet with me. Oh, I'm sorry. That didn't sound very nice. I did want to see you, too, of course. I just wish it could have been strictly for social reasons."

Suzanne didn't have time to feel offended. She was too busy worrying that someone else she knew had been dragged into her nightmare. She felt an icy jab of fear in the pit of her stomach at the idea of her father putting another friend in danger. Why had he chosen to involve Cissy? He barely knew the woman.

"He called you? That's certainly a surprise. What did he want?"

"He sounded very distraught. He said he's been doing undercover work for the Feds involving a couple of big time drug lords. They found out, and your dad barely escaped with his life. He says he has enough evidence to put them away, but he's afraid they'll kill him if he comes out of hiding."

Suzanne barely managed to keep her anger in check. Leave it to her father to make it sound like he was some kind of hero.

"He should have called me and not bothered you."

"He explained that. He said the group he infiltrated is very dangerous. They know you're his daughter, which means they're probably watching your house and may even be having your phone calls monitored in case he tries to get in touch with you. He's worried the same thing may be true with your mother. He doesn't want either of you to get hurt."

"But he didn't hesitate to involve you. I apologize for that."

"Your dad said those people would never guess he'd be calling me." She rummaged in her purse and pulled out a slip of paper. "This is the number where you can reach him. But be careful. He gave me strict instructions to tell you not to give the number to anyone else or to use your own phones."

Suzanne took the paper.

"Cissy, there's something you should know about Thad."

"I know he's not your fiancé. I have a feeling he's more than just a friend from your cruise. Right?"

"Yes, and he knows about Dad."

She squeezed Suzanne's arm.

"You can't tell him about that phone number. I promised your dad you'd be the only one to know about it. He begged me to be sure you kept this to yourself. He said you shouldn't trust anyone. Please do as he asked. I don't want his blood on my hands."

Perhaps not, but Suzanne couldn't help thinking that her father didn't mind having other peoples blood on his. She also couldn't ignore the nagging voice inside her head that reminded her despite everything this was still her father and Cissy had gone to a lot of trouble for him.

"I promise not to say anything. I can't apologize enough for him calling you."

"Just don't let anyone else know."

She looked at her watch.

"I should be going now."

"Go through the kitchen, out the back way."

Cissy clutched her purse to her chest like a shield.

"Oh! Am . . . am I going to get into trouble?"

"No. I'm just suggesting this as a precaution."

"Okay. To tell you the truth I wasn't looking forward to facing your friend again. He's a very intense person, isn't he? I sure hope you know what you're doing, Suzanne."

"Actually, I'm not sure about much of anything these days, but lucky for me, Thad is."

They hugged each other and promised to get together for a more leisurely lunch once things were settled with Suzanne's father. She watched her friend leave, praying that Cissy would be safe.

Suzanne returned to the table and told Thad Cissy had to get home to her baby. They stayed to finish their beer. He sat silently watching her until Suzanne had the feeling he was actually able to read her guilty thoughts. She wouldn't be surprised if he did. The man didn't miss much.

"Your friend seemed a little edgy."

"I don't think she's getting much sleep these days with taking care of her baby."

Thad took another slow swallow of beer and nodded toward the front entrance.

"I didn't see her leave."

"I thought it would be best if she went out the back in case someone did follow us here."

"Good idea, but I'd be interested to hear what you said to convince her that was necessary."

"It wasn't difficult. You made her nervous, and she wanted to avoid having to see you again."

"Is that so? And here I thought I was being quite charming. Are you sure there isn't something else I should know about?"

Suzanne sighed.

"Are you going to be suspicious of everyone who wants to talk to me?"

"Being suspicious goes along with my job."

"If you must know, she's having marital problems and needed a sympathetic ear."

"So you're Dr. Ruth now?"

"Of course not, but I am her friend and sometimes just having someone listen can help."

Suzanne amazed herself with how glibly the lies came, but then she'd learned from the best. No one could prevaricate any better than her father, and no one was better at using people. It didn't matter if that also included his own daughter.

Suzanne was willing to do anything if it meant he was ready to go to the authorities. If she saved her dad, she might be able to save herself. She peered at Thad from beneath her lashes. All she had to do was figure out a way to get in touch with her father without her diligent bodyguard finding out.

But how in the world was she going to keep a bloodhound like Thad off her trail when just about everything she did made him skeptical?

Six

Sometimes inspiration came from the simplest of things and at the oddest of times. Hadn't she discovered that more often than not during her teaching career? This particular brainwave came while Suzanne stood at the kitchen counter mixing up a batch of dumplings using her godmother's recipe.

"Always be grateful for whatever inspires you," Nanadoo used to say. "There's usually a good reason for it."

Suzanne recalled the words and wondered if it was okay to be thankful that she was going to lie to one man, so she could help another. Did one deed justify the other?

She was about to find out.

"Thad, I'm going to take the chicken and dumplings left from our dinner to my neighbors next door," she said as soon as they'd finished eating. "They're elderly and not in the best of health. I sometimes cook for them. I'm afraid it'd be a little intimidating for them if you join me, so I'd appreciate it if you'd let me go alone."

Suzanne busied herself loading the dishwasher and kept her back to Thad while she talked. She waited, bracing herself, expecting him to argue.

"All right."

She allowed a quiet, relieved breath to slip between her lips before she turned to face him.

"Thanks for not giving me a hard time, and don't get all antsy if I'm not back in five minutes. They like me to visit whenever I go over there."

"Fair enough. Just don't decide at the last minute to take any detours."

"As if I would."

Suzanne had to dig deep to maintain her composure as she continued to cultivate the delicate rapport they'd been

54

working on since that morning. She also had to make sure Thad wouldn't in any way be suspicious of her actions. The piece of paper from Cissy felt like a weight in her pocket. Every time he looked her way she imagined he had Superman's x-ray vision and could see right through her jeans.

She'd gone over and over in her mind different ways she could get in contact with her father since seeing Cissy, without Thad finding out and had finally come up with this idea. She wasn't happy that her plan would mean using the old couple. She hoped to God it wouldn't end up causing them any harm. Too many people had already been dragged into this calamity.

Suzanne hated herself for what she was about to do. It reminded her too much of her father. She wished she could make herself not care about him. But even in her anger she still loved him. She had to remind herself the main reason she decided to call his number was to try and get him to go to the police.

She picked up the container of chicken and another with fruit salad before walking to the door. Thad opened it for her. "Need any help carrying that?"

"No thanks, I have it. I'll see you in a little while," she said and forced herself to smile again.

"I'm counting on it."

The man answered the doorbell.

"Hi Greg. I brought you and Mary dinner. Chicken and dumplings with a side of fruit salad."

"Well, bless your heart. Come in, come in." He stepped back to let her enter. "Mary's in the kitchen right now trying to decide what to fix."

"Looks like I arrived in the nick of time. I also have a favor to ask."

"Anything."

"My house phone is on the fritz and would you believe silly me forgot to charge my cell? I was wondering if I could use your phone."

"Of course you can, darlin'. Take the one in our bedroom. It'll give you more privacy."

"Thank you, but first let's get this food into the kitchen."

Suzanne left them as soon as they sat down to eat. She felt bad enough lying to Thad, but taking advantage of these good people made her feel lower than pond scum. She picked up the phone and made her call. Her father answered after the first ring and sounded genuinely terrified.

"Thank God it's you. Are you calling from a safe phone?"

"If you mean is it bugged? No it's not, and hello to you too, Dad."

"I'm in trouble, honey. A real barrel of trouble."

"I know, and it's spilled over onto me. Thanks to your escapade I've been shot, had to hide out in the middle of a jungle, and now I'm forced to have a bodyguard move into my house to protect me."

"You have? I didn't know. Well, things are a real mess here, too. You've got to help me."

"Thanks for asking if I'm okay."

"What? Oh, yeah. I'm sorry, but you sound all right. I need you to do something for me. I'd do it myself, but I'm being followed."

She pulled in a breath.

"What makes you think I'm not? I can't even go out for a simple lunch without having someone chasing me. I want you to stop running and turn yourself in. Let the police handle this now."

"That's easy for you to say. You're not the one who'll end up in a pine box if the people I'm running from finds me."

"I'm also not the one who stole a truckload of money, either. You promised to cooperate with the authorities by giving them evidence on the Montane brothers. Why haven't you followed through?"

"How'd you find out about all that?"

"I got it from the man who's staying with me. He said you could have those men put away for good."

"I do have plenty of stuff on them, but they got wise to me. I barely escaped with my hide intact. I've decided to use the money I took to go to some nice little island and live out my days in comfort. The problem is I've got to be sure the Montanes are behind bars, or they'll hunt me down like a rabid dog."

"But not all the Montanes want to harm you. Right?"

"What do you mean?"

"I'm talking about Muriel Montane."

"So you know about her, too," he said after a few seconds hesitation. "She's a sweet girl. The only way we can be free of her family is to be sure the evidence I gathered gets to the police."

"Then mail whatever you have to them and leave me out of it, for heaven's sake."

"Well – see, that's the problem. I don't have the stuff with me."

Suzanne pressed fingertips to her eyes, willing the headache away that had started to emerge.

"What did you do with the phones?"

"I put them in a green canvas bag and tossed it into the bushes in the backyard at our old house. I knew the Montanes were getting close. I didn't have much time to think about what else to do."

"Which old house? We lived in more than one if you'll recall."

"The one on Daisy Drive. It's okay because no one's living there now. I checked. I thought it'd be easy to go back later, but I don't think I should take the chance. I've got to keep myself safe for Muriel's sake. I need you to go there, get that bag, and turn it over to the police, honey."

"I can't. I'm being watched too closely myself."

"You got to a phone to call me, didn't you? You've always been clever. I know you'll figure out a way to help your old man."

"It's kind of crappy that you're not worried about me as much as you are about your lady friend."

"Of course I'm worried about you, but Muriel has to be my priority right now."

Her shoulders sagged.

"It's nice to know where I stand in the pecking order. Why is she so special?"

"She's pregnant."

Suzanne decided she was worse than pond scum. She was the primordial ooze that seeped up from the bowels of the earth. She'd not only tricked her friends into using their phone, but she took the cell phone sitting on the dresser. If that wasn't bad enough, she swiped money out of Greg's wallet lying there because she'd had to leave her house without her purse.

Greg's phone was very basic and she knew he only used it for emergencies. This was definitely an emergency. She took it in case she needed to call for help. Her father said their old house was empty, but what if someone followed her? Something could happen to her and no one would even know where she'd gone. The only thing she could think to do was phone Heather and tell her where she was headed.

Suzanne told Heather she felt obligated to go, when her friend tried to talk her out of it. She knew her dad was using her and that hurt. Still, she hadn't been able to refuse him. Maybe she needed counseling? Why else would she allow herself to be manipulated into doing something so dangerous?

The pattern between them had been set long ago. She'd always been willing to do anything, short of murder, to please her father in an effort to win his love. But this was the first time she'd been asked to protect an unborn child. Her dad's child, she reminded herself. Well, she was his child, too, even if she was an adult now.

Thad was right when he described the kind of home she wanted. Maybe that was because she'd never had that life growing up. People who claimed you couldn't miss what you never had didn't know what they were talking about. There were all kinds of hunger in the world, and not just for food.

Thad must have discovered she was gone by now. Suzanne hated deceiving him. He'd inadvertently given her the idea to use her neighbor's yard and call a cab to meet her a few blocks away. She prayed she'd find the bag, so she could turn it over to the police before the Montane brothers ruined more lives. It made her feel better to focus on the idea that she wasn't doing this just for herself, or her father. The Montanes had done bad things to good people. If she had the power to end their reign of terror, wasn't that a noble quest?

Maybe if she succeeded it might make her father love her. Or maybe she should grow up and stop believing in fantasies. But sometimes fairytales were all there was, and not for the first time in her life Suzanne wished for something she couldn't seem to have.

She had the cab driver drop her off a few houses from her destination. She walked at a quick pace in her anxiousness to find her father's bag and get away as fast as she could. The streetlights spaced out along the route made it easy to see where she was going. But she made herself stay in the shadows as much as possible in case someone might be watching her progress.

Suzanne doubted if she would ever get comfortable with having to look over her shoulder. She enjoyed a good cat-and-mouse game as much as the next person. But not when she was the mouse.

A few stars were just beginning to dot the sky, winking like tiny rhinestones on a bed of dark gray velvet. She glanced at the houses as she hurried along. Most of them had lights on giving them a friendly, lived-in appearance. Suzanne remembered this as a neighborhood with a lot of young families. She wondered if anyone she knew still lived here.

She experienced some happy times here, but all too often they were overshadowed by unhappy moments. Like the day her father gave her precious bike to his latest paramour's little girl to impress his lover when he was in between jobs and short of cash. Or the time her mother made the one and only parent/teacher conference at school and ended up trying to seduce the young male teacher.

But she wasn't here to reminisce. Nostalgia could have no part in her return to this childhood home tonight. She found the house she sought at the end of the street in a row of houses all very similar in style.

Her old house stood out from the others mainly because of its neglected appearance. The windows were dark and without curtains. Several advertisement newspapers yellowed by the weather lay on the front walk that divided the two patches of front lawn. The grass was badly in need of mowing and weeds had taken over the flowerbeds flanking the three steps leading up to the porch.

An empty field bordered one side of the house, silent and shrouded in darkness, while the neighbors on the other side were obviously having a party in their backyard. She sniffed the air and smelled the distinctive aroma of grilling meat. Loud music, bright lights, and laughter spilled over the flimsy fence. Suzanne remembered going to a birthday party in that yard once upon a time. She wondered if the same family lived there after all these years.

The boy had been eight and in her class at school. Her mother had forgotten about the party and gone off to lunch with friends. No gift had been bought, so Suzanne shook all the money out of her Unicorn bank from Nanadoo and used the meager cash to buy a present.

She ran six blocks to the nearest Mom and Pop store and had just enough money to buy the boy a thin coloring book and a small box of crayons. She hurried back home and wrapped them in paper towels using one of her hair ties to keep the ends of the paper closed.

The boy hadn't opened her gift with the others and when she got ready to leave, she saw his mother scoop it up and toss it in the trash with the discarded wrappings from the other presents. Suzanne stood there now flinching, not wanting to remember, but unable to forget.

She couldn't help envying the people partying there now who seemed to be enjoying themselves while she had to skulk around like a thief. And skulking was a lonely business. She darted around the side of the house to the back. She skidded to a stop at the sight that greeted her. If she thought the front was overgrown, the backyard looked like a jungle. It reminded her of her time in Belize.

Whoever occupied the house last hadn't bothered to do any yard work from the looks of things. Her parents didn't do much gardening when they'd lived here, either, but the plants were young and small then. She could see everything had definitely flourished over the years. How did her dad expect her to find anything in this tangle of vegetation that seemed to fill almost every available space? She'd need a machete or better yet, a bulldozer to get through this mess.

There weren't as many streetlights this far down the street. But she had a fairly good view of her surroundings, thanks to the partying neighbors. Although it would have been a lot less difficult if the bag she had to find was any color instead of green. Leave it to her dad to make things complicated. But on the flip side, if the bag was a brighter color that would make it easier for someone else to find it. She gulped in a resigned sigh, lowered her head, and plunged boldly into the overgrown plants closest to the side of the fence by the street, hoping this might be where her dad may have tossed his elusive green bag.

This wasn't going to be easy.

But she had a feeling trying to explain to Thad why she'd lied to him was probably going to be a far more daunting task.

Thad frowned at his watch and opened the backdoor. He stepped outside to look in the yard, but there wasn't any sign of Suzanne. He was beginning to feel uneasy about her continued absence, despite her warning him that she'd be staying to visit with her neighbors. Just how long could it take to deliver the food, maybe sit and have a cup of coffee while they ate, and head back? Had she stayed to help with the clearing up and lost track of time?

He looked at his watch again. Whatever the reason for her staying away it seemed to him it was more than enough time to do what she had to do and be home by now. His restlessness increased until his whole body felt like a rubber band ready to snap. He'd waited long enough. He didn't care what the old folks thought about him showing up at their door. It was time he paid them a call.

Thad rang the doorbell. He heard a safety chain slide into place and waited impatiently until the door opened just wide enough for a man to peer at him.

"Yes?"

"I'm sorry to bother you, sir. I'm a friend of Suzanne's. I've been staying with her the last few days. You may have seen me around outside."

"Oh yes, I believe I have. What can I do for you, young man?"

Thad chuckled.

"To tell you the truth I'm getting a little lonely all by myself in the house. I was wondering when Suzanne might be coming back. We planned to watch a movie together."

"I don't understand. Are you saying she's not at home?"

Thad's stomach muscles quickly tightened.

"No she's not. I assumed she was still here with you."

"Why no. She left quite a while ago. She said she'd come back tomorrow to collect her bowls."

Alarm mixed with fury. Thad had to force himself to keep the anger out of his voice.

"Did she mention she might be going someplace else? Perhaps to visit another neighbor close by?"

"Not that I recall. Oh my goodness. Perhaps she's hurt somewhere. Should I call the police?"

Thad shook his head.

"She probably went to the store. She said something about being out of popcorn. No need to call anyone. I'll just wait for her to return. I apologize for worrying you."

"You be sure and let me know when you find her."

"You bet. Goodnight now." Thad started to walk away, but stopped. "Just out of curiosity, did she ask to borrow your car? She thought she heard a funny noise in hers today and wanted to have it checked out," he said, continuing to improvise.

"No she didn't mention the car, but she told me about her phones."

"Her phones?"

"She said the house phone is on the blink and her cell needed a charge, so she asked to use ours. Do you want to use it, too?"

Thad kept his expression bland, but anger at Suzanne's deception dug at him like razor sharp claws.

"I forgot about her phones. Mine's fine. I should have told her that. Thanks again for your help."

"Don't forget to let me know if she's all right."

"Will do."

Thad whipped out his phone as soon as he heard the door close. Frustration and worry warred inside him as he jogged back to the house. He couldn't believe Suzanne would run off after promising to come back. What part of your life is in danger did the woman not understand? He cursed himself for trusting her and cursed her even more for taking advantage of that trust.

Seven

Thad knew he probably wouldn't have discovered Suzanne's destination so quickly if he didn't have the right resources to tap into. It embarrassed and infuriated him that he'd ended up having to ask for assistance. He must be losing his edge, or she'd messed with his mind enough to make him trust her. She never should have been able to slip away from him so easily.

Either way, he vowed it wasn't going to happen again. If Suzanne thought he'd been watching her too closely before, this reckless stunt just cost her any chance at privacy. He never thought she would use her neighbors as a cover to escape him after she seemed so upset about having her other friends involved in this chase to find her father. His hands clenched on his knees, as the taxi slowed to a halt.

"This is where I dropped her off," the cab driver said, breaking into Thad's thoughts.

"At this house?"

"No. She walked down that way," the man pointed. "Looks like someone's having a party down there. I figured she was either crashing the shindig, or maybe trying to surprise someone."

"Sounds like it." Thad handed him the fare, with a generous tip.

"Thanks. You want me to wait? This extra just bought you more time on the meter."

"No. I'll take it from here."

The driver shrugged.

"Your call, Ace," he said, holding up the money. "Thanks for the extra dough."

Thad stepped out of the taxi and started jogging in the direction the driver had indicated. He kept to the shadows and stopped when he came to the party house. Once his sources had located the cabbie and this area, they'd also discovered she actually lived in this neighborhood at one time during her childhood.

Thad checked the number on the house in front of him. It didn't match the address he was looking for. Next door would if the numbers were running in the correct sequence.

He walked there, careful to stay out of the glare of the streetlights, and verified what he already knew to be true. This was her old place, but it looked deserted. Who had Suzanne phoned that she didn't want him to know about – someone at the party house? His gut told him otherwise.

He had a feeling she came to her old house to meet someone, and that person was most likely her father. Had she been lying when she said she didn't know how to get a hold of him? Was she waiting, knowing her dad would be contacting her? If he was right about that then Suzanne was a better actor than she'd accused him of being.

Her father had probably been manipulating Suzanne and twisting her emotions to his advantage since she was a kid. It looked like she was just another pawn to a man who used people for his own benefit. The idea disgusted him and made him feel sorry for her. But she was an adult now, and it was time she broke free from whatever hold her parent had on her. That'd be up to her. He had more important things on his mind than playing counselor to Suzanne's dysfunctional family.

He ducked around large bushes and headed along the edge of the lawn before he vaulted over the railing and landed on the porch. Thad wasn't surprised to find the door locked and a quick check in the front windows showed nothing but dark rooms behind the grimy panes.

Suzanne hadn't gone in this way unless she had somehow obtained a key. She'd either used a side window or one in back to gain her entry, if she actually went inside. He jumped down off the porch and slid around back checking the perimeter of the house as he went. His search didn't turn up a single clue that anyone had been here. The yard at both sides of the house needed trimming; but the back was a virtual forest of plants literally gone wild without the hand of man to cut them back.

Thad moved slowly keeping his senses alert, as he eluded the lights streaming over the fence from the neighbor's house. He'd find Suzanne if she was still here and demand an explanation. He knew she would give him some flak and that was just too damn bad. He wasn't going to back down until she told him everything. No more Mr. Nice Guy. He had let his emotions cloud his judgment, and allowed himself to have faith in her. His mistake caused him to let down his guard and forget this was a job, not a courtship.

How many times was he going to have to keep telling Suzanne it would make things a lot easier for them both if she would realize he only wanted to keep her safe and help find her father? Thad supposed this was what people meant by that old saying about blood being thicker than water. She insisted on putting him in the role of bad guy when her dad was actually more the villain in her personal life.

Thad caught a movement out of the corner of his eye and dropped to the ground. Suzanne! She hadn't spotted him. He watched and frowned, as she crawled around on her hands and knees pushing foliage out of her way, face close to the ground, obviously searching for something. That something could very well be the phones with the evidence her father was supposed to have collected on the Montanes.

He wondered how the hell anyone would be expected to find anything in this tangled mess with so little light to guide them. He made his way silently over to Suzanne, slithering through the foliage making him feel like a snake. He grabbed her and clamped a hand over her mouth before she had a chance to react. She began to struggle and fight him until he pressed her into the ground rendering her completely immobile with the weight of his body.

"Stop fighting me. I'm going to take my hand away, and if you so much as let out a squeak, so help me God I'll shove a mouthful of dirt down your throat. Do I make myself clear?" he hissed in her ear.

She nodded, and he eased his hand away.

"Are you trying to squash me to death?" she gasped.

Thad shifted, but still kept her pinned down.

"How did you know where to find me?"

"Didn't you ever hear that imitation is the sincerest form of flattery?" he said, keeping his voice quiet and close to her ear, while doing his best to ignore how good her hair smelled.

"Huh?"

"You didn't have a car. You used the same cab company I did when we met your friend."

"You found the cab driver who brought me here? I can't believe it."

"I'm here, aren't I? What are you looking for?"

"What makes you think I'm looking for anything?"

"Oh, I don't know. Perhaps it's because I just watched you crawling around with your nose to the ground like a dog trying to find where a favorite bone is buried."

"You think I'm a dog?"

Thad rolled his eyes.

"Vanity, thy name is woman. It was just a metaphor. I repeat, what are you hoping to find here?"

"Nothing."

"Have it your way. We can lay here like this all night for all I care because I'm not moving until you tell me the truth."

She wiggled restlessly beneath him.

"You're not being fair using brute force to get your way."

"Do you consider it fair that you abused my trust when I let you go to your neighbors on your own, only to have you run out on me?"

"No. And I feel awful about that, especially in using them. I took Greg's cell phone and a twenty out of his wallet," she wheezed. "Would you please get off of me? I'm having trouble getting my breath."

Thad rolled to a sitting position and grabbing Suzanne, tugged her up to sit beside him while keeping his fingers locked around her wrist.

"No more stalling. What are you doing here?"

"It's a long story."

67

"I'll take the abbreviated version."

"Oh, all right. Your instincts were correct about Cissy. Dad contacted her and gave her a phone number where I could reach him. And before you jump down my throat, I swear to you I didn't have any way to get in touch with him before. He said he put the evidence he collected on the Montane brothers in a bag and tossed it into this backyard."

"Is he expecting you to take it to him?"

"No. He didn't tell me where he's hiding. He asked me to turn the evidence over to the police. He's going to take off and live on some island with his lady love as soon as he knows the Montanes are in custody. According to Dad, she's pregnant, I might add."

"He's not exactly Father of the Year material, and now he's going to have another kid." Thad shook his head. "Do you believe he really stashed the stuff in this hodgepodge of plants?"

"Why else would he ask me to come here? I don't want to be the one to dole out his punishment even though I agree he deserves to pay for giving everyone the runaround."

"That's some kind of hold he has over you."

Her jaw clenched.

"You don't have to tell me something I already know."

"Then why don't you stop trying to save your father and concentrate on trying to save yourself?"

"I assume you're referring to the years I've spent trying to please Dad and not about escaping the Montanes. Well, I don't know how. Now are you going to help me find the bag or not?"

"What does it look like?"

"Green and canvas."

"A green bag hidden among a forest of green plants. Wonderful. Not that it matters in the dark. I don't suppose it occurred to your father that it'd be more logical for you to wait until daylight."

"Dad doesn't do logical."

"I'm beginning to think that might be a family trait."

Suzanne glared at him.

"Could you just please help me find the stupid bag, or would you rather sit here going on about fixing my screwed up genes?"

"Lady, there isn't enough Super Glue or Duct tape on this planet to fix what ails your family."

"Well, that made me feel better."

He removed his hand from her wrist.

"I'm sorry. You have my permission to take a swipe at me."

"Forget it. I can't very well deny something when I know it's true. "

"All right then, let's see what we can find here."

Thad sat back on his heels after they'd finished searching as much of the yard that was possible to reach.

"Either you misunderstood him, or your father's playing games with you."

"I know what he said. That bag has to be here."

"If it is, I don't think we're going to find it tonight. There's something else to consider."

"What?"

"Someone else knew about the bag and got here before we did."

"That means they saw my dad put it here. He said the Montanes were getting too close."

"Or he's playing this from both sides. There might be someone in the Montane camp that's willing to help your father for their own benefit."

"Which would mean he doesn't care what happens to me; as long as he gets to leave the country with the stolen cash and his woman on his arm?"

Suzanne pushed the hair out of her eyes.

"Nice of him. You'd think I'd be used to his conniving by now. He pulled the guilt trip on me again. I foolishly tried to be the obedient daughter and help him like I've always done. It burns my butt that he can still make me feel like I'm five years old. He didn't even care that I'd been shot. Well, I've had it. I came for the bag, and I couldn't find it. My conscience is clear."

"I'll have someone come back and look in the daylight. I'll need that number you used to reach your father to see if we can track him down."

"Okay, but I'd like to get out of here first. My clothes are filthy, I'm full of stickers, and I'm pretty sure there's something getting ready to crawl up my pants leg."

Suzanne walked to a pool of light coming from next door and started to brush at her clothes. The music suddenly went to an ear piercing high. Thad shoved her to the ground seconds before a tiny missile shredded the bush above their heads.

"What the hell were you doing, standing up in the light like that?"

"Please tell me that wasn't what I think it was," she said, ignoring his question.

Thad pushed her head down when Suzanne tried to take a look.

"Stay down!"

Another bullet slammed into the dirt near them making Suzanne tremble.

"Oh dear God, not again!"

"Listen to me," he commanded. "We're going to crawl to the back gate that leads to the empty field."

"It's too overgrown with tangled vines. We'll never be able to get it to open."

"Yes we will. Stay low and move away from any light. Now go. I'll be right behind you."

Suzanne swiveled her body around, encouraged by his calm confidence and headed for the gate in a commando crawl just as two more bullets hit the ground near their feet. She wiggled over thick weeds, sharp pebbles, thistles, and dirt to reach the gate in record time with Thad following inches away.

Thin streams of sweat streaked her face while she panted from the combination of fear and exercise. Thad breathed so quietly Suzanne couldn't even hear him. She had no idea how he thought they'd be able to get the gate open until she heard him attacking the vines with quick, aggressive sawing motions.

The old gate creaked opened in a surprisingly short time with enough room for them to squeeze through. Suzanne had the urge to start running across the open field. She probably would have in her desire to get away from the trigger happy sniper next door if Thad hadn't taken her by the arm and steered her to the edge of the meadow.

He led her into a nearby grove of trees amazing her with his ability to see so well in the dark. He finally stopped and leaned her gently against the trunk of a large oak tree. Moonlight played hide and seek with the clouds while a breeze wove through the woods cooling her heated cheeks. Suzanne listened and felt relief flood through her when she didn't hear the sound of bullets whizzing through the air.

"How did you cut those vines?"

"I had a knife strapped to my ankle."

"I should have known you'd be prepared for just about anything. I'm really . . ." She stopped and began to shake as reaction set in. "I think I'm going to be sick."

Thad pulled her to the ground and pushed her head between her knees.

"Breathe through your mouth," he instructed.

She closed her eyes and took a few shaky breaths. He got down on his haunches in front of her.

"All right now?"

Suzanne opened her eyes and squinted in the darkness trying to make out his face.

"About as all right as anyone can be who's been crawling around in the dark on her belly through dirt and waist high weeds. Oh yeah, and dodging bullets. That's one of my personal favorite ways to spend an evening. Can we go home now?"

"Not just yet. Whoever shot at us has probably left the party, but I want to check it out anyway."

"I know this looks like my dad set me up, and for a moment I did believe it. He may be into a lot of things, but trying to get his own daughter murdered isn't one of them. He needs me to help him with his grand escape."

"You'd know. Stay here while I go take a look."

"No problem. My legs don't seem to be working properly."

Suzanne watched him blend into the darkness and disappear within seconds. It fascinated her to see how easily he could melt into the shadows considering he wasn't exactly a little guy. She leaned back against the tree and let her thoughts drift to her father.

Was he responsible for this latest shooting fiasco? She'd told Thad she didn't think so, but she couldn't quite block out the possibility that he'd used her. Did he send her to their old backyard so some Montane hired gun could find her and appease Muriel's family? Was this an eye for an eye kind of thing? She shook her head, not wanting to accept that her father would do something so despicable.

He may not need her love, but he did need her to get that bag of evidence. Saving himself and his precious Muriel was all he cared about. It wouldn't occur to him that putting his daughter in harm's way was a bad thing. Her father wasn't picky about a relationship when someone became a tool to be used.

Suzanne sat there nursing her hurt feelings until she had the sensation that she wasn't alone. Fear rose with the chilled bumps on her arms, as she struggled to her feet. Had the sniper found her hiding place? She needed to get out of here and hoped her wobbly legs wouldn't fail her.

She'd barely taken a couple steps when a long arm snaked out and clamped on her shoulder making a scream rise in her throat.

"Going somewhere?"

She whirled around and pressed a hand to her heart. "Oh my God! I thought you were the trigger-happy jerk. You keep scaring me like that and I'm going to have to do something really unpleasant to punish you, Thad Novak."

"Punish me? Hmm, okay. I've never been into S and M, but I bet you'd look great in black leather."

"And I'm sure you'd look adorable with a whip shoved up your nose. How come you're back so soon? Did you see anything?"

"Yeah. Cops. One of the neighbors called them when the music got so loud. The couple who live there are on vacation. Their college age son was house-sitting and decided to throw a party for forty or fifty of his closest friends."

"Did the police tell you all that?"

"No. I overheard the neighbor talking to them. I have very good hearing if you'll recall."

"I've also noticed that you can see in the dark. You're like some night predator."

"What can I say? I'm a man of many talents."

She let out a sniff. "Modest, too. I hope one of those talents includes getting us out of here."

"I've called for a cab. It'll meet us a couple of streets over."

"It is okay for us to go back to my place? Or do we have to worry about unwelcomed houseguests?"

"The house has been checked out. We're good to go."

Suzanne thought of the black feather.

"But that doesn't mean someone hasn't been there while we were gone."

"That's why you have me and your new security system."

"Right." She looked down at her clothes and back at Thad. "We're covered with dirt. You must be wanting a shower as much as I do."

"Is that an invitation to share and save on water? I may not be into the S and M scene, but I'm all for environmental conservation," he said keeping their light bantering going, as they started walking away.

"I'd love to wash your back, but I'm too strung out. By the way, thanks for saving my life – again."

"You're welcome. Try not to make it a habit."

Eight

Suzanne walked into her kitchen the next morning tying the sash of her robe.

"I can't believe I slept so late."

Thad turned from the stove.

"It's the meltdown after the adrenaline rush. Your body needed the sleep to recuperate."

He poured her a mug of coffee and set it on the table before pulling out a chair for her.

"Sit down and start with that. Your omelet will be ready in a minute."

"You made an omelet? I'm beginning to think you're not such a bad guy to have around after all."

"That's what I've been trying to tell you."

He walked back to the stove, retrieved the skillet, and tipped the food onto a plate before placing it in front of her. "Eat while it's hot."

She took a bite, chewed, and swallowed.

"This is really delicious. When did you learn to cook?"

"When I realized I was hungry."

She laughed.

"The master of evasion. Well, whatever the reason, I'm grateful. Thanks."

"Don't mention it." He filled a mug of coffee for himself and sat down across from her.

Suzanne scooped up another forkful.

"Aren't you eating?"

"I already have. I've been up for a while."

They made small talk while Suzanne ate. Thad topped off their coffee cups when she pushed her empty plate aside.

"Thanks again," she said wiping her mouth on her napkin.

"My pleasure."

"I've been trying to figure out how the person who shot at us knew I would be at my old family home, since I was so careful not to leave from my house here."

"How did you leave from the neighbors? Front or back door?"

"The front door, of course, or they would have wondered what was going on."

"Do you really think the Montanes would only have people watching your house?"

Suzanne visibly paled.

"Oh God. Do you think I've sicced the dogs on them by my carelessness?"

"Hopefully not, but I'll have someone keep an eye on your friends. You must understand that every time you leave your house you're going to be followed, because you are the key to finding your father."

"Not a very comforting thought." She looked at him from beneath her lashes. "I won't blame you if you want to come with me, but I really should go next door and explain about taking their phone."

"I took care of it."

"You did? How?"

"I promised the old guy I'd let him know when you got home okay. I set their phone on a table when they weren't looking. I doubt if they'll remember where they left it last night."

"Probably not. Greg's always grumbling about misplacing things. Don't you think I need to have a phone in case of an emergency? If what's going on isn't a crisis situation, I don't know what is."

"I'll see that you get one, but I'd rather you didn't give the number to your girlfriends, hairdresser, or whomever else women seem to think they can't live without. Also, try to keep the calls to a minimum."

"I'll be careful. What about the twenty bucks I took from Greg? How did you explain that?"

"I told them you needed to buy some very important feminine products and was short of cash."

She couldn't stop herself from giggling. "You really didn't say that, did you?"

He grinned. "No, but the fib was worth it to see your expression. I put the money by the phone."

"Once again I'm in your debt. I'll pay you back as soon as I finish my coffee."

"You don't have to."

"I don't like to owe people money. How is it that you know about female products?"

"Are you kidding? A guy can't turn on TV without seeing ads for that stuff."

She got up and carried the dirty dishes to the sink.

"Did you trace that number from my father?"

"Yes. That's the only time he used it."

"A phone bought for one call? He must be buying them in quantities. So we're back to square one. What do we do now?"

"Wait until he gets in touch with you again."

"What if he doesn't?"

"He will when the contents of that bag turns up in the wrong hands. I had someone go back this morning and look for it. They found the bag, but it was empty."

Suzanne almost dropped the dish she was rinsing. "What if my dad did send me to that house to get them off his back? What if he . . ."

"Don't worry about what ifs. You've got enough to think about just sticking to the facts."

"The fact is I don't think my father gives two cents about me; and I'm not too sure about my mother, either. I guess I've always known that. It just hurts to admit it. I remember when they were getting ready to divorce. I heard them arguing over child custody. Neither one of them wanted me, you see. Oh, there were little periods of time when they seemed to care, but it never lasted very long. I hope you know how lucky you are that you have parents who genuinely love you."

Years doing his job had made it necessary to keep most aspects of his personal life private, but it didn't seem to matter now when Thad heard the bleakness in Suzanne's voice. It obviously made her feel worse to think he had it so good – time to loosen up and share a bit of his real self with her.

"I never doubted that my parents loved me. They're gone now. They died years ago in a house fire."

Her mouth hung slightly open for a moment.

"I'm so sorry. Were they good people?"

"Very good."

"I know you must have been a wonderful son to them."

"What makes you say that?"

"Because despite you insisting you aren't a nice man, I believe you are. I also think you're the kind of person who's very loyal to the people you care about."

"I'd say that description fits you more than it does me."

"Really? I guess we don't always see ourselves as others do. Did your parents live on a farm, or did you make that part up, too? I had this fantasy about you helping with the plowing and feeding chickens."

"Dad had a vegetable garden and my mom kept a few chickens."

"How about those siblings you talked about. Do they exist?"

"Nope. Sorry. There's just me, myself, and I."

"Well, there goes that illusion. You're such a good liar you really had me believing your story."

He grimaced.

"Storyteller. Please. It sounds so much less devious."

"Well, either way you had parents who wanted you. I envy that."

Thad got up and tugged her to him.

"You deserve so damn much more than either of yours have ever given you," he said, and brushed his lips over her mouth.

She leaned back and looked up at him.

"Was that a pity kiss?"

"Yeah. For me."

Thad cupped her face between his hands before lowering his head again. Suzanne moaned beneath the onslaught of his probing kiss. His hands raced over her, greedy with the desire to touch. What bit of sanity he had left warned him that he would be taking advantage of her if he made love to her now, while she was in such a vulnerable state. Thad didn't want to be like her parents, using her just to satisfy his own needs. He managed to step back, although his body clenched in protest, and it took every ounce of willpower he had to pull away from her.

He cleared his throat.

"I think you should go to your room and get dressed now."

"Why do you keep doing that?"

"What?"

"Come on to me, and then back off."

"I told you, I don't want to hurt you."

She tilted her head to one side and stared at him.

"You know what I think?"

"Dare I ask?"

"You're just a big scaredy-cat. You're really afraid of allowing yourself to get too close to anyone and letting them get too close to you. Funny, but I never would have pegged you for a coward."

Suzanne started to walk away, but Thad grabbed her and scooped her up into his arms.

"Coward is it? I can't have you thinking that; your room or mine?"

"Mine's closest."

"Fine. Your room it is, then."

He laid her on the bed and quickly stripped his clothes off while she watched. Her eyes traveled down his length. He wanted her all right, in the most obvious way. He lowered himself next to her.

"Last chance to back out, Suzanne."

"Stop stalling, or do you enjoying driving me out of my mind?"

"If I am, I'm right there with you."

He spent long erotic minutes readying her body with such tenderness Suzanne couldn't help but admire his control or his expertise. Her fingers were clawing at him by the time he eased away.

"Hold on a second. I have to get something."

"I'm on the pill," she said and drew him back down to her. "Do me. Now. Please," she pleaded.

The warmth of his lips and the heat of his body seared her skin like a brand, marking her as his own. Pleasure tore through them as they strained against each other, eager to receive and give in return. Their bodies shuddered in release moments later. Thad rolled away, holding her hand to keep their connection.

"I know I shouldn't have let you get to me, but I'd be lying if I said I didn't enjoy this."

"I may never breathe again," Suzanne panted.

"Don't worry I'm very good at giving mouth to mouth."

"Yes you are; and you're much better in bed than James. You roar. He whimpered."

Thad let out a strangled cough.

"Well, you're a very dangerous woman, Suzanne Conway."

"Me? Dangerous?" She wrinkled her nose. "I don't think so."

"You made me lose all control. That's not a good thing in my line of work."

"I don't want you to think I'm promiscuous. You're just too darn sexy for your breeches."

"Breeches? Now there's a word you don't hear very much these days."

She chuckled.

"One of Nanadoo's favorites."

"Sounds like something she'd say. Just so you know, I would never think of you as promiscuous."

"Good, because I want us to do this again."

"You sure? Did it ever occur to you that I may be using you just for the sex?"

"I thought I was the one using you."

She shrugged.

"It doesn't matter. No strings. Remember?"

"No strings," he repeated.

"This could be the beginning of a beautiful, uncomplicated relationship. Our choice, Thad."

"Sometimes there aren't any choices, but let's not go into that."

"Let's not," she agreed, kissing him on one shoulder. "You taste salty."

"And you taste delicious," he said, his mouth toying with her lips.

"You're very good at this lovemaking business."

"We aim to please, ma'am."

Suzanne propped her arms up on his chest. "I bet you've been with a lot of women."

"I'm not the kiss and tell type, if it's a confession you're hoping for."

Her phone rang. She picked up the bedroom extension at his nod.

"What's that crazy father of yours gone and done now?"

"Nanadoo?"

Suzanne shot up into a sitting position.

"Have you seen Dad recently?"

"He's crashed out upstairs with a little slip of a girl who looks like she should still be wearing pigtails. What's going on, Suz Suz?"

"My dad is at your house right now?" she said repeating the words for Thad. He leaped off the bed and hurried into the living room to pick up the phone. "I never expected him to go there."

"Sometimes the last thing you expect to happen is often the first thing that does. He showed up on our doorstep late last night."

"I hate to ask, but it's very important to keep him there. I need to see him."

"Oh my. It sounds like he's in a spot of trouble as usual."

"More than a spot this time. Just don't let him leave; and don't tell him I'm coming there. I'll get to you as soon as I can."

"What has he done to hurt you now?"

"I'll explain when I see you. I wouldn't ask you to be involved if there was any other way."

"All right. Call me when you arrive, and I'll have the colonel meet you. Be careful. I love you."

"I love you, too."

They said their goodbyes, and Thad walked back into the bedroom.

"Who's the colonel?"

The sight of him standing there naked fogged Suzanne's brain for a moment. She licked her lips.

Who had she been kidding when she said no strings attached? Remembering how it felt to be pressed against his hard body caused her blood pressure to spike to a dizzying level. She couldn't stop staring.

"Uh, Suzanne?"

"Hmm? Oh! The colonel is Nanadoo's husband," she said, scrambling off the bed.

"Is he retired military?"

"No, it's his nickname because of how he looks."

"Let me guess, a Colonel Sanders look alike?"

"Yes. You heard the conversation. I've got to get to Nanadoo's before Dad decides to take off. I'm beyond furious with him for going to them. He'll have to answer to me if they get hurt."

Thad walked into the room.

"I've noticed you're quick to want to protect your friends from your father's antics."

"I've had plenty of practice. Are you saying that's a bad thing?"

"No. I just wonder why you don't look after yourself when he uses you."

"Doesn't one of the Ten Commandments say we're supposed to honor our parents?"

"Yes, but I don't think there's anything about enabling them."

Suzanne came out of the bathroom, wrapped in a towel, her hair still damp from her shower.

"I better see about going on one of the ferries. I should have done it sooner, but I'm kind of rattled. We can either do the Catalina Flyer, which only leaves from Newport Beach. It takes a little over an hour. Or we can use the Catalina Express. It gives us more options because they go from Long Beach, San Pedro, and Dana Point. They also have like twenty-five departures a day. Tell me which one you think would be best, and I'll call to make sure the schedules haven't changed."

"Neither. I took care of our transportation while you were in the shower. We'll be using the Island Express Helicopter Service. It only takes fourteen minutes, and we have the choice of going from Long Beach or San Pedro."

She clutched at her towel.

"Did you say helicopter?"

"I did. Have you ever flown in one before?"

"No, but I'm sure it'll be way more expensive than the ferries."

"Is that your way of saying you're afraid to fly?"

"No, but I'm not sure I can afford it, that's all."

"I have it covered."

He glanced at his watch.

"A car will be here to pick us up in twenty minutes. Let me just take a quick shower."

Thad appeared less than fifteen minutes later, dressed and ready to leave. He frowned when he found Suzanne pacing in the living room, chewing on her thumbnail.

"Are you all right?"

"I'm worried about Nanadoo and the colonel."

"I told you don't go anticipating trouble. You've got enough on your plate as it is."

Suzanne barely stopped herself from pressing her nose against the window of the helicopter, as she looked at the scene below. Living in southern California made it easy for her to visit Nanadoo's home on Catalina Island over the years. But she'd always gone by boat. Viewing it by air gave her a whole new appreciation of the bay with its variegated navy blue water shimmering with colorful   hues of emerald green. Lines of various watercraft bobbed at their mooring sites. A large cruise ship sat majestically with its bright white paint glistening in the sun while the ocean rippled quietly against its graceful hull.

The island's most recognizable landmark, the circular iconic Catalina Casino outside Avalon Harbor, caught her attention. She smiled remembering the first time Nanadoo took her on a tour of the beautiful old building. Suzanne could still recall how awed she'd been staring at the rose-hued walls, arching fifty-foot ceiling, and the five Tiffany Chandeliers.

She leaned closer, studying the rocky coastline, the chewing gum magnate Wrigley's mansion, and the herd of North American Bison that had scattered themselves among the hills. The beasts were introduced to the island from a movie filmed there in 1924. Nanadoo told her the buffalo ended up faring better than the film.

Suzanne knew other movies were filmed on the island since the silent movie era and that stars still liked to vacation here. Nanadoo rarely missed an opportunity to finagle an invitation to the various movie sets and had an impressive collection of filmdom autographs and photos for her efforts.

Thinking of her godmother drew her attention away from the sights. They were getting ready to land. Her stomach muscles began to tense up, anticipating what she should say to her father. How could she convince him to give up his dangerous scheme? She hoped she would find the right words.

As soon as the helicopter touched down, Thad helped her climb out. Suzanne put her hand up to shade her eyes from the sun while she looked around.

"I don't see the colonel's golf cart."

Thad frowned.

"Golf cart? Is he planning on taking us golfing?"

"No. Golf carts are a popular mode of transportation on the island. The colonel loves driving his around. He prides himself on being punctual. He should be here by now. I'm going to phone them."

"Good idea," Thad said, and waited while she made her call.

"No one answered. I left a message telling them we're here, but I think we should go to the house ourselves."

She saw her own worry mirrored in his eyes.

"I think you're right," he said, quietly.

Nine

Suzanne gave the driver the address and leaned slightly forward in her seat, as though that might somehow make them get to her godmother's sooner. They wound their way up into the hills. Thad instructed the man to let them off a few houses short of their destination. While he paid the driver, Suzanne fumbled with her seatbelt and opened the door ready to start running, but Thad stopped her.

"Call again, and say you're still waiting to be picked up. Leave another message if you have to."

"Why? I thought we were in a hurry to get to the house."

I don't want to announce our arrival in case anyone else is listening to their calls."

Suzanne made her call and waited. One ring. Two rings. Three rings and on for six full rings. She paused, gripping the phone, and left a quick message before tucking her phone away.

"Please, can we go to them now?" she pleaded.

He took her by the hand, and they jogged the short distance until she stopped just short of the condominium, and pointed toward the Mediterranean style condo sandwiched between two other similar units. Suzanne dug a house key out of her purse and was ready to rush up the four cement steps leading to the front door.

"Hold onto it for now," Thad said. "Tell me about the layout."

"The ground level has a patio in back with a sliding glass door to the living room. The kitchen, an office, and a half bathroom are also on the main floor. The second story has a couple of bedrooms with bathrooms. Both bedrooms have sliding glass doors leading to outside decks with stairs going down to the patio on either side of the house. The front door opens into an entryway that leads into the living room. Oh; and there's also a door going outside from the kitchen."

He squeezed her hand.

"Good job. Do they have access to the beach from here?"

"Not unless they hack their way through a lot of plant life. They take the road we just used."

"All right. We'll go around back and try the door leading to the living room. Do not, I repeat, do not try to muscle me out of the way until I know it's safe inside."

"Muscle you out of the way? It'd be like trying to move a Mac truck with a toy bulldozer."

They made their way along one side of the house adjusting their feet to the gradually sloping terrain. Suzanne kept close to Thad, as he flattened his body against the wall until he could peer through a corner of the glass door. He tested the slider and found it unlocked. The door slid silently open on its track when he nudged the handle.

He eased himself into the empty living room, motioning for Suzanne to stay outside. Thad stood for a moment listening, assessing his surroundings. The house was eerily quiet for someone who was supposed to be expecting company. He inched his way down the short hallway to the kitchen.

What he saw made him feel like he'd been punched in the stomach. Had they been too late? Two elderly people sat in chairs with their upper bodies slumped onto the kitchen table. Two tea cups, one tipped on its side in the saucer sat in front of them on the table and two others were placed near empty chairs. Cookies, arranged in a neat little pile lay on a plate in the center of the table.

Thad hurried over and pressed a couple fingers gently against first the woman's neck, and then the man's. Relief flowed through him when he felt the distinct throbbing of a steady pulse in each of them. He ran from the room and bounded upstairs, going quickly knowing Suzanne wouldn't be content to wait outside much longer despite his warning for her to stay put.

Both bedroom doors stood open to empty rooms. He entered the one on the right and found everything to be in neat order and the bathroom empty. Thad didn't bother to linger, as he headed across the landing to the other rooms where he discovered an unmade bed in the bedroom and towels thrown on the floor in the bathroom.

It would seem Suzanne's father decided to take off and ruin any chance of a family reunion. Not only that, he had to go tell her it looked like they'd had a tea party before they left and spiked the old couple's brew as a farewell gesture – which just went to show some people were lousy houseguests.

Thad found Suzanne peering through the sliding glass door. She moved away when she saw him. He slid the door open and stepped outside.

"I checked the carport. The colonel's cart is gone. We must have missed him. Is Nanadoo here?"

"Yes."

She let out a ragged sigh. "Thank God. Did you find my dad and his little chickee?"

"No."

Suzanne started to push by him. Thad seized her shoulder making her scowl at him.

"What are you doing? I want to go inside and see Nanadoo."

"Your Nanadoo . . . he stopped. "What's her real name? I'll feel like an idiot calling her that."

"Nesta, and the colonel is Liam. Liam and Nesta Harold. Now will you please let me go? I'm surprised she hasn't come looking for me. She's probably wondering why I'm still standing out here."

"No, she's not. They're both in the kitchen." He kept hold of her. "They've been drugged."

She cried out. Thad made her face him, as she pushed at his hands trying to break free.

"Listen to me," he said in a sharp voice when she continued struggling. "They're alive. I'm sure they'll be fine as soon as whatever they took wears off. But you should call a doctor to have them checked out to be on the safe side. I'll take you to them now."

He held her by the hand and led her inside. Suzanne pulled away as soon as they entered the kitchen. Thad let her go. A gasp escaped her as she touched them each on their backs before looking at him again.

"I never expected my dad to stoop this low," she said in a shaky voice. "Did he take off?"

"Yes, as far as I can tell."

"Good riddance."

Thad and Suzanne sat in the living room drinking coffee. Late afternoon shadows put them in semi-darkness. The doctor came and went, satisfied with his patients' vital signs. Thad helped him carry them upstairs to their bedroom while Suzanne saw that they were comfortably tucked beneath the blankets.

She explained that Liam and Nesta hadn't been sleeping well lately and misjudged the dosage for a sleep aid. Thad hoped the doctor was convinced because the last thing he wanted right now was to have the local authorities asking questions. Enough people were already involved in this ever growing muddle.

It reminded him of a stain that just kept spreading wider and wider.

"Leave it to my dad to skitter away like the rat that he is. Wait till I get my hands on him." Suzanne set her mug down with a bang. "I think I'll go talk to the neighbors. They may know something."

"I already did. No one is home at the condo on one side, and the old woman in the other said she didn't see or hear a thing."

"Her name is Mrs. Neal. She has a little trouble seeing and hearing."

"That was seemed pretty obvious when I saw from the thick glasses she wore and the hearing aids in both ears. I damned near had to pound the door down before she answered. She thought I was the bottled water guy."

"We'll have to wait awhile until before we can question Nanadoo and the colonel. I still have to find out what happened to his cart."

As soon as they finished their coffee, Thad stood up and took their mugs. "I'll take these to the kitchen and start on our dinner."

Suzanne eventually moved off the sofa, still massaging her head with the tips of her fingers.

"I'm so upset I don't think I can eat, but I should help you," she murmured.

"I'll manage," Thad said, putting his arm around her shoulder and squeezing softly. "You go check on Liam and Nesta."

"See," she said, smiling as her body straightened a bit. "I told you that you were a nice man."

"Well, don't let it get around. I wouldn't want to spoil the tough guy image I've been cultivating."

Suzanne came into the kitchen with an armful of sheets and towels. Thad turned from the stove to watch her.

"What's all that?" he asked, pointing toward the massive bundle she carried.

"Sheets and towels my Dad and his girlfriend used. Not a very tidy couple."

Thad choked back a chuckle, coughing instead.

"How are the patients doing? Awake yet?" he asked.

"They woke up enough to talk to me a little bit."

"That's good."

"Made me feel a lot better, I can tell you." She sniffed the air. "What is that heavenly aroma?"

"My quick version of Steak Diane. The potatoes are in the toaster oven, and I threw together a salad."

"I'm suddenly finding my appetite again. Thank you for doing all that."

"It wasn't difficult. The Harolds keep a well-stocked kitchen. I hope they won't mind, but besides taking their steaks, I also raided their wine cabinet."

"They'd want you to help yourself. I'll take care of this then set the table."

Suzanne walked to an alcove in the kitchen and shoved open a folding door, revealing a washer and dryer inside.

Lifting the lid to the washing machine, she began stuffing soiled laundry inside. A few minutes later while she was setting the table, the telephone rang.

"I'll answer that in Liam's office," she said, suddenly animated as she moved toward the sound.

"Check the caller ID before you answer. Let it go if it looks at all suspicious," he yelled at her disappearing back.

Just as Thad was pouring their wine, she returned, with a satisfied look on her face.

"Now, I know what happened to the colonel's cart," she smirked. The guy who owns the golf cart rental place at the harbor found it among all of his carts. It must have been put there when his back was turned. He's going to drive it up here."

"He's certain it's Liam's?"

"Yes. He didn't even have to check. The colonel fancies himself an artist and painted some beach scenes on the sides of the cart. Most of the permanent residents recognize it."

"All right. In the meantime, let's eat while it's still hot."

Thad waited until they'd taken their first few bites of food before speaking.

"So," he queried, thoughtfully, "this guy doesn't have any idea when Liam's cart showed up?"

Suzanne shook her head.

"Doesn't he check his own stock?"

"He said he was busy with so many people coming ashore from the cruise ship to rent carts. He works alone, so once the people paid, he gave them keys, and they got the carts themselves. Dad must have driven the cart down there and took one of the ferries."

"Or he may still be hiding on the island."

She took a sip of wine and wiped her mouth on a bright red cloth napkin.

"That would be stupid now, wouldn't it?."

"Not necessarily. Haven't you ever tried to find something you misplaced only to find it was right there in front of you all the time?"

Later, Suzanne thought about Thad's theory that her father may not have left the island. She supposed it was possible they'd stayed. After all, her dad wasn't a young man, and he had a pregnant woman in tow. They were probably worn out from being on the run for so long. Still, the idea seemed kind of farfetched to her; staying on the move was part of his strategy to keep one step ahead of the Montanes.

Her restlessness drove her out of bed. She walked across the landing to check on Liam and Nesta. They were both sprawled on their backs, softly snoring. She leaned over and gave them each a kiss on the forehead before tiptoeing from the room.

Pulling open her room's slider, Suzanne stepped out onto the deck. Twinkling lights from the harbor boats sparkled like tiny diamonds in the midst of the casino's brightly lit building glowing like a giant gem. Her thoughts wandered to Thad, sleeping on the living room sofa. Being awake wouldn't be so bad if he was up here with her. But she knew he was right where he said he'd be.

"Better if I stay downstairs," he'd said, *"just in case anyone decides to come calling during the night."*

Suzanne still didn't know who he worked for and how it was he had access to so many resources. But she did know she'd never met anyone like him before. He seemed to be able to do almost anything he put his mind to. Excellent cook, fantastic lover, and a handy guy to have around when things got dicey.

And she'd been thrust into some pretty serious situations lately, no thanks to her father. The more she stood there thinking about her dad, the more she was convinced he was gone. He'd want to leave under the cover of secrecy, which meant looking for a less commercial mode of transportation other than the passenger ferries or via air transport. He'd want to go by private boat.

Suzanne straightened up and gripped the railing. Of course. Why hadn't she thought of this before? Once, when she was here visiting while on a college break, she received a call from a friend inviting her to a party in Long Beach. Her friend had waited too late to call. A boat was the only way Suzanne could get off the island.

Enter good old Captain George, a boozed up, washed out ex ferry captain with a small yacht that looked and smelled worse than he did. But he worked cheap, and if you gave him a bottle of booze, the price went down even further. He also didn't ask nosy questions.

Suzanne blushed now, remembering how Nanadoo had caught her trying to swipe the whiskey from Liam's liquor cabinet. She never made that trip, but she'd heard about other people using Captain George over the years. She didn't know if the man still had his business, or if he was even alive. But she would mention him to Thad in the morning on the off chance her father had taken advantage of this resource.

She walked slowly back inside and tumbled onto the bed. It felt good to come up with some information that might help. Suzanne also reminded herself to call Heather and apprise her of the latest development. She knew Thad didn't want her giving out her new cell number, but he couldn't have meant Heather. She was her best friend. They'd always looked out for each other.

He may not understand their special bond, so it'd probably be best if she didn't mention the call.

"It's about time you called," Heather scolded. "I've certainly left you enough messages."

"I didn't know. I haven't been ignoring you. I don't have my usual phone."

"What are you talking about? Where are you? I went by your house, but no one was home."

"I'm at Nanadoo's."

"Oh. I guess I can't blame you for wanting to get away after your aborted cruise."

"I didn't come for fun. Dad and his girlfriend showed up here."

"He did? I sure wouldn't have expected that. What about all the money he took? I hope he gave you some of it, considering everything he's put you through."

"I don't have it because he and his woman left before Thad and I got here."

"Damn that wily old devil. Did he say anything to Nesta and Liam that might help you find him? I mean, he must have left some kind of clue."

"The only thing my dad left was some dirty sheets and towels. He also thanked them for their hospitality by drugging their tea before he left."

Heather sucked in a breath.

"What a rotten thing to do. Are they all right?"

"Yes, thank the lord. They're downstairs with Thad. They haven't been able to give us much help about what happened. He thinks my dad could still be on the island. I don't agree. I hoped to talk to a guy who used to run private trips, but Liam said he died."

"Well, be sure to keep me in the loop. I get so worried when I don't hear from you."

"Thad got me another phone. I'll give you the number. But please don't share it, and I'd rather you didn't use it unless you really have to. He thinks it's safer that way."

"He's probably right. You know you can trust me. I'm so glad he's looking after you, Suzie."

"I never thought I'd say this, but so am I."

"I'll keep an eye on your house, since you don't know when you'll be back."

"Maybe you shouldn't go near the place. I don't want anyone else getting hurt because of me."

"This is all your dad's fault. I want to do what I can to help you. Do you still keep your house key in the same spot?"

"No. Thad had me move it to the garden shed." Suzanne told her the location. "You don't have to do this. Knowing him he probably has someone watching."

"Okay, if you think that's for the best. Now give me your new cell number and remember what I said about keeping me in the loop. We're in this together, girlfriend."

Suzanne gave her the number, and they said their goodbyes.

She put fresh sheets on the bed her father and Muriel used during their brief stay. She did this as quickly as possible, not wanting to linger and think about them sleeping together. Cleaning the bathroom was next on her to-do list. She certainly didn't want to leave any of these household chores to her godmother or the colonel considering how her father treated them.

Suzanne also thought it might help if she stayed up here for a while rather than be downstairs. She didn't want to be a distraction while Thad gently probed the old couple for any information that might help to find their errant houseguests.

Captain George's death created another dead end in their search for her father, frustrating Suzanne, even more. Anger swirled around inside her when she remembered how Nesta and Liam looked, slumped over the kitchen table. The painful image made her hand jerk on the sponge she was using to wipe the bathroom counter, causing a small decorative box to tip over, spilling its contents of cotton balls.

She set the sponge aside when she spied a small slip of paper under the box. Suzanne eased it out and saw a single name and a local phone number written there. She wouldn't have thought anything of it except for one very important detail.

The note had been written in her father's handwriting.

"It can't be this easy," she muttered, as she ran into the bedroom clutching the paper in her hand. Suzanne swallowed a few times, trying not to get too excited before she called the number.

"Hello?" a man's gravelly voice answered after three rings.

Suzanne's palms felt clammy, and her heart pounded like a tennis ball against the walls of her chest.

"Is this Dewey?"

"Who's asking?"

"A friend."

"I have lots of friends, lady. Just which one might you be?"

Suzanne bit her lip, hoping what she was about to say would tell her what she needed to know.

"I have a lot of friends, too. You may have met a couple of them recently."

"That so?"

"I'm referring to an older, distinguished looking gentleman and a young pregnant woman traveling together. I was supposed to meet with them on the island, but I arrived later than I expected, and we missed each other. It's very important that I talk to them. They, um, might need my assistance."

Seconds ticked by. Suzanne was about to say something else when he broke the silence.

"Meet me at the harbor where the private boats are moored. Thirty minutes. Come alone, or don't come at all," he instructed and severed the connection.

Ten

The receiver slid from her fingers and landed on the bed with a soft thud, freeing her hand to press against the front of her blouse where her heart still hammered. She breathed in deeply, holding it a few seconds, before releasing the air, taking calming breaths. Her fingers clenched around the scrap of paper. She looked down and blinked, surprised to find it still there. Was this the break she'd been hoping for? Could this man lead her to her father? The only way to find out would be to keep the meeting he'd set up.

But how could she leave here without alerting anyone else in the house about this new development? Thad would probably know if she tried to sneak out considering his watchful nature. She also realized if she didn't go downstairs pretty soon someone would be coming up here wondering what was keeping her so long. Suzanne knew she had to find a way to get them all out of the house. It'd have to be some kind of an emergency, but barring setting the house on fire, that wasn't likely to happen.

She stood up and started pacing while stealing anxious glances at her watch. The man gave her thirty minutes. Precious seconds elapsed, as she tried to think of a way to solve her dilemma. She caught a movement through the sliding glass door and walked over just in time to see a calico cat nimbly leap onto the railing outside.

She recognized the feline as Mrs. Neal's wayward pet, Toby. She knew he often wandered over here in search of food, as the old woman didn't always remember to feed him. Nanadoo and the colonel not only looked out for the cat's needs, but were also diligent about checking up on their elderly neighbor as well. The thought of their concern for Mrs. Neal's

96

welfare suddenly sparked an idea on how to get everyone away from the house. She dashed over to the phone and called Heather back.

"I have to meet with this Dewey. He may know where Dad is. Will you help me?" she pleaded after explaining how she'd found the man's name and phone number.

"You know I'd like to, but what can I do being so far away?"

"Remember Mrs. Neal, the elderly woman next door? You've met her a couple of times when you were here with me."

"You mean the old lady who can't see or hear very well?"

"Yes, that's the one. I want you to phone and tell Nanadoo that you just received a call from Mrs. Neal saying she fell and needs help. Explain that I gave her your number from your last visit. Tell Nanadoo she must have called you in confusion. I hate to ask you, but you did say you wanted to help me. Can you make it sound convincing enough?"

"That won't be problem for a drama queen like me. You just get yourself ready to leave."

"Thanks, Heather. I owe you."

"Then you won't mind when I collect my payment as soon as you find your dad."

"If I know you, it'll be a large piece of chocolate fudge cake. Please hurry. I'm running out of time."

"Hang tight for a few more minutes."

Suzanne sat on the bed digging her fingers into the bedspread, staring at the phone. She actually jumped when it rang. She barely remembered to breathe waiting until Liam yelled upstairs.

"Mildred Neal's had a fall. We're going over to check on her."

"Oh gosh, I hope it's not serious," Suzanne called back. "Better take Thad with you in case she needs lifting. I'll be right there as soon as I change my shirt. It got wet while I was cleaning the shower."

"All right."

Suzanne waited a few more heartbeats until she heard them leave. She sprinted downstairs, looked through the window to be sure they were inside the Neal condo before she ran out, and climbed into Liam's golf cart. He usually left the key inside and luckily today wasn't any exception.

She dared a peek at her watch and inhaled a quick breath between her teeth. Thank goodness the route was downhill all the way to the harbor. She should be able to make her secret appointment with the mysterious Dewey, if she drove like a maniac. Suzanne gripped the wheel and spun around a curve. It wasn't until she was halfway to her destination when she realized she had no idea what the man looked like. Thad wouldn't have let something so important slip his mind.

Thinking of him made Suzanne wince with guilt for sneaking off again without telling him. She hoped her decision to leave him behind wouldn't damage the new budding closeness they'd enjoyed since making love. Thad, on the other hand may not be so ready to forgive her once he found out about her latest trickery. And what about the colonel and Nanadoo? They probably weren't going to be too happy with her, either.

But what other choice did she have? Dewey made it clear he wouldn't help her if she didn't show up solo. Sometimes you make choices, and sometimes choices make you. Surely she couldn't be blamed for seizing this opportunity to follow up what could turn out to be a major clue in finding her father.

Liam took a moment to give a couple of courtesy knocks before trying the handle.

"I usually get after Mildred for not locking her doors, but this time I'm glad she didn't," he explained to Thad when the door swung open and they stepped inside.

"Millie? It's Nesta. Are you all right?"

No answer. She gave the two men a worried look.

"You two split up and start looking down here while I check the upstairs," Thad suggested.

Liam found her seconds later lying on a lounger outside. He yelled to let Thad know, while Nesta scurried over to peer closely at her friend.

"Oh dear. She must have fallen here and managed to crawl onto this lounger before she passed out. I just hope she doesn't have a concussion."

"I just hope she's alive," Liam muttered.

Thad joined them and immediately checked for a pulse.

"Her breathing is good," he said, "and there isn't any evidence of injuries. It looks to me as though she's asleep. Why don't you see if you can wake her?"

Nesta gave Mildred's shoulder a gentle shake.

"Millie? Can you hear me?"

Mildred's eyes fluttered open then blinked several times behind her thick glasses, as she tried to focus on the faces in front of her.

"Nesta? Is that you?" She struggled to sit up. "Did you tell me you were coming over?"

"Easy now. We don't want you doing any damage until we know if you're hurt from your fall."

"What fall? I came out here to take a nap." She pushed her glasses further up her nose. "Forgot to remove my glasses again, I see."

"We're here to find out if you're all right. I understand you took a tumble," Nesta explained.

"Tumble? What in the world are you jabbing about?"

Liam turned his head away and whispered to Thad.

"She gets confused sometimes."

Thad nodded and got down on his haunches next to the lounger. "Hello, Mrs. Neal. Do you recall seeing me here before?"

She squinted her eyes. "Oh yes. You're the nice young man from the water company. I don't need a refill just yet."

Nesta patted the woman's hand.

"He's not from the water company, Millie. He's a friend of Suzanne's. They're visiting us right now."

"That's nice. How is your daughter? Such a sweet girl."

No one corrected her that Suzanne was the goddaughter. The main priority had to be finding out whether or not the woman had fallen and didn't realize it.

"Suzanne is fine. We just received a phone call from a friend of hers saying you contacted her because you'd fallen and needed our help."

"What nonsense is this? I didn't have a fall," she said, moving her legs off the lounger.

Thad stood up and helped her.

"Are you saying you didn't call a friend of Suzanne's?"

"I did not. If I needed help I'd call Liam and Nesta myself. I don't have numbers for any of Suzanne's friends. Why would I?"

"Why would you, indeed?" Thad looked at Liam and Nesta. "Speaking of your goddaughter, in case you haven't noticed she's conspicuously absent."

"She said she had to change her blouse."

"Well, it's certainly taking her long enough," Nesta added.

"Yes, and I think I know why. Liam, it's time we check to see if your golf cart is still here."

"I don't know why it wouldn't be."

"Did you leave the key in after the last time you used it?"

"I always do."

"I suppose Suzanne is aware of that."

"Yes. Did I do something wrong?"

Thad flashed him a frustrated sigh.

"No, but I did."

Suzanne brought the cart to a shuddering halt arriving at her destination three minutes late. She flipped off the seatbelt and hopped out, landing with both feet smacking against the smooth asphalt. She made sure she parked close to the harbor. It was the only way she could think to connect with this Dewey.

She fisted her hands on her hips and looked around. The area emptied out pretty fast once the cruise ships left taking the hundreds of tourists with them. She could see a few people walking in front of the shops and several men dressed in gray pants and shirts cleaning up litter.

A pelican landed on a nearby rock drawing her attention. The bird flapped its large wings to dry them out. He stretched his neck and wiggled his head back and forth, causing the gray pouch hanging from his beak to flop back and forth like an empty laundry bag. She watched as he folded his wings snug against his body, closed his eyes, and settled down for a nap.

Suzanne turned from the bird to focus her attention on the harbor when a small takeout food box landed at her feet making her jump back seconds before a long handled grabber picked up the carton.

"We tend to frown on littering here, miss."

Her head jerked up at the sound of the gravelly voice. Suzanne realized she was staring at one of the cleanup men. He stared back, scrutinizing her shorts and sweat streaked blouse, with his dark eyes lingering long enough to make her cross her arm over her breasts.

She wanted to go, but steeled herself to stay. She'd gone to a lot of trouble to find out if this creepy looking man might be able to tell her something about her father. Suzanne shifted from one foot to the other, bringing her a bit closer to the cart. She'd left the key in the ignition. At least she wouldn't have to fumble around for it if she ended up having to leave in a hurry.

Suzanne gave him what she hoped came across as a confident look, as she lowered her arms to point at the tool he'd used to lift the dirty box into the bag he carried.

"I don't litter, but you obviously know what it's like to have to clean up messes other people leave."

He nodded.

"Yeah, and sometimes those people leave a long, dirty trail of garbage."

"Yes they do. So tell me. What can you do to help me clear up my particular mess?"

"I have a boat. I dropped them off in San Pedro."

She gulped in a quick breath.

"Did you ask him where he was going exactly?"

"He paid me not to ask questions, but I heard the woman say something about staying with friends there named Martinez."

"Did the man look all right? I mean, as far as you could tell, he wasn't hurt was he?"

"There are all kinds of ways of being hurt, lady. Some just showed themselves more than others. But he looked okay as far as I could tell. Maybe a little tired, but not bad otherwise."

"Thank goodness."

"Aren't you going to ask me about the girl?"

"No. She's nothing to me. I don't know her, and I don't want to know her."

He lifted bushy brows.

"You sound pretty sure. How do you know if that won't change someday?"

"It won't if I have anything to say about it. I appreciate your help, but I don't have any money to pay you. I should have thought about that. I'll bring you something later. Where can I find you?"

His hand tightened on the bag.

"I don't want your money."

"Then why did you agree to meet with me?"

"Because I know the kind of things the Montanes do to people who cross them."

Suzanne couldn't stop herself from raising her own eyebrows.

"You know the Montanes?"

"Yeah, and they know me."

She caught the unmistakable sound of bitterness in his voice and watched the almost savage way Dewey rammed his stick against the bare ground.

"What did you mean by *the kind of things they do to people*?"

He shook his head.

"Forget it."

"Tell me. Please."

He surprised her by thrusting his face so close to her that Suzanne could smell nicotine on his breath. She stumbled back bumping her hip against the side of the cart.

"You don't want to know. Ever."

He turned around and walked away, leaving Suzanne's insides shuddering at the implication of his harsh words.

Eleven

Suzanne sat on the sofa between Liam and Nesta, as Thad paced in front of them. His long legs carried him from one end of the small living room and back again in rapid spurts of restless tension. He finally stopped directly in front of her and crossed his arms over his chest. Anger rolled off him in undulating waves. Suzanne stared down at her hands clasped in her lap, unable to face his fierce scowl.

She felt like a little girl at school, preparing herself to receive a scolding from the principal. She knew she deserved it, but wished she could be anyplace else at the moment.

"Did I, or did I not tell you, no more going off on your own?"

She lifted her head and gave Thad the benefit of her full attention.

"Yes you did, but I . . ."

"No buts, Suzanne. What you did was very dangerous."

"You did take an awful risk, honey," Nesta agreed.

"I already told you; Dewey insisted I meet him on my own. I'm fine, so why are you all so upset?"

"You didn't know what was going to happen when you left here," Thad insisted.

"I'm sorry I worried everyone. But instead of bawling me out, you might try to remember that I did get some valuable information. It could help us find my father."

Thad jammed his hands in his pockets.

"How valuable it is remains to be seen. Do you have any idea how many people by the name of Martinez there probably are in San Pedro?"

"No, but we can get out the phonebook and start making calls."

"What if they have an unlisted number? I don't suppose that entered your mind?"

Suzanne shot to her feet, fueled with her own anger now.

"What entered my mind was I finally had a clue to my father's whereabouts; and if you'd stop criticizing me long enough, you'd know it's more than we had this morning."

She looked at Liam and Nesta.

"I wanted to do something to help without involving anyone else."

"If that's true, then why did you drag Heather into your little scheme?" Thad taunted.

Suzanne did her best to mask her surprise.

"How did you find out about that?"

"Did you think I wouldn't?"

"Okay, have it your way. I called her earlier to let her know where I was, and she offered to do anything she could to help me."

"Why do you find it so necessary to apprise her of your every move?"

"I told you, she's a worrywart. Friends take care of friends."

"What about your friends here? Do you even give a damn about our feelings?" he said, taking his hands out of his pockets to point at himself and then to Liam and Nesta.

"Of course I do. That's why I'm trying to fix things the best way I know how."

"You can't fix stupidity," Thad growled.

Nesta started to protest the insult, but Liam squeezed her hand and stood up, pulling her with him.

"I think it'd be a good idea if we went into the kitchen, my love. Let's give the kids some privacy."

Suzanne waited until they left. The room had gone as quiet as a tomb.

"I know you're angry, and you think I did a dumb thing. I'm sorry that I can't be what you want, or follow your carefully laid out plans for me. But if it makes you feel any better to call me stupid, then be my guest. You aren't the first person to do so, and you probably won't be the last."

Thad ran a hand around the back of his neck.

"I meant your father when I made that crack about stupidity. Do you have any idea what it does to me when I don't know whether or not you're safe? It nearly tore me apart when I realized you'd gone off on your own again."

She stared at him, rendered speechless by his unexpected confession. Was there anything more surprising than a strong man admitting that he could be weak? That something could break inside him, and you were the one responsible? Suzanne sensed Thad wanted to keep his feelings bottled up because he didn't want to confess to needing anyone. But she knew that sometimes emotions filled a person so full they couldn't be contained, no matter how tightly you tried to screw on the lid.

"I do care about your feelings, Thad. I don't try to worry you on purpose. I really did feel awful when I left here without telling you, but I had to do what I thought was right for my dad. If I had told you and let you make the decision for me, it would be a lot easier to face you now, because then I could blame you if things go wrong."

Suzanne went to him and put her arms around his waist, burying her face against his chest. He resisted her for a moment, before gathering her to him and resting a cheek on top of her head. They stood there quietly drawing comfort from each other. Their anger was gone now, faded away as the energy that fed it evolved into another emotion.

She'd been prepared for anger, not this new, raw emotion from Thad. She'd wondered if his feelings for her were more than just physical; and now, she had her answer.

"I think I may be falling in love with you," she whispered, and felt a shudder go through him.

"And I think I may be falling in love with you right back." He moved away a little, so he could look at her. "I'm sorry I came down on you so hard."

"I deserved it. I need to learn to be a better team player."

"It would help. Have you always been so sneaky?"

"No. It's a recently required skill."

Thad let out a low groan.

"God help me."

"I suppose you'll have to think of a way to get even."

He fingered a lock of her hair and gave it a hard yank. "How's that for a start?"

"Ouch! That wasn't what I had in mind, but I hope it made you feel better."

"Not even half close, but it'll have to do for now."

Thad may be falling in love with her, but apparently that didn't take away the fact that he was still smarting from her latest deception. He called her sneaky. The word left a bad taste in her mouth. Had she inherited one of her father's less than admirable traits?

Suzanne didn't like the idea of that. But sometimes you have to embrace their habits, in order to capture the bad guys. She didn't like the idea of thinking of her father as being one of the bad guys. But so far he wasn't exactly behaving like someone who should be wearing a white hat, either.

Wendell Conway wiped beads of sweat off his brow with the back of a hand. A very shaky hand he noticed. No surprise there. He'd been living on his nerves for weeks, and the stress was taking its toll, robbing him of a little more stamina each day. His eyes shifted to Muriel, lying curled up, asleep. His expression softened.

She looked as exhausted as he felt. Who could blame her – the way they'd been forced to hopscotch all over the state, trying to steer clear of her vindictive father? They had to be so cautious, watching every move they made because Caesar Montane was not a forgiving man, not even to his own daughter.

Daughters. Lovely gifts to be cherished. Wendell thought about Suzanne. He hadn't missed the hurt in her voice during their brief conversation. He couldn't blame her, knowing he was largely responsible for that pain. Was he any better than Caesar – the way he deliberately used his own daughter as bait, when he sent her to their old house looking for the green bag?

He'd lied when he said the phones were there. But the ruse became necessary to shift some of the focus away from him. God knows he hadn't wanted to set Suzanne up, and he'd prayed they wouldn't hurt her. He'd been desperate. He had to be so careful who he could trust. Too many people were waiting in line to betray him. He swore the Montanes must have eyes and ears everywhere, not to mention arms that reached out like deadly tentacles ready to squeeze the life out of him.

Wendell closed his eyes wishing he could forget how Suzanne said she'd been shot. Guilt pressed heavily against his chest. He'd unleashed an evil force when he ran out on Caesar; and the man wouldn't stop until he had the evidence Wendell carried, along with the daughter he considered a traitor.

Opening his eyes, he reached for the glass of water from the nightstand, wishing instead for a generous serving of hard liquor. He gulped down a few swallows of the cool water in an effort to bring some much needed moisture into his dry mouth. A cough cleared his throat; and he returned the glass, noting that his hand shook worse than before.

Yes, he'd put his daughter in harm's way, and God forgive him, he was about to do it again. Wendell fingered the phone in his hand, stared at it for another moment, and made his call before he could change his mind.

Relief filled him at the sound of Suzanne's voice

"Hi, honey. I had a feeling you'd be at Nesta's. I'm glad you answered the phone. Can you talk?"

"Yes. I'm upstairs on my own. I can't believe you'd have the nerve to be calling here after what you did to the colonel and Nanadoo. It's bad enough you're using me, but I'll never forgive you for taking advantage of them," she scolded, grinding the words out with the force of her anger.

"I needed a place to stay. We were only there for one night and used some bedding and towels. I hardly think that, and a couple of meals, is enough to make you act as though I've taken advantage of them."

"How can you be so nonchalant about the fact that you put them in danger by coming here? Not to mention the dirty trick you pulled when you drugged them."

"Drugged them? I don't know what you're talking about."

"Stop trying to weasel your way out of this. They were both slumped over their teacups when I got here, thanks to your little tea party."

"Oh lord. Suzanne, listen to me. I did not drug Liam and Nesta. I don't know how you think I would do such a thing."

"It's not too difficult. Are you going to continue lying when I saw the cups on the table and had to call a doctor to make sure they were going to recover okay?"

"We were about to have tea with them, but Muriel and I went upstairs when the bottled water guy knocked on the door."

"What is it with the *water-bottled guys* around here?" she mumbled.

"I'm not sure what you mean."

"Never mind. Just tell me what you know."

"I decided it would be better if we left the house using the back stairs. I didn't want anyone to see us there. Liam and Nesta were perfectly fine when I walked out of the kitchen. I swear to you I didn't put anything in their tea."

"Well someone did."

"You might try checking up on that water guy. I could see he was pretty big when I looked through the window. Nesta didn't recognize him. I heard her ask where their regular deliveryman was. This man said he was a substitute. Obviously he came to do more than deliver water."

"Why didn't she or Liam tell me that when I questioned them? Neither of them mentioned anything about some man delivering water."

"Well, they are old, honey. Maybe they suffered a bit of shock from being drugged. Or maybe the drug not only put them to sleep, but it might have wiped out part of their memory."

"That would be a handy alibi for you, wouldn't it?"

"I don't blame you for being upset with me, sweetheart."

"I've gone way beyond upset; and don't call me sweetheart, because I'm not feeling very sweet at the moment. Thanks to you, you've got me chasing after green bags, putting Liam and Nesta in danger, and being forced to arrange secret meetings with shady characters."

Wendell shifted restlessly on his chair.

"What's this about shady characters?"

"Dewey. Ring a bell?"

"Oh Dewey, yes. I took a chance by leaving his number in the bathroom as a little test. I knew you'd figure out what to do if you were the one to find it. You've always been my smart little Suzie."

"Cut the flattery," she snapped. "Dewey warned me about the Montanes. It sounded personal. Why?"

"It's a long, ugly story that I don't want to go into right now. But my phones will do him good."

"This whole hornets' nest you've stirred up is ugly. How is it that Dewey just happens to be working here on the island right when you needed his help?"

"I asked him to go there and check things out. I knew he had a boat, which would get him there and also be a way for me to get away without anyone else knowing."

"Covering your rear end, as usual, I see. Okay, you couldn't give Dewey the phones because you left them at our old house. I get that, but what about the green bag? Did you know it turned up empty? I'm surprised you're still running around loose. I assumed whoever found the phones you put in there either turned them over to the police, or the Montanes."

Wendell grabbed the glass for a hasty drink, wishing more than ever it was something stronger.

"I, um, didn't put the phones in the bag."

"What! Well that just tears it. Give me one good reason why I shouldn't hang up on you."

"Now, now, Suzie. Take it easy. I told you I was pretty sure people would be watching your house knowing you're my daughter. I had a feeling they would chase after you every time you went anywhere. I needed the diversion."

She squeezed the receiver and swallowed down the hurt his confession caused.

"You used me as a lure to get them off your back? That's pretty darn low even for you, Dad,"

"I didn't want to do it, and it makes me sick that I was forced to use you like that."

"Well, you're not the only one who felt sick. I ended up having to dodge bullets again."

Wendell nearly dropped his phone.

"Oh God! I had no idea that would happen. I wouldn't have sent you there if I did. I assumed they'd follow you and nothing else. I'm so sorry."

"Sorry is an empty word coming from you. I'm sure you won't hesitate to use me again to protect your girlfriend."

"You have a right to feel the way you do, but there are things you don't understand about all of this."

"I don't want to hear any more of your sob story. If you really do have those phones, turn them over to the police. Or did you lie about that, too?"

"They exist; and there's enough stuff on them to put the Montanes away for the rest of their lives."

"Then stop procrastinating and mail the phones to Mom and me like you originally planned. We'll get them to the proper authorities, so we can bring this madness to an end once and for all."

"I can't mail one to your mother because I think the man she's with could be a Montane plant."

Suzanne sank down onto the bed suddenly feeling very weak. "Oh no. Do you think he'll hurt her?"

"Not as long as I don't mail her the phone."

"Then mail both phones to me, and I'll take them to the police myself."

"I don't think that's a good idea, either."

"Why not?" she demanded. "Are you saying you don't trust me after all I've done for you?"

"On the contrary, you're one of the few people I do trust. But I'm not so sure about that bodyguard of yours. What do you know about him?"

"Thad? He's been helping me."

"Is that so? Who hired him?"

Suzanne hesitated.

"I don't know. I've asked, but he won't tell me."

"And that doesn't bother you? Funny how he just happened to show up right around the time I started my running."

"Hold on. Are you implying he could be a plant like the guy who's with Mom?"

"Or a rogue trying to get the money for himself. The Montanes will pay plenty to get my phones. The lure of big money tends to make a person ambitious; and sometimes, the wrong kind of ambition can be dangerous. They're all liars, honey, no matter what label they use to make people think otherwise. They're grand manipulators twisting everything to benefit themselves, and they're very good at it."

"Not Thad – no way," Suzanne said, shaking her head.

"Are you sure?"

"Absolutely. Why would he bother to save me in the jungle when those men shot at us?"

"He saved you?"

"Yes he did," she replied with some indignation, feeling the need to defend Thad.

"How do you know if those men weren't trying to save you from him?"

Twelve

Her father's words made Suzanne feel like she'd been socked in the stomach, knocking the wind out of her. Thad, a betrayer? No, he couldn't be. She'd slept with the man, trusted him with her life, and the lives of the colonel and Nanadoo. Had she exposed her friends and neighbors to what could turn out to be a treachery far worse than what she'd accused her father of doing?

Was she destined to become a pawn for every man she let into her life? The thought sickened her and made her stomach twist into a gut wrenching knot. Rubbing a slender hand across her warm, tingling forehead, Suzanne gently messaged the aching skin. It actually felt feverish. Did Thad fool her with his handsome face, sense of humor, and sexy body? He said he was falling in love with her. Was that another lie? He certainly had a talent for saying whatever he needed her to hear. Was he protecting her? Or could he be using her, as her father suggested?

"I can't get my brain to accept what you're saying. I truly believe Thad cares about me. You haven't witnessed how upset he is whenever I've run away from him."

"Of course he'd be upset. He needs you to get to me. He hasn't told you who he works for. Don't you think that would be pertinent information from a bodyguard? God only knows what else he's keeping from you."

"I'm not saying I agree with you, but if Thad isn't on the up and up, what do you suggest I do?"

"Come to me, but don't tell anyone. I can't emphasize enough how crucial it is that you keep my whereabouts a secret. I'm trusting you with my life and the life of Muriel and her unborn child."

"Don't forget it's your child, too."

She heard him sputter into the phone.

"Whatever gave you that idea?"

"You didn't contradict me when I called her your girlfriend and you slept together at Nanadoo's."

"I slept on the floor. Muriel is not my girlfriend. I'm old enough to be her father for heaven's sake."

"Since when has that ever stopped you?"

She held her breath, wondering what he would say. It took him several seconds before he replied.

"Oh, honey. I've really been a terrible father to you, haven't I? It's no wonder you think of me the way you do. But I want you to know something, Suzanne, and it's something I should have said to you a long time ago. What I feel for you goes beyond love. It's difficult for me to express just what I do feel for you. I admire you. I respect you, and I'm in awe of you."

"How do I know you're not saying these things just so I'll help you?"

"I don't blame you for doubting me because of the way I've acted in the past. I'll understand if you decide not to help me now. But it won't make me love you any less because I'd rather lose my life than your love."

Suzanne fully expected him to defend himself, but his surprising reply left her reeling. Tears thickened in her throat and she swallowed several times, unable to speak. A long neglected yearning began to stir inside her. How many times over the years had she imagined hearing her father say he loved her only to be disappointed again and again?

"Why did you wait so long to tell me something I've wanted to hear all my life?" she whispered.

"I just took it for granted that you knew. I haven't any idea how this fix I'm in is going to turn out, and I meant it when I said you can back away if you want. But I won't lie. I'm hoping you'll do as I ask, if not for me, then for Muriel's sake."

Hearing her father's concern for the girl irritated Suzanne. She wanted to savor this new-found declaration of his love for her without being forced to share the precious moment with a stranger.

"Why are you putting yourself in such danger to protect her if she's not your girlfriend, and the child she's carrying isn't yours?"

"Guilt. I admit I started taking small sums of money from the Montanes. They hired me to keep their books because they saw I was good with numbers, and I didn't ask questions about where those numbers came from. They have so much dough I figured they wouldn't miss some of it.

But Muriel's boyfriend, Tony got wise to me; he threatened to tell her father, if I didn't take a huge chunk and give it to them. What I didn't know at the time was that Caesar Montane wasn't aware of their relationship; and he had another man picked out for Muriel to marry."

"He sounds like a real old-fashioned father."

Wendell snorted into the phone.

"Nothing could be further from the truth. He's a monster. Makes me look like a saint. Muriel is terrified of him. When she and Tony discovered she was pregnant, that's when he came up with the idea for me to steal enough money, so they could get away. I, um, decided to take a little extra for myself. I also started gathering as much information as I could about the Montane's criminal activities as a kind of insurance plan."

"I understand your motive now. Where's her boyfriend? Why is she with you instead of him?"

He breathed a heavy sigh into the phone.

"That's where my guilt comes into this. Caesar caught the three of us sneaking out one night. Tony got shot when he threw his body in front of Muriel and me. How could I not help her when I'm partly responsible for Tony's death?"

Suzanne found her animosity toward the girl lessening now that she knew the tragic circumstances.

"So you want me to go to you without telling anyone and deliver the phones to the police?"

"Yes. I don't want to mail them and take the chance they might get lost."

"I see your point. Will you stay with Muriel once I've delivered the goods into safe hands, or do you plan to part ways? I can't help feeling sorry for her knowing how terrible her father is. Is it possible for you to see her safely settled someplace?"

"Remember I told you I'm going to go to an island and retire there? Well, we're going to go to St. Kitts in the Caribbean. She has friends there who are willing to help. They hate her father and will do everything they can to keep her safe."

"Do you trust them enough to believe their protection plan will include you?"

"Yes I do. I got to know Muriel very well while working for the Montanes. She's a sweet girl who through no fault of her own happened to be born into a rotten family."

"What about her mother? Where is she in all of this?"

"Dead. Caesar murdered her when he caught her sleeping with one of his so-called associates. But she got off easy, which is more than anyone can say about the guy who was bedding her."

Suzanne couldn't stop the chill that ran down her spine at the implication in his words. Her parents may not have given her the fairytale upbringing she wanted, but she'd never felt in danger from them.

The pity she'd begun to feel for Muriel grew and deepened for the unfortunate girl.

"Dewey said he overheard you say you'd be staying with someone named Martinez in San Pedro."

"We let him think that on purpose. We're actually in a motel in Long Beach." He gave her the address and room number. "I'm counting on you, honey. I'm worn out from running, and Muriel isn't having an easy time of it what with the grief over losing Tony and being pregnant."

"I'll do my best, but it's not going to be easy. Thad barely lets me go to the bathroom without him since I tricked him to go after your canvas bag and again to meet with Dewey."

"Well, whether or not you can help me, I'd advise you to put as many miles between you and your shadow as soon as you can in case he is in this for his own gain."

"I'm still not sure you're right about that, but I'll do my best for you, so your phones can get to the proper authorities."

"That's my girl."

"Dad, there's one more thing I need to ask you before we hang up. It's kind of melodramatic, but some guy shoved a black feather in my hand while I was on the cruise and said it was a warning."

Wendell groaned.

"You want to watch out for those. It's the Montane's calling card. You get one, and you know something bad is going to happen."

"I had a feeling it was something like that. Someone left another feather on my bed the day I finally got to go home after the cruise, and I've run into trouble after each one."

Something she hadn't contemplated before suddenly came to her. Thad was on the ship when she got the first feather, and he'd gone into her house ahead of her that first night back. He could have easily left that feather on the pillow. Maybe her father was right to be suspicious about Thad's motives.

"All right, you win. I'll start thinking of a way I can leave here."

"Thank you. Oh, and just to be on the safe side, you'd better not use Dewey again. He's probably being watched now. Be careful because even your best friends can be your enemy in a situation like this."

"My friends I trust. It's the glib talking strangers I should have been more concerned about."

Suzanne ended the call and stood there staring into space while she went over the conversation.

Everything her father said about Thad's so-called protecting her made sense now. He had resources; and he used them to plot and orchestrate his every move, so she would let down her guard enough to betray her dad. He'd probably kept her in that Belize jungle house all that time for just that purpose. What about the day they went to lunch with Heather? He could have arranged that car chase to scare her into believing he was the only one who could keep her safe.

117

He'd seduced her not only with his body, but also with the aura of mystery he cultivated. But what woman wouldn't be taken in by a handsome, mysterious stranger? It'd be tantamount to waving catnip under her nose, if she happened to be a cat.

Suzanne already knew Thad was an impressive ally. She had a feeling he'd be an even more formidable adversary, which meant she'd have to be very clever to outwit him. The surprising thing was having his own words help her. He accused her of copying his idea to get to her old house the night she went for the green bag. This time she'd use what had happened to Liam and Nanadoo. Drugs.

She suggested the others adjourn to the living room while she prepared the after dinner coffee. She slipped sleeping pills into their cups. She hated having to include Liam and Nesta in this, but didn't feel an iota of guilt while adding an extra pill to Thad's cup. He was a big man and she wanted to make sure he stayed knocked out. But even then, he took so long to go completely under she had to rush to get away.

Suzanne waited until they fell into their drug induced sleep before taking all the money from Thad's wallet. She used Liam's golf cart and drove to the harbor to catch the last ferry off the island. Leaving Nanadoo and the colonel in such a state filled Suzanne with remorse, which in turn made her anger against Thad intensify. This wasn't just between him and her. He'd made her hurt people dear to her because of his duplicity.

Thad. Fake friend. Fake lover. Now it was his turn to be on the receiving end of being duped and dumped. Let him see how he liked it.

She stood at the railing of the ferry watching the dark mass of the island grow smaller and smaller, wondering if she would ever be able to trust a man again. She'd taken a bite of an apple that looked perfect on the outside, but had she gone deeper, she would have found decay. Unbidden tears filled her eyes as a testimony to promises made and future dreams lost.

Her ex-fiancé's disloyalty had damaged her self-confidence.

Thad's deception felt more like a mutilation of the soul.

118

The first thing Thad thought when he opened his eyes the next morning was he must be suffering the aftereffects of a very bad hangover. The second thing that registered in his foggy brain was how quiet the house seemed. He sniffed the air and smelled the lingering scent of the vanilla candle Nesta burned last night. But not a hint of coffee aroma or any breakfast food being prepared. He looked outside and could tell by the position of the sun it was much later than he was used to waking up.

Had his hosts both overslept, too? Or could they have decided to go out to eat and didn't want to wake him. What about Suzanne? He rolled off the sofa and staggered a bit while pulling on his jeans. What the hell was the matter with him? His head pounded, and his mouth and throat felt like he'd swallowed a bucket of sand.

Maybe he was coming down with something. He almost groaned. He didn't have time to be sick. He made his way to the kitchen and found it empty. He pulled on the hand railing literally dragging himself upstairs to the bedrooms. Since when had climbing a few steps become a trek to Mt. Everest?

Liam came out of his bedroom looking disheveled just as Thad arrived on the landing. Nesta still lay in bed sleeping soundly. The two men greeted each other with a barely perceptible nod.

"I thought I heard someone. Nesta and I must have overslept." Liam pressed a hand to his forehead. "I have a devil of a headache."

"That makes two of us. Let me check on Suzanne."

Thad knocked, opened her door, and peeked inside.

"Her bed's empty. I'll check the bathroom."

He returned to Liam seconds later.

"She's not here."

"Perhaps she went for a morning walk. She does that sometimes."

Thad shook his head, instantly regretting the motion when it felt like someone was pounding spikes into his eyes.

"Her bed hasn't been slept in."

119

"Oh my. Shall I go see if my golf cart is still here?"

"I'll do it. You stay here with Nesta in case she wakes up while I'm gone."

Thad found the carport empty. His search around the outside of the house didn't reveal any clues. He went back to Suzanne's bedroom. He looked in the closet and the dresser drawers. Her jacket and purse seemed to be the only things missing. Traveling light; or in too much of a hurry to pack? On her own? Or taken? Either way, the grim reality was, she was gone. Again.

He walked out of her room. Liam met him on the landing and held up a small prescription bottle.

"Nesta woke up and found this in the bathroom when she went to take her shower. Sleeping pills." He popped off the plastic lid. "Some are missing. We're careful to keep count. As much as I hate to accuse Suzanne, I'd say our girl may have laced the coffee last night."

Thad eyed the bottle. "I'd have to say you're probably right, considering how late we all slept and how lethargic we feel. By the way, your cart is gone."

"Why would she do that to us?" Liam said, shaking his head at the distressing thought.

"She wouldn't want to do anything to deliberately harm you unless it was absolutely necessary, which means I was probably her main target."

"But why do you suppose she felt it was so necessary to go on her own?"

"Good question.

She hadn't forgotten her father's warning about not telling anyone his whereabouts. But Suzanne knew they'd all have to find somewhere to stay for the time being. It'd be too dangerous to use her own house. She had in mind what she felt certain would be a safe place, but first she had to find out if the house was empty. She pulled her cell phone out of her purse.

"Heather."

"Hey, girlfriend. I've been thinking about you. Are you okay? You sound kind of weird."

"Maybe that's because I feel weird; and to answer your question, I haven't been okay since I got off our cruise ship in Belize, but let's not go into that again. You said you wanted to be kept in the loop."

"I meant it. That's what friends are for. Has anything happened since we last talked?"

"Yes. Is your parents' beach house still empty?"

"Why do you want to know? Oh wait, I get it. You and your hot man want to be alone. I don't imagine you've had much opportunity to share a bed at your godmother's."

"He's not my hot man. He's a backstabbing liar," Suzanne snapped, cutting through her friend's chuckle.

"Whoa, what happened? It'd be a shame if you had a lovers' quarrel. Things were going so well."

"Well for him. He's been lying to me, so he can get those phones from my dad and use them to bargain with the Montane brothers for a big fat reward."

She blew out a breath.

"Busted! Who knew all that gorgeous man flesh would turn out to be the skin of a rat? Are you still at your godmother's?"

"Thad is. He doesn't know I left. I'm on a ferry right now."

"He doesn't know you're gone? How'd you shake him?"

"I put sleeping pills in his coffee."

Heather laughed out loud.

"Hot damn! Good for you. Did Liam or Nesta give you any flack?"

"I had to drug them too. I feel sick about that."

"I bet." Heather paused. "But you know, sometimes you have to do things to people you care about that you wish you didn't because there's no other way. So you want the beach house for yourself?"

"Not just for me. I need it for my dad and Muriel, too."

"Oh my gosh! Does this mean you know where they are?"

121

"Yes, he called this afternoon. They're staying at a motel in Long Beach. That's where I'm headed. I'd really appreciate it if you could meet me and take us to your parents' place."

"Sure, but I thought you hated his girlfriend."

"She's not his girlfriend. I don't have time to go into it. But she is a friend, and she needs our help."

"I see. Does your father still have those elusive phones?"

"Yes. I'm taking them to the police as soon as I get to him. Then we'll have to hide for a while."

"Okay. Tell me the name and address of the motel."

Suzanne gave her the information.

"Aaron and I will meet you there. You haven't told anyone else where your dad is, have you?"

"Of course not. I have to be careful who I can trust. Thank you, Heather. I'm more grateful for your help than I can say. Now I owe you another slice of that double fudge chocolate cake."

"Oh, more than that. You may as well know that I expect to have the whole thing."

Suzanne knocked on the door of her father's motel room and waited several seconds. She frowned at the closed door and checked the number to be sure she had the correct room. She knocked again, a little harder this time. She supposed she shouldn't be too surprised that her father didn't answer her summons right away, since it was well after midnight.

More seconds dragged by. She tried to peek in the window, but the drapes were drawn. Someone should have answered her by now. She made a fist and pounded on the door.

"Dad!" So much for trying to do this quietly. "It's Suzanne. Let me in."

She moved over to rap on the window, calling out again, only to be met with more silence. She looked around, wondering what to do next. She didn't have long to think about it when the motel manager came hurrying out of the office.

"I've had three calls complaining about all the noise you're making out here. What's your problem?"

"I need to talk to the people staying in this room."

"They obviously don't want to talk to you. You can come back in the morning to see your friends, but I can't have you standing out here yelling and disturbing the other guests."

"You don't understand. I'm his daughter," Suzanne said pointing to the door.

"Lady, I don't care if you're his fairy godmother. It's almost one o'clock in the morning. I want you to leave right now or I'll call the police and have you arrested for disturbing the peace."

"He has a woman with him. She's pregnant and . . . and having complications. They phoned me to come here. All I'm asking is that you let me check to see if they're all right."

"If the woman's having complications like you say, then why haven't they gone to a hospital?"

"They don't have any medical insurance or credit cards, and they're short on cash. Please just let me make sure nothing is wrong."

Suzanne thought he would refuse her when she heard him mutter a few derogatory words under his breath. But he surprised her by stepping forward to knock on the door.

"Sir, this is the manager. We have someone here who is concerned about you. She says she's your daughter. I'm going to unlock your door. If you'd rather we didn't enter you room, please let me know."

He looked at Suzanne and took out a master keycard. "It'll be on your head if this doesn't go well."

"Please just hurry," she urged, peering over the man's shoulder.

He swung open the door and flicked a wall switch instantly bathing the room with a harsh light. Suzanne blinked against the brightness and felt her body clench with disappointment when she realized the room was unoccupied. The manager walked over to the bathroom and snapped on another light.

"I think you should see this," he said, motioning to her.

Suzanne rushed over and stared in horror at a bloody towel on the counter with more blood splattered in the sink and on the floor. Her eyes followed the trail of blood across the floor to the gaping hole that once was the bathroom window. Several pieces of broken glass lay strewed across the floor.

"I knew they made the bathroom windows too big when they built this place. This is the second time this month I've had someone go out this way. The last guy didn't make such a mess of it, though."

He continued to speak, but the words faded into unintelligible murmurs inside Suzanne's head.

"I'm sorry. What did you say?" she asked after several seconds had elapsed.

"I said, it looks like your father and the woman should be in a hospital, if all that blood means anything."

Thirteen

"Suzie? Are you here?"

Suzanne spun around at the sound of Heather's voice when she and Aaron came running into the room. They stopped, mouths gaping open, as they stared though the open bathroom door.

"What the hell is going on here?" Aaron yelled.

"That's what I'd like to know," the manager said. "Someone's going to have to pay for this mess."

"You're a real sensitive guy, aren't you?" Heather glared at him while pulling Suzanne away. "You'd better sit down before you fall down. You look kind of green around the gills, hon."

Suzanne allowed herself to be guided back to the main room where she sank down onto a chair upholstered in an ugly shade of yellow fabric that she imagined must be making her complexion look even worse. Aaron and the manager followed.

"Where's your father?" Heather asked.

"I don't know. No one answered when I knocked on the door. Oh God Heather, all that blood."

"Take a deep breath," she advised rubbing Suzanne's shoulder. "Did you find what you came for?"

"I haven't had a chance to look."

Heather nodded toward Aaron, and he immediately began opening drawers.

"Just what do you think you're doing?" the manager demanded, as Aaron headed for the closet next.

"I need to find something that happens to be very important." Aaron got down on his knees to look beneath the bed and pulled out a couple of small suitcases.

"Stop that right now. I can't allow you to search a guest's room. I'm calling the police. That broken window and all the blood tells me something obviously isn't right here. We may be talking foul play."

Suzanne gripped the arms of the chair and slanted Heather a look of pure panic.

"You needn't bother the authorities, sir," Heather assured him. "The man who was staying here suffers from depression. He's been suicidal lately. He called his daughter to come here because he realized he needed help. My husband is looking for the pills he threatened to take."

They all stared while Aaron opened each piece of luggage and dumped the contents on the bed.

"Damn! Nothing here except clothes and a few toiletries," he said, flinging a shirt onto the floor.

"What about the pregnant woman you mentioned?" the manager asked Suzanne.

"Oh, um, she's . . ."

"The pregnant woman is his girlfriend. She's a little mental herself," Heather explained, rushing to fill in the awkward silence.

"They sound like a lovely couple." He pointed to the bathroom. "I'd still like to know who's going to pay for that damage."

"I will," Aaron said "Why don't we go to the office while my wife takes our friend outside? I'm sure you'd rather not have a fainting woman on your hands."

The manager looked at Suzanne where she sat, pale and shaking.

"All right."

Heather tugged Suzanne to her feet.

"Let's get out of here. The smell of blood is starting to make me nauseous."

The cool night air brought back some of the normal color to Suzanne's cheeks. She sucked in a deep breath, anxious to free her nostrils from the room's sickening stench. She stumbled into the car and turned to Heather as soon as they sat down.

"I can't believe how fast you came up with that story about Dad."

"I can lie with the best of them when I need to."

Her comment reminded Suzanne of Thad's glib tongue. She forced the comparison away knowing it was mean-spirited to compare her loyal friend to a good-for-nothing false friend like he turned out to be.

"What do you think happened to my dad and Muriel?"

"Something or someone must have spooked them, which isn't too surprising since they seem to have a small army of people chasing them."

"I'm worried. I can't help thinking all that blood must mean one or both of them suffered bad cuts."

"I know. They might need stitches. I'll have Aaron swing by a couple ER rooms in the area. We shouldn't hang around here too long in case the guy changes his mind and ends up calling the cops."

"God forbid. I guess it's a waste of time to go to the beach house now."

"Aaron and I decided that wouldn't be a good idea anyway because you're too closely connected to us. We have another plan in mind, and I'd say it's a good thing considering what just happened here."

Suzanne frowned at Heather.

"What is your plan, and am I going to like it?"

"I don't know if you'll like it or not, but I strongly suggest you consider what we propose. We'll hide you where no one would think to look and wait for your dad to get in touch with you again."

"I may have lost my last chance for that ever happening."

"Why? He's going to want to talk to you if for no other reason than to tell you what happened here."

"Not if he thinks I'm the one who gave away his hiding place."

"Suzie, I . . . ." Heather said, but stopped and caught her bottom lip between her teeth.

"What?"

Heather shook her head and looked away.

"Nothing."

Suzanne pressed her forehead against the car window and stared at the *No Vacancy* sign hanging in the manager's office window. The red neon reminded her of the blood smeared bathroom. She closed her eyes wishing she could block out the awful scene. Her father probably needed help more than ever now, but how could she help him if she couldn't find him?

Thad would know what to do.

But asking him for assistance would be like inviting him to help write her father's obituary.

Thad jumped down from the helicopter and jogged across the tarmac. His brain hummed with the few facts he'd managed to glean from Suzanne's latest stunt. Someone called her at her godmother's and she had a lengthy conversation with them. Unfortunately, he didn't know who that someone was. But if he had to guess, he'd say it was probably her father.

He went through her room again looking for the phone he'd given her, but came up empty handed.

He'd also discovered all the money he carried in his wallet had disappeared. Suzanne had probably helped herself, while he was passed out on the sofa.

Thad decided she must have left the island last night, considering the timeframe from when he last saw her and until he awoke this morning. Liam went with him to check with the man named Dewey. He insisted he'd neither seen nor helped her in any way. Thad's only clue was Dewey telling her about the people named Martinez in San Pedro.

Nothing came of that, but he hadn't expected it to. A man and woman on the run wouldn't be dropping clues to their whereabouts like Hansel and Gretel's breadcrumbs. The phone call Suzanne took at her godmother's had to be the catalyst that threw her into flight mode. Drugging him wasn't such a surprise, but Thad knew she had to be pretty desperate to leave without anyone knowing, when she chose to drug Liam and Nesta as well.

He had her house checked. She hadn't shown up there. Thad had no idea where Suzanne might be. But he knew someone who probably did.

Thad stood on the porch of the modest bungalow and rang the doorbell. He studied the front of the small house while he waited. The two terracotta pots of bright red germaniums standing on either side of the black door lent cheery color to the stark white walls and black trimmed window frames.

He heard the click of a lock seconds before the front door swung open.

"Hello, Heather," he said and smiled.

No smile in return. Not a good sign for a guy hoping to get some information.

She glared at him.

"What do you want?"

"I'm sure you already know the answer to that. Where is she?" he asked, dropping all pretense that this might be a friendly visit.

"Suzanne's not here if that's what you're thinking."

"I'm sure she isn't. That would be too easy. But I do think you know where I can find her."

"You're wrong."

"Your attitude says otherwise."

"I don't care what my attitude says. Even if I knew where she was, I wouldn't tell a louse like you."

Thad tugged on his earlobe.

"So I'm a louse now? What has Suzanne been telling you?"

"What makes you think she's been in touch with me?"

"Maybe it's the fact that you're acting like a mother bear protecting her cub."

"Of course I'd be protective. Suzanne is my friend."

"Yes, I've noticed how friendly you can be, especially the day we all had lunch together and your hand somehow kept finding its way under the table to my crotch."

Flames of color streaked Heather's cheeks.

"Shut up!"

"Tell me where she is and I just might do that."

"I told you, I don't know. The last time I heard from her she was at her godmother's, and you were with her. Now you're telling me she's gone and you can't find her? Some bodyguard you are."

"I'm here to correct my shortcomings. Every minute Suzanne is out on her own puts her in danger. You'll help me keep her from harm if you really are her friend."

"You've got a lot of nerve coming here whining to me about your mistakes. You blew your chance to protect her. I wouldn't trust you to keep my dog safe. Now get away from here and don't come back."

"I'm not going anywhere unless it's where Suzanne is. Now tell me what I need to know."

"You can go to hell!"

He slapped his hand against the door when she started to shut it.

"I'll be taking you there with me if anything happens to Suzanne."

"You'll have to find her first, won't you?" Heather sneered.

The screaming woke her. Again. Suzanne shot up in bed, drenched in sweat, her heart pounding. No need to wonder who emitted the ear-splitting screeches. She already knew, and she had the aching throat to prove it. Hopefully the yelling didn't wake up any of the other guests in the inn.

Moonlight streamed into the room, bright beams cutting through the darkness. Suzanne climbed out of bed on shaky legs, abandoning any attempt to fall back to sleep. Experience told her it'd be a waste of time to try. The nightmare hadn't varied in the three nights since she began this latest venture.

Images of her father covered in blood, crawling over broken pieces of glass, begging her to take the phones continued to plague her. She tried, but she could never get close enough to grab them. A faceless woman stood weeping in the background. Was it Muriel?

Other people came. Faceless. Menacing. Suzanne didn't know who they were, but she had a pretty good idea when they started throwing black feathers at her. She didn't want to stay, but her legs refused to carry her away. She stood there helpless, not knowing what to do, so she screamed until she woke up.

She padded across the room on bare feet to shove the window open and made herself take in deep gulps of sea air. She'd spent hours in the car with Aaron after leaving the motel. They drove along the Pacific Coast Highway heading ever further north stopping each night in a different seaside town.

Aaron held onto the car's steering wheel as though it was a life preserver in a storm tossed ocean. He spent almost as much time looking in his rearview mirror as he did keeping his eyes on the road in front of him. Suzanne couldn't say that she blamed him. She felt edgy, nerves hanging by ragged threads.

Aaron finally decided to let her stay at this particular inn. The building stood on a high cliff, but she could still hear the waves below. Sometimes she could even feel the remnants of sea spray if the wind blew in her direction.

They were both too mentally and physically exhausted to have a normal conversation by the time he left. Aaron's last words were strict instructions to contact him as soon as she heard from her father. He made her register under an assumed name and told her not to call anyone but him or Heather. He also warned her against talking to people insisting that every stranger could be a potential threat. She'd felt alone before, but now she felt completely ostracized from society.

Suzanne knew she would be enjoying this pretty inn and the scenic location if she didn't have to be here under such distressing circumstances. Her room was cozy and the owners friendly. Their smiles when she checked in were warm and welcoming. The woman offered her a little dish of mints wrapped in shiny green paper decorated with tiny white flowers. Suzanne didn't know why, but that little bit of kindness made her want to cry.

Her stay here reminded Suzanne of the time in Belize. That place had a different kind of beauty, which she'd also been unable to appreciate because of the events that brought her there. But she did have the luxury of being able to talk to people then. People, mainly as in Thad.

She pressed fingertips to her tired eyes. Her weary brain cautioned her not to think about him. The conflict flared up inside her, as a reminder of the disparity between them. She trusted. He lied. She gave. He took. Greed. So many people all wanting the same thing. Strange how money could twist lives into a pretzel of need and wanting so strong nothing else seemed to matter.

Suzanne stood there until the night air chilled her, but she still didn't move until someone knocked on the door making her jump. She turned away from the window, eyes wide with fear.

"Miss? It's Mr. Kenny, the proprietor. Can you hear me?"

"Ye . . . yes."

"My wife thought she heard screaming coming from your room. Are you all right?"

"I'm fine."

Talk about a misnomer.

"Are you sure you don't need a doctor?"

"No. I'm all right."

More lies. Suzanne squeezed her eyes shut, mentally begging him to go away.

"Please don't hesitate to let us know if we can do anything for you."

"I had a nightmare. I apologize for disturbing you."

"That's all right. I hope we'll have the pleasure of your company at breakfast."

Aaron's warning flashed in her head. Don't tell anyone your plans. Always keep them guessing.

"I'm . . . I'm not sure. Please don't wait for me."

"Oh. Well, I hope you'll be able to sleep better now. Listen to the rhythm of the waves. That helps me sometimes."

"Thank you. I will."

Suzanne hurried across the room and pressed her ear to the door listening until she heard his footsteps fade away. She turned and sagged against the wooden panel. She'd have to start stuffing a sock in her mouth before she went to bed if she was going to continue waking up screaming every night

132

She pushed away from the door and looked around her. The room had suddenly become very claustrophobic. Maybe a walk along the beach would help relieve some of her strain. The moon was bright enough to light the trail that led away from the inn, and she could always hold onto the railing provided to guide her.

She dressed quickly, looking forward to be doing something physical. Aaron couldn't object since she'd have the beach to herself this time of night. Heather must have known Aaron would be heading to cooler weather when she packed boots, warm socks, sweatshirts, jeans, and a coat with a hood.

Suzanne arrived on the sandy beach minutes later and started walking. She kept on the alert, watching to make sure she was alone. But so far the only movement came from the waves. The wind blew harder here and it wasn't long before her cheeks stung from the cold. She didn't care. It felt invigorating and helped to clear the cobwebs from her brain. She shoved her hands into her pockets and headed for an outcrop of rocks further up the beach.

She'd talked to Heather earlier and wasn't surprised that Thad went there looking for her. According to Heather, he tried to bully his way into gaining information and insisted he wasn't giving up trying to find her. He'd turned out to have a one-track mind like everyone else. They all wanted her father's phones, so they could get the reward money from the mob.

It did worry her that Thad might somehow use the colonel and Nanadoo as pawns to force Heather to tell him what he demanded, but thankfully he hadn't. So far. Suzanne could only pray he wouldn't change his mind and go back to the island. She confessed her worries and as usual her friend promised to help.

Heather called them. They were all right, but expressed concern about Suzanne's surprising disappearance. Heather delivered the apology for drugging them. She assured them things were under control by mentioning something Nanadoo had taught Suzanne when she needed to know everything was okay during her turbulent years being shuffled back and forth between her irresponsible parents.

The words were simple and in this case probably a good thing since no one else would probably pay attention to the odd code. The message varied depending on Suzanne's situation. The rose blooms meant everything was fine. The rose is wilting let Nanadoo know she needed to check on her goddaughter. The rose is losing its petals signified things weren't going well and she should take Suzanne home with her. But if she said the rose won't be picked, that indicated a problem, but she wanted to handle it on her own.

Heather delivered the latter words to Nesta. She suggested they could give Suzanne peace of mind about their safety if they left the island for a while. They promised to go on a mini vacation to ease her fears, but pleaded to be kept informed of her wellbeing.

Suzanne thought about so many people leaving their homes, including herself, as though they'd been shot out of a cannon like a bunch of cartoon characters who were now running all over in several different directions. The moment of amusement vanished when she remembered the ever present danger that made the fleeing necessary. The Montane brothers were wicked men without a drop of compassion between the two of them.

Once again she felt thankful she could rely on Aaron and Heather to come to her aid. She longed to go back home to her normal life and her little house. Nothing she'd ever done before could be considered exciting, but at least she could go out to lunch without being tailed by some lunatics or enjoy a tranquil visit with her godmother and not have to end up hurting the people she loved.

Suzanne looked up and saw twinkling stars. They reminded her of stubborn fireflies defying the night. The wind chased a few clouds across the sky. Half a dozen tiny sand crabs scurried out of her way. The waves rolled into shore dragging foamy fingers over the sand. Random droplets of water split off in a frantic little dance before swirling into the air to disappear. White lights, no more than mere dots, blinked from a ship far out to sea.

It made Suzanne think of the cruise she'd allowed Heather to talk her into. She wished she'd never boarded that ship because then she wouldn't have met Thad. Of course, knowing the situation now he probably would have found another way for them to connect. Suzanne knew she couldn't blame Thad entirely for their lovemaking at her house because he told her it wasn't a good idea. He even gave her a chance to back out; and she still grabbed him like he was the last donut in the box, and she couldn't wait to take a bite out of him.

Her body quivered now recalling how good it felt to have his hands on her. His manly scent. The perfect ten build. His expertise. No strings they said. Of course he didn't want any permanent relationship with her. He just wanted to get her father's phones and sell them to the highest bidder, and she'd made it so easy for him. How embarrassing to know she begged him to make love to her. What a fool she was.

Suzanne reached the outcrop of rocks. She stepped behind a large boulder, grateful to be out of the wind and protected from the salt spray. She knew she would have to make her way back to the inn eventually, but it felt nice to be out on her own without having to worry about any strangers accosting her.

She settled back, enjoying the serenity until she felt a chill creep up her spine that had nothing to do with the cold weather. Suzanne stumbled back, as a large, dark form slowly began to emerge from behind a boulder. She whirled around ready to run. But she was too late.

A hand whipped out and grabbed her arm in an iron grip.

Fourteen

"Hi, honey, I'm back," a familiar deep voice taunted in her ear. "Did you miss me?"

Shock slowly faded to recognition. Thad! Suzanne clawed at his fingers until he moved his hand away. The wind had tousled his hair into an untidy mass. He needed a shave. Tiny lines of fatigue fanned out from either side of his eyes. His clothes were wrinkled, as though he must have slept in them for days.

But much to her chagrin she still thought he looked very sexy; and if her pulse was any indication, her traitorous body thought so, too. Damn the man. How could his mere presence make her desire him when she knew he represented a walking, talking liar?

Suzanne drew on her anger as the only defense she had to fight this frustrating attraction.

"How did you find me? Do I have a tracking device in my uterus for Pete's sake?"

"I'm happy to see you too, babe."

"Well, I'm not happy to see you, and stop calling me those stupid names."

"So I guess that means I don't get a hello kiss."

She scowled at him.

"Not while I'm working on goodbye."

"Aw, didn't you miss me even just a little bit?"

"Yeah, about as much as I'd miss having an infectious disease," she snapped.

"You know, you really do need to work on your people skills."

"I don't have a problem with people, just two-faced rats like you who use others for their own gain."

Thad scratched the stubble on one cheek. "Well, that explains a lot. What makes you think I'm in this for personal gain?"

"I'm not going to stand here and explain the obvious. I'm trying to get over the fact that I made the biggest mistake of my life by sleeping with you."

Thad yanked her back when she started to walk away. "Is that what this is really all about? You're upset because you think I took advantage of you? I gave you the chance to back out. But you wanted me just as much as I wanted you. We're two consenting adults who happened to sleep together and enjoy it."

"I . . . I didn't like it."

"Sure you didn't," he mocked. "You were there with me all the way in that bed, sweetheart."

Suzanne didn't want Thad to think her surrendering to him was the real reason for her rejection. How could she when giving herself to him was pure pleasure rather than any sacrifice? He was right about that.

"You used me."

"Like hell I did." He let go of her arm and reined in his temper. "Do me. Now. Please. Any of that ring a bell?" he taunted, repeating the words she'd used when begging him to make love to her.

Suzanne's face heated with embarrassment. "I'm not talking about being used for sex. I meant that you've been with me just so you can get to my father. You want his phones to sell to the Montanes for the money they'll pay you."

"Of all the things I expected you to say for running out on me, that sure wasn't one of them. Where the devil did you come up with that idea? I neither want nor need their dirty money. I'm being paid very well by a legitimate party to find your father. Someone, I should add, who doesn't have any ulterior motives to hurt him. My client wants to keep your father just as safe as I do."

"That's news to me. You've never told me who hired you. Every time I tried to get information all I got was another evasion or more lies. Why wouldn't I suspect you?"

Suzanne watched him and lifted her brows, challenging him to answer her.

"You're right. It's time I gave you an explanation." He sat on a rock and patted the spot next to him.

She shook her head.

"Do you want to hear this or not?"

"How do I know you aren't getting ready to tell me more lies?"

"Because by taking you into my confidence I'm risking losing my job. My client requested that I not share a lot of information. I'm not working alone on this, Suzanne. You've seen me make calls asking for assistance. Many man hours have gone into this case long before I came in contact with you."

"I still don't know if I can believe you."

"I understand, but give me a chance. I know you want to help your father, but you can't do that by running away. I'm the best bet you have for finding him."

He patted the space again.

"If you really want answers about my involvement then you'll hear me out."

Suzanne moved slowly to the rock and sat down, but refused to look at him.

"Okay, I'm listening. But bear in mind I've had it with all the lies I've had to deal with, so you'd better make this good."

Thad nodded.

"I'm an investigator for a prestigious private security firm."

"Is that so? What's the name of this so-called prestigious firm?"

"You wouldn't know if I told you. The company prefers to operate under the media radar. We specialize in investigating cases and protecting prominent people who choose to have our services remain anonymous. Our clients have included political figures, diplomats, and movie stars, among others. The person currently responsible for paying my salary is a very wealthy man who would give every cent he has to see Caesar and Marco Montane locked away for good."

This finally earned him her sincere attention. Suzanne didn't know what else he was going to say about why the client wanted the Montanes so badly, but she instinctively knew it was going to be awful.

"What did they do to him?"

"They kidnapped his nineteen year old daughter."

"Why?"

"He outbid them on a major real estate transaction. They convinced themselves that he won the contract because he exposed some of their less than legal business practices. My client didn't, but they decided otherwise and took his daughter as a way to punish him. He paid their astronomical ransom, but instead of returning her, they sold her into sexual slavery. By the time we found her it was too late."

Suzanne's eyes widened. "She . . . she died?"

"Yes." His voice roughed. "Murdered when she tried to escape."

"That poor girl! I feel so sad for her father. No wonder he wants the Montanes locked up."

"My client is a widower, and this was his only child. His daughter meant everything to him. Your dad would be a hero to him and more people than you can imagine if we can get those phones. He also wants to talk to Muriel."

An unexpected urge to protect the girl seized Suzanne. "Why? According to my dad she's an innocent pawn and is terrified of her father. I know he's lied about a lot of things, but I believe he's telling the truth about Muriel. Surely your client doesn't want to punish her for losing his daughter when Muriel is a victim herself."

"He doesn't want to punish her. He wants to rescue her. He's a good man, Suzanne. Muriel Montane was his daughter's college roommate. She was there the night her friend was taken. She didn't know anything about the kidnapping until it happened. Her father had his thugs rough her up to make sure she wouldn't cooperate with the authorities. He's a monster."

"My dad said as much."

Suzanne looked at Thad and knew she owed him an explanation for drugging his coffee and fleeing. She scraped her toe in the wet sand, gathering her courage to make her confession.

"I left Nanadoo's because my father called and said he was ready for me to come and get the phones. He thought you might be after them for yourself. I couldn't take the chance that he was right and have you following me."

"Hence the drugged coffee."

"It was necessary. I felt terrible about having to drug the colonel and Nanadoo."

"They weren't too thrilled about it themselves. We all felt like zombies when we finally woke up. I noticed you didn't mention feeling guilty about slipping that crap into my cup."

"Well, I do now. But I didn't at the time because I thought you were . . ."

"A rat. Just because I don't express my feelings the way you think I should doesn't mean I don't care. People show their emotions in different ways. I'm walking a fine line trying to be loyal to my client and get the job done. I've had to juggle that with my personal feelings for you. You got to me, Suzanne. You know that. I can't afford to indulge myself as much as I would like until this is over. But I would have helped you if you'd given me the chance instead of running out on me."

She exhaled a deep sigh.

"I've been so upset over all this business with Dad and he scared me even more when he said the man with my mother works for the Montane brothers."

Thad shook his head.

"He's wrong. It's understandable that your father would suspect everyone, including me considering that I haven't been upfront with you. The man is on the run from some very dangerous people. But just so you won't worry, the guy with your mother works for my agency."

"Really? That ought to be interesting. My mother never stays with a man for very long unless she can sleep with them. This guy must be darn good in bed for her to keep him around."

"Our agency doesn't encourage us to sleep with clients, but he'll do what he has to do to protect your mother. And before you misconstrue my statement, do not for one minute think I made love to you because I felt obligated."

"At least you didn't say it was just sex. My mother, on the other hand is very interested in the sexual prowess of her male companions."

"I've seen pictures of your mother. I'm sure he's coping."

Suzanne's lips thinned.

"My mother's had a lot of help in that department. Her little black book has the names of some very talented plastic surgeons. I guess I sound catty, but I don't want to be like her in looks or in any other way. She has very definite ideas of what she wants; and when she sees it, she takes it. I'm more of a *make it up as I go along* kind of person, and most of the time I think I'm wrong."

"I wasn't comparing you to her. As for you thinking you're wrong, you've been doing a pretty good job of convincing yourself you're right, or you wouldn't keep running out on me."

"I haven't always felt comfortable with my decisions. My biggest worry is who to trust, including you. You may as well know, if you don't already that my dad called and told me he and Muriel were staying in a motel in Long Beach. But when I got there they were gone. They must have felt threatened by someone because they went out the bathroom window. There was broken glass and blood everywhere."

"Broken glass and blood? That doesn't sound good. Did you tell anyone else about this motel?"

"I called Heather and asked her and her husband Aaron to meet me there."

"I was afraid of that."

Thad swore under his breath. Suzanne immediately rushed to defend her friends.

"I know what you're thinking about my dad saying to keep it a secret, but we were going to need a place to hide out. Heather is my oldest and dearest friend. I thought we could stay at her parents' beach house. They were going to set everything up for me."

141

"But that all changed when you couldn't find your dad and Muriel."

"Yes. Aaron and Heather felt it would be safer to get me out of southern Cal in case whoever scared Dad away might come after me. Aaron drove me up here. He had me stay in a few other places first."

"I know. I've been following you two and sleeping in my car."

"You have? No wonder you look so terrible."

"Thanks, I needed that."

Suzanne gave him a sympathetic look. "Sorry."

He shrugged.

"You're entitled. I've seen myself in the mirror. So, I take it you're still here because you haven't heard from your father."

"That's right; and I'm going out of my mind imagining him being somewhere slowly bleeding to death. I've even had nightmares about it. Aaron believes Dad will contact me again, and he insisted that I don't tell anyone else but Heather or him what's going on."

"Well, we can keep it our little secret that you told me. Now that you know how desperate the situation is I'm going to ask you not to tell Aaron or Heather if your dad calls again."

Suzanne had to take a few moments to mull over Thad's suggestion. Not keeping her friends informed was going to make her feel as though she'd lost a very important link.

"Aaron and Heather are just trying to help. They've already done so much I hate shutting them out."

"They're drawing too much attention to you, and that's not good for you or your father. The Montanes know your connection to your friends, and they will exploit that to the nth degree."

She rubbed fingers over her eyes.

"I'm not thinking very straight right now. I haven't slept well since I left Nanadoo's. I guess you haven't slept a lot lately yourself."

"Not much."

"Would you like to come back to my room with me? It has a queen size bed."

"Are you inviting me to share it with you even though I'm a rat?"

Suzanne tried to smile, but she felt too tired to even do that. She hopped off the rock.

"I don't think you're a rat, but right now you do smell like one. I have my own bathroom with a shower. May I suggest you use it?"

"I'd be happy to oblige."

Thad slid off his perch. He reached for Suzanne's hand, but she moved away.

"You look cold. A hot shower may be just the thing you need to warm you up."

"It does sound good," she agreed.

"I know something that sounds even better."

She looked at him. "What's that?"

"That we share the shower."

"I invited you to my room to bathe and sleep. It wasn't an invitation for anything else."

Suzanne slumped down onto the bed and dragged her clothes off feeling too tired to shower. She slipped into her nightshirt and crawled beneath the quilts, shivering. She laid there waiting for Thad. The cold wasn't the only thing making her tremble. He climbed in beside her a few minutes later.

"God, you're like ice," he said pulling her against his nakedness.

"I told you I don't . . ."

"Relax. I just want to keep you warm while we both get some much needed shuteye."

She had to admit she was grateful to have Thad there when her dreaded nightmare returned. He held her in his arms whispering reassuring words. Somewhere in the nooks and crannies of her mind Suzanne knew that voice – knew she had only to follow the sound, and she'd be safe. She settled more fully against him and drifted into a less troubled slumber.

They awoke facing each other. Some of the fatigue had lifted from their eyes. But a shadow of wariness still remained between them. How could it not? His entry into her life marked the beginning of events rivaling any soap opera. She would have written herself out of the script long ago if it had been in her power to do so. Thad wasn't the author, but he had more experience in handling complex plots.

He wanted her to believe he wasn't a nice man. Was that because he'd been forced to do bad things in the past as a result of his work? Suzanne knew he fought his attraction to her. Had he been tempted by other women on other jobs? He said his firm sometimes protected movie stars. She didn't have to remind herself how beautiful most of them were. Not to mention, talented, rich, and able to give a man like Thad anything he could desire. She wondered if any of them had ever touched his heart.

Whether or not he'd succumbed to some famous woman's charms was irrelevant. He was in her bed now. Suzanne had a feeling he was waiting for her to make the first move after her chilly reception last night. What would be more important, quality or quantity? Both, actually because once you had the best, the more you wanted to repeat the experience. She might never see Thad again once this job was finished. Wasn't that reason enough to savor their time together?

She reached up and palmed his cheek.

"Do you believe in taking what you can get when you can get it because you may not have a chance to have it again?"

"You just said a mouthful, but to answer your question, yes I do. It's practically my theme song."

"I thought so," she said and gave him a light kiss. "Would you like to sing it to me right now?"

His brows drew together.

"Let me make sure I understand you, so there won't be any confusion. Am I seducing you, or are you seducing me?"

Suzanne sat up and pulled off her sleeping shirt. "How about we seduce each other?"

"That'll work," he said, tugging her down into his arms.

Fifteen

Suzanne lay with her head resting on Thad's chest. She heard the steady rhythm of his heart thumping strongly against her ear. He kissed the top of her head and brushed fingertips down her cheek.

"Now that's what I call a very nice welcoming home gift."

"You call this home?" she said looking around the little room.

"I haven't had a real home in years, so yeah."

Suzanne positioned herself, so she could see his face. He sounded like a man who'd been lonely for a very long time. Suzanne understood why her father doubted Thad because he didn't know him. But she should have shown more faith. Thad had proved to her more than once that he may have lied about a lot of things, but never about wanting to keep her safe.

"Sometimes having a home isn't all that great."

Thad threaded his fingers through her hair.

"I know. Your parents didn't do a very good job."

"Neither did James."

"I hope you got even with him somehow."

"I couldn't do anything really big, but I did some stuff when I suspected he was cheating on me."

"Like what?"

She shrugged.

"Oh, little things like putting too much hot sauce in his food, letting the cat pee in his car, cleaning the toilet with his toothbrush, and . . ."

"Cleaning the toilet with his toothbrush?" Thad narrowed his eyes at her. "I left my toothbrush in plain sight for you to help yourself when you were sore at me. Is there something I should know?"

Suzanne laughed.

"No, no. I swear on my favorite pair of shoes that I never did that to you."

He grunted.

"I'll have to take your word for it, but I might watch when you clean the bathroom."

"Okay. Maybe we can make a real home together some day?" she said, keeping her tone light.

"My life hasn't exactly been very conducive for putting down roots, Suzanne."

His disappointing reply tumbled her back into the old familiar crater of self-doubt. It seemed no matter what she did, she couldn't get him to make any real promises for a future with her unless it involved his job. He'd obviously do the physical part of a relationship, but shied away from any deep emotional commitment.

Embarrassed, she rolled away and turned her back, so he wouldn't see how much his words hurt.

"I misunderstood. I thought you sounded as lonely as I feel. But then, why would you want to spend any more time with me than necessary? I'm just another job and another faceless person in the crowd."

Thad grabbed her shoulders forcing her to face him again.

"Stop talking about yourself as if you're a nobody, damn it!"

"I try not to, but you know the saying about some days you're the statue and some days you're the pigeon. Well, most of my life I've felt like the statue, especially when it comes to my dad and mom."

"I hate what your parents have done to your self-esteem, but you have to get over that now. You think I don't see you? Well, you're wrong. You are more special than you know. There may be millions of grains of sand on a beach like the one last night, but it only takes one grain inside an oyster to make a pearl. You are that pearl, Suzanne."

Her lips formed a silent O, awed by his words.

146

"I can't promise a future with you because I don't know what the future is going to be. But that doesn't mean I don't fantasize about being with you, especially at night lying in the dark missing you so damn much that I ache for your touch."

"Oh Thad, I've ached for you, too. Maybe we can start by taking baby steps. You told me a lot about yourself. I'd like to know more."

"What kind of more were you thinking about?"

She looked into his eyes.

"Well, let me see. Where do you live when you're not on a case?"

"Motels, hotels, unless it becomes necessary for me to stay at a client's home."

"What about friends? Is your relationship with Linc and Maya for real?"

"It's real. We met in college and have remained friends over the years. The connection is as important to them as it is to me. But we don't get a chance to be together too often. At least not under what you would call normal circumstances."

"How about family? I know you're an only child and your parents died. Are there other relatives?"

"No."

She raised her brows. "Nobody?"

"None that I know about. My parents were both only children themselves. Their parents died before I was born. I never heard them talk about any other family."

"So not a lot of leaves on your family tree just like mine." She wiggled herself into a more comfortable position.

"Do you remember telling me you weren't a nice man?"

"Yeah."

"Did you say that because you've had to do some unpleasant things in your work?"

"You're getting into some dicey territory now," he said, shifting his eyes away from her.

"I know what happened to those men chasing us in Belize. I assumed that was unusual. I mean, guarding movie stars surely doesn't involve getting shot at, unless you get in the way while they were posing for a camera on the red carpet," she joked. "It seems like your job would be kind of glamorous."

"I don't get those types of assignments," he said looking at her. "I generally get the messier ones."

"I take that to mean the more dangerous cases. You remind me of those guys in the shoot 'em up movies. That kind of thing never seemed real to me until you were forced to kill the men in Belize. Have there been others?"

"It's not something I like to talk about."

"I suppose not. But if you're doing what you have to do to protect a person or yourself, that doesn't make you a bad man. It just means you're good at your job."

"I try to tell myself that. It doesn't always work. But thanks for your vote of confidence."

"Why don't you quit and do something else for a living?"

"I never had enough incentive."

Suzanne framed his face, splaying her slender fingers over his cheeks.

"I know we have to wait until this situation we're in right now is finished. But you should know when it's over I'm going to do everything I can to give you that incentive."

"You're already doing a pretty good job of it," he said and kissed her.

The kiss was long and sweet and probably would have led to something more intimate if Suzanne's stomach hadn't chosen that moment to let out a loud rumble. Thad laughed and pulled away.

"Talk about killing a guy's romantic notions."

She grimaced.

"I've been so nervous lately I've hardly eaten. I guess that's my stomach's way of letting me know I'm feeling better now."

"I haven't had a decent meal myself in the last few days. What do you say we go out for a bite?"

"I won't say no to that, but I'm going to have to explain you to the management here."

"Tell them I'm your boyfriend. We had a little tiff. We made up over the phone, and I decided to join you here."

"That ought to be interesting."

He gave her a puzzled look.

"Because?"

"Aaron told them he was my boyfriend and wanted me to stay here while he went away on a business trip. I'm afraid if it looks like I'm having different men coming and going out of my room the owners are going to ask me to leave. Or hang a red light over my door with a sign, Open for Business."

Thad chuckled.

"That might not be such a bad idea. The leaving part, that is."

"You want us to go to another place?" she asked, surprised.

"Now that you mention it, yeah I do."

"Why? Aaron and Heather are the only people who know I'm here. No one's going to find me."

"I found you."

"Not everyone is as clever as you. How did you find me, by the way?"

"I knew damn well Heather was lying about not knowing where you were, so I used my agency to help me track down her husband when I called his work and found out he'd asked for a few days off."

"I still don't know how you managed it."

Thad shrugged.

"I knew the kind of car he drove and the license plate. He left a paper trail because he charged all your meals, rooms, and gas."

"Your agency is able to access credit card information? It sounds more like the FBI or CIA."

"We do our best, and it's probably only a matter of time before the Montanes track you down, too."

Mentioning the Montanes made her shudder.

"You convinced me. What do I tell the people here?"

Thad decided it'd be better if he snuck away from the inn unnoticed while Suzanne checked out on her own. She told the owners her boyfriend had taken ill on his business trip, and she was going to join him. Lies and more lies. Where would it all end? Suzanne was beginning to feel every time she lied she was taking something away from the truth of who she really was. Every lie felt like a nick on her soul.

She wondered if people asked for forgiveness for their wrong doings would that guarantee them a better afterlife than people who said they had no regrets for the way they lived or the things they'd done. Was her father really sorry that she'd been dragged into his conspiracy? Or did he have a clear conscience because he believed he was doing the right thing?

Suzanne knew there was a very good chance she might never find out because of what happened at his motel. She still grappled with the nagging worry that her dad was too wounded to get in contact with her. Thad looked at her closely when she joined him.

"You look upset. Did you have trouble checking out?"

"No. That went fine. I can't seem to get rid of the feeling that Dad seriously injured himself at his motel. It'd take more than a few nicks to leave a bloody trail like I saw in that bathroom."

"Hopefully Muriel would get in touch with you if your father was in a bad way."

"She hasn't so far, unless she's worse off than my dad. God, I didn't think of that until now."

Suzanne pressed a hand to her head.

"I've worried myself into a headache."

Thad gripped her elbow.

"You're also hungry. Come on, let's get out of here and find something to eat. Who knows, you may get that phone call by the time we finish."

Suzanne's phone did ring while they were in the restaurant, but it wasn't her father. She wrinkled her nose and looked across the table at Thad.

"It's Heather. She calls two or three times a day. You'd think it was her dad who's missing."

"Don't tell her I'm with you and don't mention that you checked out of the inn."

"Okay." Suzanne answered the persisted chime. "Hi."

"It's about time. What took you so long?" Heather demanded.

"I'm eating and needed to swallow a mouthful of food."

"Nice to know stuffing your face is more important than taking my call."

Suzanne's lips tightened. "That's not a very nice thing to say, Heather. I need to eat."

"All right, all right, don't get all snippy on me."

Suzanne felt like mentioning she wasn't the one who sounded snippy. But she wasn't in the mood to argue. She also wasn't in the mood to listen to her friend's badgering her yet again about forgetting something that could help lead them to her father.

"I still haven't heard from Dad. I keep telling you I'll let you know if and when I do."

"He expected you to be smart enough to find him before. Maybe that's what he's waiting for this time. Think, Suzanne. Where might he go? You must know some of his haunts. I don't think you're trying hard enough. Aaron left you there in that inn, so you'd have the peace and quiet to concentrate. We can't believe you haven't come up with something."

"I've told you I've been trying. May I remind you that I'm the one who's had her life turned upside down? Do you really think I haven't whacked my brain over this? If I had anything to say that might be useful you would have heard about it by now."

"Calm down. I'm just trying a little tough love. I thought if I could get your adrenaline going, it might kick something loose. Aaron wants me to remind you not to call anyone else and don't talk to strangers."

"I know, I know, zero contact. Stop worrying. You're the only people I've talked to on the phone and I haven't even looked at a stranger."

She gave Thad a little smile across the table feeling proud of her clever evasion.

"Good. Keep it that way. I'll check back with you later today."

"Please don't take this the wrong way, but I'd rather you didn't. You're making me feel more uptight with all your calls. I know you mean well, but every time the phone rings it makes me feel worse."

"How do you think I feel when you never have anything worthwhile to tell me? Yours isn't the only life that's been turned upside down, Suzanne. Aaron and I are putting ourselves in danger to help you. The least you can do is put up with a few phone calls from us."

"I do appreciate everything you're both doing for me. But I can't help being on edge."

"Well, you're not the only one. There's a lot at stake here. If we don't get your dad's phones, we're going to suffer, too."

Suzanne's brows lowered in a frown. "What do you mean by that? How are you going to suffer?"

"Never mind."

"Well I do mind. Is there something you're not telling me?"

But Heather had already ended the connection.

"I take it everything isn't copacetic," Thad said.

Suzanne dropped the phone into her purse and shook her head.

"It's not. I made her angry and probably hurt her feelings as well. I didn't mean to. It's just that they keep calling and bugging me so much I'm to the point I dread hearing from them. I suppose because they're helping me they feel I've given them the right to make demands. But they've turned into control freaks."

"Could be because they think they have something to lose if you don't find your father."

"It's odd that you should say that because Heather just said something similar."

Thad decided to drive Suzanne back to the southern part of the state without further delay. He didn't want to add to Suzanne's concerns, but her friends' behavior bothered him. Why were they so anxious to know if and when she heard from her dad? And why were they hiding her away and insisting they be her only contact? She'd convinced herself that they were protecting her. Thad knew it hadn't occurred to Suzanne, but they could be keeping such a close eye on her because they were using her to get to her dad for their own ulterior motives, which was ironic when this was exactly what she'd convinced herself he'd been doing.

He had a feeling the Martin's didn't care so much about Wendell Conway's welfare as they did for their own. Thad knew if he was right about his suspicions he had to find out the reason. How much protection would they be willing to give to Suzanne once they got what they were after? Suzanne believed she could trust the Martins with her life. He wasn't so sure about that. Were they worried about Suzanne's welfare, or more concerned for their own skin? He very much feared it was the latter case, especially after listening to her conversation with Heather.

Aaron drove along the coast when he brought Suzanne up north. Thad opted to head inland to make their way back down south. He took them through lush forests with trees so tall they sometimes blocked out the light. Where pristine rivers meandered carving their silver paths over rocky beds and around big boulders sometimes larger than their vehicle. He guided his truck out of the cool mountains of the gold country and entered the warmth of the wine valley where mile after mile of grapes wound their long spindly vines over rows of trellises lining either side of the road.

Suzanne appeared to be enjoying the scenery as he drove. Thad kept up an easy flow of conversation with her while he continued to silently ponder over his ever growing suspicions about her friends. He told her he needed to stop for gas and a stretch, when they still had a couple hundred miles to go.

Thad waited until she left the car to use the restroom before he pulled out his phone. He hoped it wouldn't turn out to be a call he should have made sooner.

"I need you to run a background check on Suzanne Conway's friends, Aaron and Heather Martin. Find out everything you can about them and especially if there's any way they could somehow have a connection to the Montanes."

He knew it sounded crazy, but sometimes crazy turned out not to be so crazy after all.

Suzanne came back to the car a few minutes later.

Thad smiled at her. "All set?"

"Almost. Would you mind if I ran into the minimart for a bottle of water? I'll get you one."

"I already took care of it," he said and held the door open for her.

"You must be a mind reader."

"Nope. Just thirsty; and I had a feeling you would be, too. I also bought you a Snickers candy bar."

"Okay, you really are scary."

He slid in behind the wheel and started the car.

"I am? How come?"

"Because as it happens I was craving something chocolate, and Snickers is my favorite candy bar."

"Lucky guess."

She studied him for a moment.

"You probably have a dossier on me."

"Not about your favorite foods.

I read somewhere that women like chocolate."

"Hmm. I have a feeling there are very few things you guess about, because you already seem to know so much. I wonder what else is going on in that very active brain of yours."

He couldn't very well tell her that he was thinking her friends weren't as altruistic as she believed.

"What's going on inside my head isn't anything too earthshaking. I'm thinking I'd much rather be drinking a cold beer, which I can't because I'm driving."

"You're always so cautious, but I know you have to be given the nature of your work. I bet you hate it when you make mistakes."

"No one likes to make mistakes, and in my business it can cost a life, especially when I'm supposed to be protecting someone."

"Sounds like you're speaking from experience."

"Are you?" she asked when he remained quiet.

"Everyone has experiences."

She waited.

"You're shutting me out again," she said, when he didn't elaborate.

"Yes I am, and we'll leave it at that."

They drove in silence. Suzanne's head buzzed with questions, but she made herself respect Thad's obvious desire not to say anything more on the subject. Several minutes elapsed before she worked up her nerve to speak again. She drank deeply from her bottle and cleared her throat.

"I'm sorry for the times I ran out on you. It won't happen again. I know you're just trying to help me." She recapped the bottle. "I kind of got mixed up on who I could and couldn't trust."

"Keep that in mind."

She gave him a sharp look. "I hate it when you drop those cryptic bombs. Don't forget I've been walking through a minefield of liars lately, and you were right there with the rest of them. I'm not accusing you," she hastened to add. "But you have to admit I'm right."

"The only reason I've lied to you is to keep you safe. I'm just reminding you to be cautious."

"Well, you're making me wonder again who to put my faith in when you say things like that."

He gave her a brief glance before returning his eyes to the road.

"It'd be a good idea to keep that in mind, too."

Suzanne couldn't help thinking there was more meaning in what Thad wasn't saying than his actual advice. She toyed with the idea of asking him to go into greater detail, but abandoned the thought, knowing he probably wouldn't' tell her anything more. Several sentences could say a lot, but only one word would make a real difference here.

Truth!

And there didn't seem to be an abundance of that going around in her life lately.

Sixteen

Suzanne stood in the living room of the house where Thad had taken her. The luxury home was part of an exclusive gated community filled with large custom built houses. Movie star fancy, as Nanadoo would say. One look told Suzanne that no money had been spared to create such opulence. They'd taken their shoes off at the door. She curled her toes into the thick carpet.

"I've never been in a house with white carpeting before. This place is beautiful, but it's way more space than I need. The rent has to be astronomical. It's bound to put a serious dent in your expense account. Why not take me someplace less expensive?"

"The client I told you about is paying for it. He suggested I bring you here."

"Really? Is this his house?"

Thad shook his head.

"No. The owner is a friend of his and has moved to another state. The house is for sale. He worked out something with the owner's permission to hold off on the sale for a while. My client wants to do everything he can to make sure you're comfortable and well protected."

"I'm thinking I'd like to meet this gentleman some day."

"I'm sure he'd like to meet you, too. I told you he's a good man. He's experienced the pain of losing his daughter. He doesn't want anything happening to either you or Muriel. He already knows her, of course. I'll see if I can arrange something when this is over to bring you two together."

"I'd like that. Will you be staying here with me?"

"Yes. Is that going to be a problem?"

She wrinkled her nose at him.

"Not this time. I was too angry with you before to believe I shouldn't be alone."

"I'll stay when I can, and you'll be well taken care of when I have to be somewhere else."

"Why here, other than the fact your client's footing the bill?"

"Being a gated community gives extra security. We also want you to be able to tell your father you have a secure place with plenty of room for him and Muriel to stay when he calls you again."

"If he calls, you mean. He said he loved me. I don't want to lose that, but I'm beginning to think I already have. I just wish . . ." she stopped when her voice began to waver midway through her sentence.

Thad pulled her into his arms.

"Don't. I realize the not knowing is difficult, but your dad has proven himself to be a pretty resilient man. Try to focus on that."

He held her, rubbing her back in slow, gentle circles. She nuzzled her nose against his chest sighing while her body relaxed from the effects of his soothing touch. She stepped away after a few minutes.

"Thanks for the pep talk – and the backrub."

"Always happy to oblige. Why don't I show you the rest of the house? I think you're going to especially like the master bathroom. It has a Jacuzzi tub big enough to host a national convention."

"I don't care about a convention as long as the tub has enough room for the two of us. If you'd be interested in joining me, that is," she said with an impish grin.

"You definitely have my aye vote on that."

Thad's phone rang in the middle of the night. He bolted up in bed fully alert, while Suzanne took a little longer struggling to rouse herself. She listened, wondering why the caller found it necessary to phone at this hour. A sudden, unwelcomed thought stopped her in the middle of a yawn. Didn't bad news often come at inconvenient times like this? She listened closely to the conversation trying to garner clues from Thad's brief replies.

"Who was that?" she asked, as soon as he finished.

"One of the other investigators. He found your father."

"He did? Is Dad all right? Where is he? I want to see him."

She started to launch herself out of bed when Thad's hand on her shoulder held her back.

"Suzanne, wait. Let me answer your questions first."

She squeezed her eyes shut.

"Oh God, please, please don't tell me he's dead."

"No, but he is very ill."

Her eyes sprang open.

"He hurt himself escaping the motel, didn't he?"

"Yes. Both he and Muriel cut themselves climbing out the window. Her cuts were minor, but your father wasn't as lucky. He suffered deeper wounds that turned septic. They made it to another motel where she tried to treat him. She had to call for help when he started getting worse."

"Why didn't Muriel contact me?"

Thad pressed his fingers into her shoulder.

"They think you were the person who betrayed them."

"I guess I should have seen that coming," she said with a weary sigh. "Who helped them?"

"Muriel called Dewey. He came and took them to a doctor's house who happens to be a good friend. My agency had a man keeping an eye on Dewey since he'd helped your dad before, and followed him."

"Thank God it wasn't the Montanne's lynch mob on his tail. Is Dad still at that doctor's house?"

"No. He's been moved to a private clinic where he'll receive excellent care and be well guarded."

"What about the phones? Did your people find them?"

"Unfortunately not, and your father is too delirious to tell anyone where they might be."

"I had a feeling it was going to be bad when I didn't hear from him. I thought he'd at least want to call and bawl me out. I want you to take me to him. He may not want me hanging around, but if he's angry enough with me my voice may make him respond. I'm also going to have words with that girl."

Suzanne climbed off the bed and began grabbing her clothes with quick, jerky movements.

"You can't talk to Muriel," Thad informed her, as he rose to stand by her.

She whirled to face him, fury in her eyes.

"Who says I can't? I have every right to question her. My father risked his life for that woman. The least she can do is help me now. I also need this opportunity to try and convince them I wasn't responsible for what happened at their motel. She owes me that."

"I'll take you to your dad, but you can't question Muriel because she's disappeared."

Suzanne lowered the tee shirt she was about to pull over her head and stared at him.

"She's gone? That doesn't make sense. She stayed with my father all this time; and now she left just when they're finally in a safe place. Why would she leave when Dad needs her the most?"

"I don't know, but I sure as hell hope we can find out."

Suzanne had to force down the lump in her throat when she walked into the room where her father lay, pale and silent. She hurried over to him and stared, noting the sterile dressings covering his wounds.

"Oh, Dad," she whispered between trembling lips.

Thad pulled a chair close to the bed. She sat down and called to her father, louder this time wanting him to know she was there. He opened his eyes and looked at her, but showed no signs of recognition. He mumbled incoherently in disjointed sentences. Suzanne heard her name and sometimes Muriel's, but most of what he babbled didn't make any sense.

Thad left her alone, returning later to check on her before leaving the room again. Nurses came and went silently doing their job. Deep shadows filled the room when Thad came back for one last time. He tugged Suzanne to her feet. She stumbled, her body stiff with sitting so long in the same position.

159

"You've been in here for hours. You need to eat."

"I'm not hungry and I don't want to leave Dad."

"You aren't going to help your father by making yourself sick. You need to walk around a bit and get some sustenance into you. They have a small cafeteria here, so you'll still be in the clinic."

The grip on her arm left little doubt that he wasn't going to allow her to refuse.

"All right, but I don't want to be gone too long."

Thad tucked her hand in the crook of his arm.

"We won't be."

She ate a small bowl of chicken noodle soup under his watchful eyes and sat sipping coffee.

"Has anyone been able to glean anything helpful from Dad's mumblings? I certainly haven't."

"No. Maybe if they can get his fever down he'll be able to communicate better. He hasn't been here very long, Suzanne. Give the medical team a chance."

"I hate seeing him so ill, and it's almost more than I can bear having him think I betrayed him. I just wish he'd come around enough for me to at least tell him the truth about that."

"That's my hope for both of you."

Suzanne finished her coffee and looked at her watch. "I've been gone long enough. I want to go back to Dad's room. I'm going to keep talking to him. Hopefully he'll recognize my voice eventually."

"Are you prepared to handle his possible rejection?" Thad asked in a gentle voice.

"You know, the strange thing about that is the way I've felt kind of rejected by him most of my life. Then he said something so lovely to me on his phone call that I knew I'd always been loved. That's why it hurts so much now to feel like I've lost him all over again. I know I'm risking losing that love if I can't convince him I'm not the person who betrayed him, but I have to try."

Thad stood up and took her by the hand.

160

"I know this has been one hell of an ordeal for you. I wish for your sake it could have ended long before now and spare you all this anguish."

"I'm not the only one who's suffered, by the look of my dad. He's aged ten years since I last saw him."

"Isn't there an adage that says something like, out of great suffering comes great triumph?"

"If there is I would have liked us to be spared the suffering part."

Suzanne stayed by her father's bed pleading, consoling, even chastising in an effort to break through his delirium. But nothing she did appeared to be reaching into his fevered brain. She grew hoarse from talking and still she pressed on late into the night, even when she couldn't recognize her voice as her own.

Thad came into the room and insisted she needed to go back to the house for some rest.

"You go. I'm not leaving Dad until he wakes up and tells me he'd rather I go jump off a cliff."

"All right, then. I'll stick around here to catch you if you end up falling."

He walked out of the room and leaned against the wall a few feet away. He'd handled a lot of different assignments in his career, but never one with so many twists and turns as this case. The whole thing hinged on finding those phones of Suzanne's father before the Montanes got their hands on them.

Now Wendell was finally here in safe hands for all the good it was doing anyone since he couldn't communicate. Had he stashed the phones somewhere for safe keeping when he felt himself becoming so ill? Did Muriel have them? Was she intending to take them to the police? Thad couldn't imagine what else she'd want to do with them. Surely she'd want to have her relatives behind bars, so they wouldn't keep coming after her.

He'd worked with the team searching the doctor's house where Dewey took Suzanne's father. Everyone went through the place inside and out until it looked like a warzone. But they came up empty-handed despite their diligence. Dewey and the doctor swore they had no idea where Muriel could be.

Were they telling the truth? Hell, he didn't know. This entire assignment was fraught with liars from the beginning, himself included. He'd spun some tales on other cases to get the job done and that never bothered him, but lying to Suzanne did. He'd meant it when he told her she'd gotten to him.

He'd known from the first moment he felt his control slipping that things were going to be different for him this time. Thad almost wished she would have refused to sleep with him; and then maybe he wouldn't be so personally involved. Yeah, right, his brain scoffed. He wanted her to reciprocate as much as he needed to draw air into his lungs.

He switched his thoughts, mentally listing the general facts of the situation up to this point. Wendell was now safe, but too ill to be of any help. Muriel's disappearance might or might not be a good thing. He didn't know where the phones were and the Montanes wouldn't let up their relentless search no matter how many people they had to hurt.

"A damn soap opera," he muttered under his breath and headed back to Wendell's room.

He found Suzanne still sitting in a chair, sound asleep with the upper half of her body slumped over the side of her father's bed. He shook his head and lifted her into his arms receiving a mumbled protest.

"Don't wanna."

"Hush now," Thad softly scolded, as he laid her on the cot he'd asked for earlier.

She curled on her side and pressed her head into the pillow. He slipped off her shoes, covered her with a blanket, and left the room as silently as he'd entered. He walked down the hallway, nodded to the man standing guard, and stepped outside for some fresh air.

Thad looked around him. The clinic was more like an exclusive resort for people who wanted a private place to recover from whatever ailed them. Hidden in the mountains, the building sat amid thick foliage surrounded by a spiked wrought iron fence with security cameras and a twenty-four hour guard at the gate. It might seem like a prison to some, but for others the place meant more of a sanctuary. He supposed it depended on why you were here.

There could be healing behind these walls, or there could be heartbreak.

Which one, Thad wondered, would it turn out to be for Suzanne?

Suzanne pressed the pillow against her ears trying to ignore the persistent ringing. She knew the sound came from her phone just as she knew it would be either Heather or Aaron. A quick glance at her watch let her know it wasn't even dawn yet. They'd been calling and leaving text messages each more frantic than the last. They told her they contacted the owners of the inn and knew she'd left.

Suzanne groaned wishing she could have told the proprietors to lie and say she'd gone for a day's outing. But that wouldn't have satisfied her friends for long. Now that they realized she'd left they were going out of their minds wanting to know if she was all right. Suzanne sat up knowing she couldn't avoid talking to them any longer.

She looked down at the cot wondering how she got there. She supposed she was so sleepy she must have crawled in here without thinking. She stared toward her father's bed. His eyes were closed in sleep. She grabbed her purse and shuffled her way to his bathroom hoping to revive herself.

Suzanne swallowed and grimaced. Her mouth tasted like she'd licked a shag carpet. She set her purse on the counter before turning on the water to rinse her mouth out. She splashed water on her face, rubbing the last residue of sleep out of her eyes before combing her hair.

She pulled her phone out of her bag and held it in her hand for a few seconds wondering if she should wait for Thad to be here before she called Heather back. She shook her head. She knew he hadn't been getting much sleep himself. She didn't have the heart to call and wake him up just to subject the poor man to Heather's dramatic ranting. She steeled herself and made the call.

"Hello, Heather."

"Suzanne!" The name came out in a shrill yelp.

"Thank God you called. You can't know how upsetting it's been for us knowing we couldn't call the police. Where are you? Why did you leave the inn? Did the Montanes find your hiding place? Why haven't you gotten in touch with us before now?"

Heather riddled her with questions making Suzanne wish she could put the phone away from her ear.

"I can't tell you where I am, but I'm in a safe place."

"What do you mean you can't tell me? This is Heather you're talking to, remember?"

"It's safer for all of us if you don't know. But I will tell you I'm with my dad."

"You found him? Thank the lord! What about the phones? Do you have them?"

"No."

"I hope you're not lying to me, girlfriend."

"Heather, for heaven's sake. What a thing to say. Why would I lie to you?"

"What do you expect me to think when you left the inn without telling me and waited so long to call? Aaron and I have tried to help you in every way we know how and this is how you thank us."

"I'm sorry. I didn't mean to upset you."

"I've gone way beyond being upset and since you've shown so little regard for my feelings I'm going to tell you something I've been trying to avoid. Maybe then you'll understand where I'm coming from. We both know your father likes to gamble. He came to our house just before he disappeared and said he owed the Montanes a lot of money for his losses. He said they were going to kill him if he didn't come up with the cash."

Suzanne sucked in a shocked breath.

"Why didn't you tell me this before?"

"Because I know how much he's hurt you over the years. I didn't want to add to that pain. Wendell begged us to help him. Aaron withdrew every cent out of our savings, plus we took a second loan on our house and gave him all the money."

"My God, how much did he owe?"

"It's quite a lot."

"How much, Heather?" Suzanne insisted, and gasped at the amount. "You're right, that is a lot. I'll give you what I have in my savings and take a loan on my house."

"I wish to God we'd never fell for your dad's sob story and got mixed up in this."

"I wished you hadn't, either. I'll never be able to find enough words to thank you."

"Words aren't going to do much good. We need those phones. Are you going to help us get them?"

"I've already promised to pay you the money Dad took. What are you going to do with the phones?"

"Give them to the Montane brothers."

"Heather! You can't be serious."

Suzanne's legs felt so shaky she had to lean against the counter.

"Oh yes I am. Thanks to your ungrateful parent, the Montanes have threatened to kill us if we don't get those phones for them. They know we're friends with you. We tried to protect you. That's why Aaron took you away. Now I'm asking you to help us before we end up wearing cement boots."

"Please don't say such things. I'd give the phones to you, but I meant it when I said I didn't have them. Thad helped me."

Heather hissed into the phone.

"I thought you said he was a double-crossing rat."

"My dad had me jumping to all the wrong conclusions. Thad really is trying to help me. His people found Dad. He's very ill, Heather. Remember how worried I was when I saw all that blood at the motel? Well, Dad suffered some serious cuts from that broken window, and then he got an infection. He's delirious, and so far I can't get anything out of him about where the phones might be."

"What about that Muriel? Have you asked her?" Heather demanded without offering a word of sympathy for Wendell.

165

But Suzanne supposed she couldn't blame her friend after what her father had done to them.

"I would have, but she ran off before I got here to Dad."

"Well, isn't that wonderful? It's nice that you and your daddy are both safe while, Aaron and I are left here just waiting for the Montanes to pounce."

"Heather, I'm so sorry. What if I took a picture of my dad showing how sick he is? You could send it to the Montane brothers. They'd only have to look to know he's really out of it."

"They don't want a damn picture, they want those phones!"

Suzanne recoiled at her friend's desperate shriek.

"I'm just trying to think of what I can do to help."

"I have an idea if you really mean what you say."

"Of course I do."

"The Montanes might get off our backs if we gave them a token of goodwill."

"I don't have a lot of money and I certainly don't know what else we could offer them besides Dad's phones."

"I do."

Suzanne frowned.

"What?"

"You."

Seventeen

Suzanne wandered out of her father's room feeling sick with worry for her friends and scared to death for herself if she did succeed in going to the Montanes. She thought it'd be impossible to get out of here without being noticed, until she went outside for some air and saw a bakery van.

She swore her brain must be on automatic pilot when she hoisted herself up and climbed into the van before she even registered what she was doing. She wedged her way between the rows of shelves holding covered trays of donuts, Danish rolls, and wrapped sandwiches. She wondered if the driver locked up every time he left the truck. She got inside with surprising ease, but getting out might be more difficult.

Suzanne didn't know where she'd end up, but at least she'd be out of Thad's reach. Her heart ached for what she was doing to him again. Would he ever forgive her even if she explained that she had no choice but to put her friends first after what her father had done to them? Could she make Thad see that while she cared for him deeply, she'd only known him for a short time compared to Heather who'd been part of her life for years?

Suzanne was pretty sure Thad would be hounding them as soon as he'd discovered she was gone. He'd want to stay in touch despite their mistrust of each other. She could only hope he would understand why she ran away from him once Heather explained the situation. Thinking of what she'd promised to do for Heather made her body prickle with nerves.

Caesar Montane wanted the damning phones, but he also wanted his daughter back and would stop at nothing to have his revenge on her for running out on him. God only knows what he would do to the daughter of the man who threatened to destroy his criminal empire. Would offering herself as bait bring Heather and Aaron the reprieve they needed? Perspiration glossed Suzanne's skin, as she tried not to think about the terrible things Thad and Dewey said about the Montanes.

Was she about to embark on a mission of mercy for her friends, or end up taking a path to her death?

It didn't take much time searching the premises for Thad to know that Suzanne had left the clinic. The only vehicle coming through the security gate during the time she must have disappeared was the bakery van making a delivery to the cafeteria. It looked like the driver had driven away with yesterday's stale bread and one very resourceful lady.

So, as much as Thad hated to admit it, his run away woman had run away again. This made three times now that she'd managed to elude him. Three times was a strike out and it looked like he was on the losing side. He didn't like losing and he especially didn't appreciate being made to look like a fool, which thanks to Suzanne outwitting him was exactly how he felt.

Thad decided he'd better rethink his profession if he couldn't do any better than this. Maybe Heather wasn't so far off when she said she wouldn't trust him to watch her dog. And speaking of that woman, he knew she was trying to locate Suzanne herself. Would the two women be in touch with each other?

Suzanne had gone to her friend before when she needed help in getting away from him. Now that they'd finally found her father she gave every indication she wouldn't run away again. So why did she leave without telling him? What was so important it couldn't wait?

Thad had deliberately left word with both the guard and nurses on duty that he planned to spend the night on one of the couches in the waiting room at the clinic in case Suzanne needed him. The only thing they could tell him this morning was that Suzanne had come out of her father's room shortly after dawn saying she was going to the cafeteria for some coffee.

Thad knew a machine provided that when the place was shut down for the night. They assumed she'd stayed there. He didn't chastise the guard, although it would have helped if someone bothered to tell him when Suzanne left her father's room. Thad knew it was the man's job to watch Wendell, while he was personally responsible for keeping tabs on the slicker than slick Suzanne.

He yanked his phone out of his pocket and called the front gate, fighting down his anger.

"This is Novak. Has the bakery van left yet?"

"No, but I see him coming right now."

"Don't let him leave. I have reason to believe he's carrying something I'm looking for."

"Do you want me to do a search?"

"No, that would be my job."

Thad jogged out to his truck just as his phone signaled a call from his office. "Novak."

"I did that background check on the Martins you ask for and if they might have any connection to the Montanes," a female voice said. "I think you'll be interested in what I found."

Thad listened and the more he heard, the tighter his hand gripped the phone.

The van slowed down and stopped. Suzanne could hear the driver and the guard talking, but she couldn't make out what they were saying. Several seconds ticked by. Why was it taking so long to get going again? The driver made daily deliveries, so he must have full clearance to come and go without this much delay. Suzanne pushed herself back trying to scrunch her body into tight space when the back doors suddenly flung open bringing in a rush of cool morning air along with Thad's chilly sounding words.

"I know you're in here, Suzanne."

"Listen mister, are you sure the woman you're looking for is hiding in my van?" the driver said. "I've got a schedule to keep, so I can't be hanging around here all day."

"She's here. Come out on your own, or I'll come in and drag you. Which is it to be?"

169

Suzanne peeked out from behind a box and began to crawl toward the exit, trembling as every inch brought her closer to the two men with very different expressions. The wide eyed driver turned to Thad.

"I hope you don't think I knew about this. I had no idea she was in there."

"I know you didn't," Thad ground out, grabbing Suzanne by the arm and jerking her to the ground.

"I can explain," she said, wincing in pain from his hard fingers.

Thad ignored her and motioned to the driver. "You can go now. I'm sorry for the inconvenience."

His hand tightened on her arm as he forced her to walk to his truck where he shoved her into the cab before climbing in behind the wheel.

"I can explain," Suzanne said again. "I called Heather. She and Aaron are in danger. They loaned my dad a huge amount of money to pay off his gambling debts to the Montanes. They need my help. I know you two don't trust each other, so I hid inside the van because I was afraid you wouldn't let me leave."

The words tumbled out of her in a rush. A muscle tweaked along Thad's jaw while he stared straight ahead. He stopped, yanked open the door, and practically lifted Suzanne bodily off the front seat. He marched her into the clinic and down a hallway where he shoved her into a janitor's closet.

"Stay," he ordered, pointing to a stool.

He gave the one word command as though he might be speaking to a dog that had disobeyed him.

"In here? Thad, I can't. I told you about Heather. I have to help her. She's counting on me."

"I suspect you'll be receiving a call from her in a while. Don't use your phone until then."

Suzanne lunged forward as he started to close the door.

"You can't leave me in here," she yelled and pounded on the door when she heard the sound of a lock being clicked into place. She staggered back and plopped down on the little stool.

"Now what?"

Heather cowered in one corner of her couch cringing at the rage in Thad's eyes, as he leaned over her. He looked ready to tear something apart. Mainly her.

"I want to know what Suzanne planned to do for you, and I want to know now."

"I . . . I don't have any idea."

His big hands balled into fists.

"I've never hit a woman before, but so help me God if you don't give me some answers pretty damn quick you're about to become the first."

"I really don't know where she is."

Heather hurried on avoiding his question.

"Suzie was supposed to call me if she could get away from you. I haven't heard from her. I swear."

Thad had the information from his agency and he remembered what Suzanne had told him, but he wanted to hear Heather's version.

"I asked you what she was going to do to help you, not where she is. Why did she want to leave on her own and without me knowing?"

Heather licked her lips.

"Aaron and I are having some problems. Suzie offered to help us."

"Where is your husband now?"

"He's passed out in our bedroom. Had too much to drink. We need a lot of money. Suzie said she'd pay, but what we're really after are the phones her dad is carrying."

"Why?"

"Aaron is addicted to gambling. I've begged him to get counseling, but he won't. He didn't realize the loan shark he's been involved with was affiliated with the Montane brothers. When they found out I'm such good friends with Suzanne, they began to threaten to kill us if we didn't get those phones. That's why we kept hoping her dad would call her again. We thought we had him when she confided to me that he and Muriel were at that motel."

171

"So you're the reason they left in such a hurry. Did you tip off the Montanes the day we had lunch? Is that why Suzanne and I were followed?"

She nodded and twisted her fingers together.

"What were you planning on doing when you went to the motel where her father was hiding?"

"We weren't going to hurt them. We just wanted the phones. I told her dad it was me when I knocked on the door. I said we wanted to help him. It's . . . it's not my fault he got all cut up like he did. He's known me since I was a child. I never expected him to run like that."

"Maybe he had enough horse sense to recognize when a barn is full of manure, and he didn't want to be around the stench. What did you tell Suzanne to con her into offering to help you?"

"I knew her dad liked to gamble. He's nothing like Aaron; but I made her believe he'd gotten worse, and we loaned all that money to Wendell. I told her the Montanes knew my connection to her and threatened to kill us if we didn't get those phones. I convinced her to help us because we helped her dad. She said he was too ill to tell her where the phones were, so I came up with an idea I thought might make the Montanes hold off for now."

Thad fought for control when every instinct made him want to throttle her.

"What was your idea to save your husband's sorry ass?" he demanded.

Heather swallowed several times.

"I . . . I suggested she offer herself to the Montanes as a kind of collateral until her dad reveals where he stashed the phones."

Thad had to step back then. He knew if he didn't, he really might grab her by throat, as she sat there quietly weeping now. He took in a couple of deep breaths and looked at Heather like she was something that had crawled out from beneath a rock. He clenched and unclenched his fists.

"There aren't enough ways to describe how much you disgust me. You call yourself a friend? How could you even think of allowing Suzanne to put herself in such danger? Have you no conscience?"

"I didn't know what else to do. I'm trying to save Aaron," she sobbed. "You . . . you have no idea what the Montanes threatened to do to him before they killed him if we don't get those phones."

Thad grabbed her by the upper arms and lifted her off the couch making her cry out in pain. He knew his hands would leave marks. He didn't care.

"Holy God woman, what the hell do you think they'd do to Suzanne?" he snarled, hands tightening.

"You're hurting me!"

"You have no idea how much I want to hurt you. You're going to call Suzanne and tell her the truth about your husband needing the money and above all, you do not want her going to the Montanes."

"What about the car chase and the motel incident? Should I tell her about that, too?"

"She's going to have to deal with enough right now. Where's your phone?"

She pointed toward a table across the room. He shoved her there and snatched it up with one hand while holding onto her with the other.

"Call her. Now, damn it!" he demanded when she hesitated.

Heather made the call with one hand while wiping away tears with her other hand. Suzanne answered on the first ring.

"Heather! I'm so glad you called. I can't . . . ."

"Suzie, listen," she said, interrupting her. "There's been a change of plans." She gave Thad a wary look. "I . . . I have a confession to make. Please hear me out before you say anything. I lied when I said it was your dad who had the gambling problem. It's Aaron. Your father never asked us for any money."

Various emotions played over Heather's face while she listened to Suzanne. Thad watched her closely when she began to speak again.

"I'm sorry I tricked you. I've been scared beyond scared, but it was wrong of me to put you in danger by telling you to go to the Montanes. Please, please don't even think of doing such a thing. What did you say? You're locked in a storage closet? How did that happen?"

Heather jerked her head toward Thad, as she listened to Suzanne's explanation. She gave him a questioning look and he gestured for her to continue.

"Thad probably did it to keep you safe. I also wanted you to know, so you won't worry about us that I've decided to ask Aaron's boss if he'll loan us the money to pay off the gambling debt. Maybe then I can get Aaron to go for counseling. Hopefully if we pay them the money the Montanes will agree to just keep watching while they wait to see what happens about the phones. I'll leave it up to you what you decide if your dad does wake up and tells you where they are. All I can say again is that I'm so, so sorry I took such advantage of your willingness to help us."

Heather listened.

"Yes, I'm sure Thad was pretty angry when he caught you trying to sneak away. But I bet he won't stay mad because I just told him why you were trying to leave without him. I have to go now. We'll talk some more later. I love you."

Heather looked up at Thad as soon as she was done.

"Suzie didn't say she loved me back."

"You were going to throw her to the wolves. What did you expect, gratitude?"

Suzanne slid the phone into her purse, shaking in reaction to her friend's shocking confession. She had no idea how long she sat there trying to take it all in when she heard someone unlocking the door.

What if it was a custodian? How was she going to explain what she was doing sitting here among the buckets and mops? The door swung open and a man she didn't recognize stood there.

"We're going to leave here together. Nice and easy. No noise. No scene."

174

She gave him a thoughtful look. "Did Thad Novak send you? If he didn't, I'm not going anywhere with someone I don't know."

"I have a knife that says you are," he answered, and flashed the blade.

Suzanne backed away.

"Take my . . . my purse. I have cash, credit cards. You can have them all."

"Thanks for the offer, but it's you I want. Now shut up and move."

He steered her outside to a service alley where he ordered her into the back of a van. Suzanne struggled to climb in causing the man to shove her. She gasped in pain when her hands and knees hit the hard metal. There wasn't any pleasant aroma here like her last van ride. This vehicle was filled with tools and reeked of grease and exhaust fumes strong enough to irritate her nostrils and make her eyes water.

The doors banged shut, and Suzanne felt the van rumble away seconds later. What would Thad think when he got back and found her gone? Probably that she'd gotten out and run off again. He must be thoroughly sick of chasing after her by now. She wouldn't blame him if he didn't bother to come looking for her this time.

Another distressing idea made her stomach lurch. Heather didn't say so, but she may have already let the Montanes know about Suzanne offering herself to them. Her phone call said to scrap the plan, but the mob might not be so willing to abandon the idea.

Could this mean she was on her way to the Devil's Den after all?

Eighteen

The van's momentum tossed Suzanne about like a lone marble rolling around inside a large box. She clawed her way over the hard surface, scooted around a toolbox, and managed to reach an area where she pulled her knees to her chest and leaned back to brace herself.

Who was this man who so boldly snatched her out of the clinic in broad daylight? A man who was now driving like a maniac, she noticed. How had he managed to get through security? Suzanne winced when her shoulder slammed into the wall, as the van took a sharp turn.

She supposed she couldn't blame Heather for going to such lengths to help Aaron. Fear. Desperation. They had all been there in her friend's voice. Suzanne realized Heather wasn't thinking any clearer than she was, but for different reasons. She and Heather may have been friends for a long time, but in a situation like this the husband had to come first. Still, knowing that she was being used didn't make it any easier to bear.

Suzanne had no idea what this man was going to do with her, but if she did end up at the mercy of the Montane brothers the first thing they were going to ask about were those cursed phones her father had hidden. She pressed her forehead to her knees. Would they believe her when she said she didn't know where they were? What means would they use to get her to talk?

She felt the vehicle rumbling to a stop a few seconds later. They hadn't paused at the gate, which told Suzanne they couldn't have left the grounds. Were the Montanes waiting in the woods? She sucked in a quick shivery breath realizing just how the thought of that name gripped her with a sickening dread. She must have taken leave of her senses to let Heather talk her into going to the mob.

The doors yanked open.

"Get out," the man ordered. "Don't even think about trying to run away." He held up his knife until the long slender blade gleamed in the sunlight. Two aborted van rides in one day. How would this one end? Suzanne eased her body to the edge of the van and jumped out, grimacing when her feet hit the ground jarring her sore muscles. She had a feeling she was going to be sporting a few colorful bruises by tomorrow.

If she was still alive.

The man motioned her to step away from the van. He looked to be in his late twenties with shaggy, sandy colored hair, average height and build. His denim shirt and jeans made him look like an innocent looking guy who just happened to be carrying a not so innocent looking knife. She saw he'd pulled the van off the road and parked among a grove of trees.

"What do you want?" she demanded, trying to force some strength into her voice, as she struggled to keep her fear at bay.

"Actually, I don't want anything from you, but my friend does," he said and pointed to a woman stepping out from behind a nearby tree.

Suzanne judged her to be barely out of her teens, if that old. Petite, like herself, but with jet black eyes to match her long dark hair. She wore a pair of faded jeans and a man's plaid shirt. Her body appeared on the thin side with the exception of her protruding stomach.

Muriel. Suzanne felt sure this was the girl her father had fought so hard to protect. Her body looked soft and vulnerable while her expression held a mixture of hardness and hostility. Suzanne made herself smile while bracing herself against the open fury in the girl's eyes.

"Are you Muriel? If you are you didn't have to go to such lengths to get me. I wanted to meet you."

"Why did you betray your father?" the girl demanded, brushing aside Suzanne's query.

Suzanne shook her head. "I didn't."

"Yes you did! I was there," her voice shook with the force of her anger. "You sent those people to our motel. You were the only one your father told where we were."

"Muriel, listen to me, please. The people I told were friends. They know my dad. I needed their help to get you out of there and into a safe place. But when I got to the motel you were already gone. My friends arrived after I did."

"You're wrong. You're so-called friends came first. They threatened to call my father when we didn't open the door. That's why we had to escape out the bathroom window. It's all your fault that Wendell is so sick. His blood will be on your hands if he dies."

It took Suzanne a few seconds to process what Muriel was telling her. Had it really been Aaron and Heather who got to the motel before her? Why didn't she say so when she was confessing to her other lies? Muriel must be mistaken.

"Whoever came to your motel had to be someone else."

"I heard the woman say their names, Aaron and Heather Martin." Suzanne caught her breath on an audible gasp while Muriel continued. "Your father didn't open the door because he didn't trust them. He told me they'd borrowed money from him on several occasions to help pay the man's gambling debts. He helped them because the woman is your friend. But they kept asking for more and never paid him back, so he stopped giving them money several months ago."

Suzanne felt as though an icicle had just stabbed her in the chest. Her entire body went cold, as the last remnant of her relationship with her childhood friend snapped and died like a rotten branch falling from a tree. She forced down the anger swelling inside her as she tried to separate the old caring Heather from this new deceitful person.

"I didn't know. I swear on my life. Heather said it was my dad who borrowed money from them. She said your father was going to kill them if they couldn't deliver the phones to him. I was going to help by turning myself over to your father as security until I could get my dad to tell me where the phones are."

Muriel uttered a harsh laugh.

"You're not as smart as your father says you are if you really thought that would appease my relatives. They would have killed you as soon as they found out you couldn't give them what they wanted."

"Then we must get those phones to the authorities. None of us are going to be safe from your family until they're locked away. Did you take the phones when you left my father?"

"No."

"I see." Suzanne pressed her lips together. "Will you tell me where my dad hid them?"

"I can't."

"Please, I'm begging you. It's for your own good. I want you to be safe; and I know that's what my dad wants for you, too. Help me to put an end to this, so we can all stop running. I'm sure you're getting tired of having people chasing you all over the place. I know how you feel and I . . ."

"You have no idea how I feel," Muriel sliced through the words causing her face to flush with color. "You think these last few weeks have been hard because you've had to look over your shoulder? Well, welcome to my world. Every day of my life has been like that."

Muriel wiped away tears trickling down her cheeks. The gesture caused Suzanne to experience a flood of pity so strong she longed to reach out and offer comfort. But she knew any such gesture would be refused. She may not be the girl's worst enemy, but neither had she been accepted as a friend.

"You're going to have to trust someone else now that my dad is so ill. I know he's very concerned about you and your unborn child. He told me so during our phone conversations."

"I have people I can trust." She nodded toward her friend nearby. "I'm not so sure about you."

"I understand, but I really do want to help. Please tell me where those phones are. If not for me, then do it for my dad."

"I said I can't, not that I wouldn't."

Suzanne studied Muriel. The truth slowly began to dawn on her. She walked away and paced back.

"You don't know where they are, do you?"

"No, I don't. I would have turned them over to the police if I did. Your father must have put them somewhere before he became delirious."

"Are you sure he didn't tell you anything?"

"He didn't, and since you don't know where the phones are either, you aren't much good to me."

Muriel motioned to her friend and he began to amble toward Suzanne, the knife still clutched tightly in his hand. If they were desperate enough to drag her out of the clinic they might be desperate enough to do just about anything. She had to find a way to convince them she really meant them no harm. They needed her help, but she needed theirs even more.

"Let me tell you something, Muriel. I've spent years trying to prove to my dad that I was worthy of his love. I thought he never cared about me up until very recently. Now that I know he does I don't want to lose our newfound connection. He loves both of us in his own way, and right now he needs both of us. Take me back to the clinic. Come inside with me. We'll talk to him together, and hopefully hearing us will coax him out of his comatose state. I'm asking you to trust me for my father's sake."

Muriel pushed back the sleeves of the man's shirt she wore to reveal several small bandages on her slender arms. "This is what I ended up with the last time I trusted you and your friends. I just met you, and you want me to trust you with my life."

She shook her head.

"I don't think so."

"I don't blame you for feeling that way. I'm having my own trust issues. I just found out a person I've known since childhood was willing to let me risk my life for her own selfish reasons. While on the other hand, a man I only met a few weeks ago has put himself in danger to save me more than once."

"Why would he do that?" Muriel asked, her smooth brow furrowing into a frown.

"He's been hired by a man to bring down the Montanes and put them away for good. They kidnapped the man's only daughter and sold her into sexual slavery where she died. He wants justice for her, and he wants to help you, too. You know the girl I'm talking about, don't you?"

Muriel sighed, and pushed her sleeves down."

My college roommate. My family has hurt or killed so many people over the years it sickens me. Did you know my father even killed my mother?"

"Yes. I can't imagine how awful it had to be for you. The man who's been helping me mentioned it."

"Did he also mention that my dad murdered my baby's father?" she whispered, touching her swollen belly.

"Yes, I know about that, too. I'm so sorry."

She couldn't stop herself from giving Muriel's shoulder a gentle squeeze. The girl stiffened, but didn't pull away; and this time when she looked at Suzanne, her eyes were filled with surrender.

"I've been surrounded by hatred and greed my whole life. I often wondered why I had the bad luck to be born into a family so lacking in moral decency. I want to go somewhere and have my baby and find some peace. Is that so much to ask?"

"No it's not. I'd like to help you find that peace and while we're at it, I wouldn't mind having a bit of it myself. Will you go with me to the clinic now and see if we can convince my dad to wake up?"

"All right. I'll do this for your father, but I'm still not sure about my feelings for you."

"I understand. Um, what about your friend? I hope he's not still thinking about cutting me."

"He never would have. I am not my father. I just wanted to scare you."

Suzanne couldn't suppress a nervous little laugh.

"He certainly did that. What will he do now?"

"He'll go home."

"How did he get the security guard at the gate to let him through?"

"We've been watching and waiting for our chance. We saw the plumber's van coming, and I sat on the side of the road holding my ankle. The driver stopped. He said he was on his

181

way to the clinic to fix a plugged toilet, and would take me there. My friend snuck up behind and knocked the guy out. He took the van and told the guard he was the plumber. He saw you being put in that storeroom. The rest you know."

"You're very resourceful."

"You would be too, if you grew up in a family when every day might be your last."

Thad stared at the empty closet where he'd left Suzanne and raked a frustrated hand through his hair.

Where in the hell had she gone now? What ruse had she used to get someone to let her out? He looked around. Could the Montanes have anything to do with her release? God, he hoped not. But anything was possible considering how many people they had on their payroll.

Did someone snatch Suzanne away in broad daylight? It'd be an odd twist for them. They were more used to masterminding something like this under the cover of darkness and in a place without people, so there wouldn't be any witnesses. They reminded him of rats running through sewers. They carried their vileness with them, gnawing and biting as they went along, not caring that they destroyed everything and everyone getting in their path.

He could check back with the Martins, but the more Thad thought about them being involved in Suzanne's latest disappearance the more he dismissed the idea. Who else would want to get in touch with Suzanne? Her mother? Maybe, but the last he heard she was still lying by the pool at her hotel in Mexico playing footsies with her companion.

He'd have to wait and hope that Suzanne would show up. It wasn't going to be easy. But one thing he did know, and that was how he'd failed one more time to keep her contained in a safe place. He'd earned a big fat F in protection, if anyone was grading him.

Suzanne entered the private waiting room at the clinic later that afternoon. Thad didn't turn around when she opened the door, but she knew by his body posture he was aware of her

182

presence. He stood at the windows with his back to her, his arms crossed over his chest.

A full minute ticked by, and he still didn't move. His continued silence made her uneasy. She'd been back long enough sitting in her father's room with Muriel to have Thad come and talk to her. Suzanne knew he'd been informed of her return, but he continued to stay away. She decided to go look for him.

She didn't blame him for being angry, but it wasn't her fault that she wasn't where he'd left her when he returned. She'd come here to explain to him how she'd been whisked away without a chance to let him know what had happened.

She was perfectly willing to apologize if that's why he was giving her this silent treatment. Anything to break through this strain she felt between them that was making her feel more uncomfortable by the second. Suzanne approached him carefully, not sure of her reception.

"Thad, I'm sorry. I know you're . . ."

"Don't bother." He turned to face her. His voice sounded flat, and his expression revealed no emotion at all. He looked at her as though she might be a stranger.

"I've asked to be assigned to another case. I'll be leaving here as soon as my replacement arrives."

She blinked in surprise.

"Why? I thought I had become more than just another case to you."

"You had, until you broke your promise to me once too often. I can no longer protect you because I've lost my objectivity where you're concerned. I let myself become too personally involved. I actually believed you when you said you wouldn't run off again. Bad judgment on my part. Obviously."

"I know Muriel told you about how her friend came and took me, but you never gave me a chance to explain what really happened with Heather. She made me believe she and Aaron were in trouble, and that it was my dad's fault. I had no idea she was lying. How could I?" she asked, tears welling in her eyes.

"No, but you could have told me about her call, and given me the opportunity to decide what would have been the safest course of action. Trust. That's what you promised me and that's what I gave you in return. The problem is you didn't keep up your end of the bargain. I might have seen that about you if my instincts were what they should be where you're concerned. But they're not. You made me soft, and that in turn made me careless. That's why you need someone else to be in charge of your welfare."

Tears ran down her cheeks now.

"I don't want anyone else. I've never had to run from anything or anyone before, but since all this happened with my dad, all I've done is run. I've been trying to do the best I can. You know that. I thought you understood. You . . . you can handcuff us together. Clip me to a leash. Put tracking devices on my ankles. I'll accept any and all of that. Please, say you'll stay."

"It's too late for that. I no longer want to be with you. By the way, if my replacement happens to tell you your life is in danger, it might be a good idea if you gave him the benefit of the doubt."

"You . . . you mean you're leaving right now?"

"I already have."

His eyes moved over her, letting her know he was distancing himself mentally and emotionally. Suzanne reached a hand out to him, but lowered it when he stared at her, his expression cold and remote. He walked to the door and stood there with his back to her, shoulders hunched, and with his forehead pressed against the panel before straightening up and yanking the door open.

"Goodbye, Suzanne," he said in a hoarse whisper, and left without looking back.

The soft snap of the door shutting sounded like a thunderclap inside her head, making her flinch as though she'd been physically struck.

Nineteen

Suzanne stood shaking, unable to believe Thad really meant to abandon her. She stared at the door, fingernails digging into her palms until the realization hit her that he really wasn't coming back. She slumped down to her knees, pressed her hands to her face, and wept until she was straining to draw air into her tortured lungs.

Full darkness encased the room by the time she groped her way to the small couch and sagged back against the cushions. Her heart struggled to accept that Thad didn't care enough about her to stay. She knew she needed to go back to her father's room, but her legs felt like lead. In fact, her entire body felt heavy and mired in misery. She blamed herself for this; and self-blame was the hardest to bear, because one had to take the full brunt of the burden. Bad decisions had cost her dearly.

Trying to put all the blame on Heather didn't ease her own guilt. Suzanne felt like kicking herself for not telling Thad about her phone call. She'd rushed off ready to try and be Ms. Fix-it. She'd allowed herself to be sucked into Heather's lies and ended up having a lifetime of friendship shattered within a few hours. But the pain of losing their relationship paled in comparison to how she'd trusted Heather to help her father and ended up putting him in a hospital instead.

Suzanne stood up and groped her way through the dark ready to return to her father's room, when the door abruptly flung open. Someone snapped on the light switch flooding the room with brightness, causing Suzanne to blink against the glare.

"Here you are. What are you doing in the dark? I've been looking all over for you. Your father looks like death, and I must say you don't look much better."

Suzanne gawked in surprise.

185

"Mom! What are you doing here?"

Bobbett Conway sailed into the room on a cloud of heavy floral perfume and settled herself on the couch. She crossed her legs exposing a great deal of bare thigh in the bright blue mini skirt she wore. She reminded Suzanne of a peacock bringing a burst of color to the drab room. The couch could have been a throne the way Bobbett draped herself over the modest furniture. But Suzanne knew her mother could be sitting on a dried dung heap and make it seem like a perch fit for a queen.

"Sit down before you give me neck strain."

"What are you doing here?" Suzanne repeated, sinking down next to her mother.

"Well, you can darn well bet it's not my choice. Davy received an urgent summons to come right away, so he could babysit you."

"Babysit me? Who is this Davy?"

"As far as I knew he was just my vacation companion until a few hours ago. But it turns out he works for a fancy dancy security outfit. I thought that sounded exciting until he told me the one watching you was assigned elsewhere meaning Davy had to take his place. I'm not pleased to have you and your father drag me into this mess you two have whipped up. You've interrupted my vacation."

"Your vacation? Is that all you can think about? You said you saw Dad, so you know how ill he is. Doesn't that bother you at all?"

Bobbett flipped a strand of long bleached blond hair away from her tanned face.

"Your father stopped bothering me a long time ago. Oh do stop glaring at me like I'm the one who pushed him out that window. Why are you angry with me? He's the one who stole money for his pregnant girlfriend."

"She's not his girlfriend."

Bobbett waved her hand in the air.

"Whatever. The point is I've been forced to come here because Davy's company thinks your father's antics have put me in danger. Little wonder that I don't have any sympathy for his predicament. What I want to know is why did the guy watching you ask to be reassigned? Did you bore the poor man to death with your pitiful tale about James deserting you? I swear I don't know what your problem is that you can't hold onto a man."

Suzanne surged to her feet. Listening to Bobbett's complaints and insults was the last thing she needed right now. She'd rather be in a room with a sick man too delirious to make sense than stay here, subjecting herself to her mother's cruel barbs.

"I'm going to go check on Dad."

The door opened at that moment revealing a deeply tanned man. He wasn't as tall and muscular as Thad and looked to be a little younger, but he was big enough to crowd the space with his presence.

"Here's my Davy now," Bobbett cooed.

He held out his hand to Suzanne.

"David Hamilton. I'm happy to meet you, Ms. Conway, although I wish for your sake it could be under less stressful circumstances."

His handshake was as warm and friendly as his words. His polite manner felt like a soothing balm to her bruised heart after losing Thad and having to face her petulant mother.

"Thank you. I'm sorry you had to cut your vacation short."

"You needn't apologize. It's part of my job."

"I understand you've come here to look after me. I want you to know I'll do whatever you think is best to make your job easier," Suzanne said, remembering Thad's words to be more cooperative.

"I appreciate that. I'm here to help you in any way that I can. I hope I'm not interrupting this mother/daughter bonding time."

Suzanne almost laughed at the idea of ever being able to have any kind of bonding with her mother.

"You're not interrupting anything important."

"You can say that again," her mother echoed.

David's gaze shifted uneasily between the two women. "I, um, came to tell you that you're wanted in your father's room."

The blood drained from her face. "God, is he . . .?"

"Oh, no, no. I didn't mean to upset you. Sorry. Apparently he's showing signs that he's becoming more coherent. The doctor thought you may be able to decipher some of what he's saying."

"Thank you. I'll go to him right away."

"I'll have to go with you," he said, his tone almost apologetic.

Suzanne couldn't help thinking how different he was from Thad. He pulled Bobbett to her feet.

"You have to come, too."

"Why?" she pouted. "I've already seen him. I don't want to go back in there. His room smells like antiseptic," she whined, wrinkling her nose.

"Well yeah, hospitals have a tendency to do that. Be a good girl and do this for me."

Girl? Suzanne barely held back a snort of laughter. Despite telling everyone she was in her late thirties, Bobbett was actually a couple of months away from shaking hands with fifty. But she managed to pull off the lie thanks to the miracle of plastic surgery and a deft hand with makeup.

"But Davy . . ."

"I'm just trying to do my job, and having you in that room is going to make it a lot more pleasant."

Suzanne raised her brows at the clever compliment. He'd certainly learned how to handle her mother. He opened the door and gestured for them to exit the room ahead of him. Bobbett pursed her lips.

"I'll do it for you. But I'll expect a reward for my sacrifice."

"Later," he winked.

Suzanne had a pretty good idea what that reward was going to be. What was his company's policy? Do what you had to do to keep the female clients happy, even if it meant sleeping with them?

Maybe he wasn't so different from Thad after all.

The first thing Suzanne noticed when she entered her father's room was that he seemed to be much less agitated. She walked over to his bed and took hold of his hand, careful to avoid the dressings.

"Hi, Dad. How are you doing? Can you talk to me? Muriel and I sure would like that."

Muriel held Wendell's other hand.

"Yes please, Wendell. Come back to us. We both love you."

He opened his eyes and looked at Suzanne. His eyelids fluttered while he struggled to focus on her. His lips began to move. She smiled in encouragement and leaned closer.

"Do you want to say something to me?" she asked, hoping with all her might that his first words wouldn't be to call her a traitor.

"Unicorns can't fly," he whispered in a croaking voice.

At first it seemed as though this would be another one of his senseless babbling remarks until a long ago memory gradually worked its way into Suzanne's head.

"But Pegasus can," she whispered back and watched his mouth lift in a brief smile.

Her heart raced with elation. Surely he must have forgiven her if he was willing to give her this vital clue. Everyone looked at her, clearly baffled. Bobbett exhaled a loud, impatient breath.

"What a stupid thing to say, but you two always had your silly sayings." She reached over and tugged at David's hand. "Come on, let's get out of here. He's still not making any sense."

"No, wait." He looked at Suzanne. "Did what your father say mean something to you?"

"I'm wondering the same thing. Do you know what he's talking about?" Muriel asked.

"Yes. Unless I'm mistaken, I believe he just told me where he hid the phones."

189

She stared at Suzanne. "Unicorns? Pegasus? I'm afraid I still don't get it."

"That makes two of us," David chimed in.

Wendell's eyes were closed again. Suzanne wasn't sure if he had fallen back to sleep, but she continued to hold his hand letting him feel the contact. She brushed a wave of hair off his forehead.

"I went through a period when I was growing up where I had a real thing for unicorns. I . . . ."

Bobbett rolled her eyes.

"I'll say. I remember you having posters of them plastered all over your bedroom walls. I wanted to be a ballerina at that age, which I might add was certainly a lot more normal than your obsession with things from fairy tales."

"This isn't about you," David said in a surprisingly stern voice. He nodded at Suzanne again. "Please continue. What were you saying about unicorns?"

Suzanne looked from one to the other momentarily shocked that he'd actually snubbed her mother in order to listen to her. She could see his rebuke didn't sit well with Bobbett, who now stood glaring at him. Suzanne knew her mother wasn't accustomed to having a man use that scolding tone with her. She rushed to answer him hoping to stop what could become an unpleasant backlash.

"I collected anything I could that had to do with unicorns besides the posters my mother just mentioned. My dad knew this, and sometimes would buy something to add to my assortment. One time while I was staying with my godmother, Dad came to pick me up there. I was playing with one of my small stuffed unicorns pretending it could fly."

"Oh, I get it now," Muriel said, brightening.

"He told you unicorns can't fly. Right?"

"Yes, and then he brought his arm from behind his back and handed me a beautiful stuffed Pegasus. It was white with golden wings and hooves. My godmother suggested I leave it at her house because it was too large to pack in my little suitcase and might get dirty if I tried carrying it."

"That's a sweet story, but what does it have to do with the phones your dad was carrying?"

"I was about to ask the same thing," David confessed nodding toward Muriel.

"I haven't thought of it in years, but as far as I know the Pegasus is still at my godmother's house, which I assume means it was there when you and my father visited."

Muriel shook her head. "I never saw anything like that."

"Nanadoo knows how important that toy was to me, so she wouldn't have gotten rid of it without asking me first. She probably packed it away someplace and my dad must have found it."

David scratched his jaw.

"I think I may be getting the drift of where you're headed with this. Am I correct in assuming you're of the opinion your father may have hid the phones inside this Pegasus?"

"That's exactly what I think. It has plenty of room and enough stuffing to protect them."

"Okay. I say it's worth a look. We'll go to your godmother's house. It's on Catalina Island, right?"

No need to ask how he knew that. He probably had access to the same information on her that Thad used. She immediately forced all thoughts of Thad out of her head when she felt her throat tighten.

"Yes, but they're away right now. I'll have to call her and find out where she put the horse."

David nodded.

"I'll make arrangements for us to go check it out, as soon as you know."

Bobbett plopped down onto a chair and crossed her arms over her breasts, which had been enhanced by a couple of very impressive implants and currently straining the fabric of her skin tight red tee shirt.

"I'm not going to that dinky island, and no one is going to make me. It's so boring there."

Suzanne felt like a parent being forced to explain something of obvious importance to a recalcitrant child who refused to cooperate. Good God, was this how Thad felt about her when she'd refused to obey his instructions? No wonder he became so exasperated with her.

"Mother, you only went once and spent the entire time in the house. You never gave the place a chance. But that doesn't matter now. We're going for the phones, not for fun."

"Exactly my point. That's why I want to go back to Cabo. Suzanne doesn't need us, Davy. She can dig around for those stupid phones and turn them into the cops all by herself."

"You're forgetting that part of my job now includes protecting your daughter."

"You knew me first," she reminded him with a proprietorial air.

"That's right, which means I'll still be watching out for you as well."

She shook her head.

"I'll wait here and twiddle my thumbs until you get back. This place has security guards. If you ask me you're taking a chance by leaving. Why don't you get someone else to go in your place?"

"Because part of my assignment is to locate those phones. I can't afford to pass up any opportunity or overlook any clue that might lead me to them. I'm not supposed to let you out of my sight if you'll remember; which is why you'll be going with us."

"Oh, all right. But I don't appreciate the fact that you're making those phones more important than I am. You'd better take me back to Cabo pretty damn soon if you expect to have me continue our vacation together."

"I won't be going to Mexico, or anywhere else if I lose my job."

"So? I'm sure you could find another one."

"I happen to like what I do."

"Why? Because you get a kick out of playing at being a cop? I'll buy you a toy gun and a tin badge."

His body visibly tensed.

"I'm not playing at anything. This may be a game to you, but not to me."

"Have you forgotten what a good time we were having together until we had to come here?"

"Life isn't made up of just good times."

"It can be if you work it right. We were happy in Cabo. You can't want to give that up."

Suzanne didn't want to spoil her mother's fantasy, but once David had turned the phones over to the authorities, he wouldn't be on this assignment any longer. If he went back to Mexico it was going to have to be on his own time and at his own expense. She wondered if he cared enough about her mother to be willing to do that.

She couldn't help noticing he wasn't looking quite as lover-like as he had when they first arrived, now that her mother was revealing how she could be when she didn't get her own way. No big surprise there. Suzanne was used to it. Bobbett expected the world to revolve around her. She had a way of filling herself up while draining the life out of every relationship she'd ever had, including her role as a parent.

Suzanne gave herself a mental shake. Who was she kidding? Her mother had never been a parent.

They were blood relatives, but that was their only real connection. Bobbett Conway may have given birth to her, but she had never been maternal by any stretch of the imagination.

She looked at her father. He may not be voted Father of the Year, but at least he'd admitted to loving her; and sometimes he did do nice things for her when she was growing up. Maybe when this difficult situation they found themselves in was over they could actually begin building a solid father/daughter relationship. He'd trusted her enough to tell her where the phones were even after thinking she had betrayed him. She wasn't about to abuse that trust, no matter how much her mother complained.

She took her phone out of her pocket.

"I'm going to call my godmother now. I think we should go out into the hallway and let my dad rest," she told David. "I'll let you know what happens, Muriel."

"Thank you. I'll stay here with your father."

David motioned to Bobbett to follow them from the room.

"I'll want us to leave here as soon as possible if your godmother says the Pegasus is at her house."

Suzanne nodded while her mother pressed a hand to David's arm.

"I just remembered I got seasick on the ferry ride going to the island. I don't want to go through that again. You can swing by here and pick me up when you get back."

"We'll be taking a helicopter."

"A helicopter? I have a feeling that'll be even worse. Count me out."

"I'm not giving you a choice, so make no mistake, you will be going."

Suzanne's brows rose at the sound of the determination in his voice. She watched, waiting for her mother's reaction. Bobbett's eyes narrowed at him seconds before her cheeks flamed an angry red.

"You can't tell me what to do!"

"Yes I can when it comes to doing my job. You may think what I do is frivolous, but I take my work very seriously. I'm one of the people being paid to solve this case and protect you while I'm at it. We've had some good times together as you said. Let's not spoil that by fighting now."

"Your attitude just ended any chance of repeating those good times."

She flipped a strand of hair over her shoulder in a gesture of angry defiance, while she continued to scowl at him. "I'll go with you to the island, but once you have those phones, you can forget about us. We'll be history."

Suzanne thought she saw a hint of relief on David's face. Trying to keep her mother happy was a fulltime and usually thankless job. If Thad thought she was difficult to guard how would he have managed to get along with her mother? Beneath all that silicone and skillfully applied makeup beat the heart of a truly self-absorbed woman.

Suzanne made her call. Nesta assured her she and the colonel were doing fine soaking up the sun and spiritual atmosphere in Sedona, Arizona. That and the fact that she hadn't thrown away the stuffed Pegasus was good news. The bad news was she couldn't remember where she'd put the toy. She gave some possible locations when Suzanne told her it was urgent that she find it. They said their goodbyes with Nesta's apologizing for being so forgetful.

David put his hands on his hips and stared at Suzanne. "Well?"

"She's not quite sure where she put my Pegasus."

"What'd you expect?" Bobbett pointed a finger at her head. "She's half senile."

Suzanne glowered at her.

"She is not!"

She looked at David. "She did give me some ideas where to look. The condo isn't that big. I'm sure it'll turn up with three of us searching."

"Why do I have to help? This isn't my fiasco. I just want to go back to my normal life."

Suzanne wanted to tell her mother she'd been dodging bullets while Bobbett was lying by a pool sunning herself. Not to mention that she couldn't go back to her own house, and she may not have a job if they didn't find those phones soon. But none of that would probably make a difference to a woman whose sole mission in life centered on bending people to her will.

The truth of that had been difficult to accept when she was growing up. Now with so many others hurting, her mother's lack of concern for their welfare made Suzanne feel like she'd swallowed a stone that refused to be digested. But why would she expect her mother to care about anyone else when she didn't even care about her own daughter? Suzanne had always known she'd been born to a woman who thought of her as an inconvenience. Just once she wished her mother would look at her and see a daughter, instead of a burden.

David's voice broke into her troubled thoughts.

"I said you're going."

Bobbett tilted her chin toward him.

"Fine! What are you waiting for? Go ahead and make your super-secret spy arrangements. Just don't blame me if I end up puking all over your precious helicopter."

He stared at her for a moment and shook his head before taking his phone out of a pocket.

It was too late to leave by the time all the details were finalized. Plans were made to go in the morning, which meant they would stay at the clinic that night. Suzanne ended up having to share a room with her mother and listen to her constant complaining. The bed was too small and too hard. The sheets smelled like bleach and the room reeked of disinfectant.

She was sure David was probably having a much better night's sleep without his nagging bedmate.

"Trade me pillows," Bobbett demanded. "Mine's too soft."

Suzanne barely managed to stifle a groan. She'd just as soon pass, if this was supposed to be an example of mother/daughter bonding.

Twenty

Suzanne had a splitting headache from lack of sleep and tension trying to cope with her mother, when morning finally came. She opened the door to David's knock. He didn't look as fatigued as she felt, although she thought he seemed a little on edge. Maybe he missed sleeping with her mother after all. Or perhaps he was merely anxious to get started looking for the coveted phones. She knew she certainly was.

"Ready?" he asked. "The car is waiting."

"Yes." Suzanne turned to her mother. "Mom?"

Bobbett swept through the doorway, stubbornly ignoring them. David rolled his eyes at Suzanne and led them outside. His arrangements included a chauffeur driven limousine complete with good coffee and an assortment of breakfast rolls, all of which helped to mollify Bobbett for the time being.

The helicopter ride made Suzanne recall the one she'd taken when Thad brought her to the island. It seemed like a lifetime ago. So much had happened since then, and so much still needed to happen. She glanced at her mother and couldn't help feeling a pang of sympathy.

Bobbett hadn't been kidding about her problem with motion sickness. Her face was tinged with a sickly pallor. She kept her eyes closed and her fingers fisted in her lap during the flight. Thankfully, she didn't throw up, much to everyone's relief.

David hired a cab to take them to Nanadoo's. Suzanne couldn't contain her little start of surprise when she realized the driver turned out to be Dewey. But he acted as if he didn't know her, although her own greeting was warm and friendly. Perhaps he thought she had betrayed her father, too. She sat in the back with her mother and made no further attempt to talk to him, but her insides churned with the need to defend herself.

She found the spare house key in a flowerpot on the patio and almost smiled when she thought of what Thad would have said to Nanadoo about her hiding place. David barely gave them time to get inside before he insisted they start looking for the toy Pegasus.

Suzanne thought it was odd that he didn't ask about the layout of the house or offer to go check inside first like Thad always did before he entered an unfamiliar place. She also instinctively knew he wouldn't have used a limo as their transportation because it brought too much attention to them.

But Thad was gone. The responsibility for her protection now lay in David's hands. She knew she would never get over Thad if she kept thinking about him so much. Her time with him had ended. She would have to learn to put the past behind her and move on like he was most likely doing.

Maybe it would help if she could keep remembering her mother's words to David last night about them being history. But it was easier for her mother, because she was the one who walked away from a relationship. Suzanne knew she'd personally had more experience at being the one who got left behind.

They searched in all the places Nesta mentioned without any luck. David became increasingly uptight, flinging things aside, and muttering. Suzanne didn't miss the fact that he wasn't as sweet natured as she'd taken him for when they'd first met. She supposed she couldn't fault him for that. He'd been on the case from the very beginning and probably catering to her mother's every whim. That alone would be enough to make any sane person's patience begin to wear thin.

Suzanne suggested they take a break and resume looking after lunch. David agreed, but refused to have them leave the house to eat out. She ended up rummaging in the freezer and found a packaged noodle and chicken dish along with some bread rolls. She emptied the chicken mixture into a frying pan, buttered the bread to be toasted in the oven, and poured a jar of pickled mixed beans from the cupboard into a bowl to complete the meal.

Her mother's contribution, after some prodding was setting the table while David sat there, scanning his phone. Once again Suzanne couldn't help comparing him to Thad who had cooked an entire gourmet meal, while David sat there complaining that he preferred red meat and potatoes to chicken and pasta.

"You must have misunderstood your father," David said when he finished eating. "Call the clinic. Ask them to put him on the phone. Maybe you can get some more information out of him."

Suzanne did as he requested and wasn't surprised when Muriel said Wendell was asleep and hadn't revealed anything new. She hung up and shook her head at David.

"No luck. Dad's asleep and the doctor left orders not to disturb him. Muriel couldn't add anything."

David scraped back his chair and got up to pace. Suzanne watched as he walked back and forth repeatedly slapping the flat of a hand against one thigh, until he stopped and faced her again.

"Are you sure you remembered correctly about the horse? Maybe he was talking about another toy."

"No. It was the Pegasus."

"How can you be so positive?" he insisted.

"Because it's one of the few happy memories from my childhood."

Bobbett's head snapped up.

"What's that supposed to mean? I used to take you shopping."

Her mother had taken her shopping on rare outings, but most everything she bought was usually for herself. God only knows what she would have ended up wearing, Suzanne thought, if it hadn't been for Nanadoo's timely arrival when she'd needed clothes for each new school year.

And thank heavens for birthdays and Christmas when that good lady consistently provided her with toys and other gifts. It wasn't as if her parents never bought her anything, if she was fair. It just never occurred to them that children liked to receive presents from their parents on special occasions. But she'd learned to take what she could get whenever they chose to think of her.

"We're going to have to go back to the clinic, so you can question your father in person again," David said cutting short her reminiscing. "I still think you must have missed something."

"You heard him mention the Pegasus and nothing else. It's got to be here."

"Well, we've looked everywhere your godmother said it could be. Not that she's been any help. That's the trouble with old people. They forget. She probably got rid of it and didn't bother to tell you."

"I told you she wouldn't do that. I can continue looking if you'll load the dishwasher, Mom."

"Since when am I your servant?"

David rounded on her.

"Just do it for God's sake, so we can get the hell out of here."

"There's nothing I'd like better. You've turned into a real drag, Davy."

"That makes us even," he retorted. "I'm going to make arrangements for our return trip."

"It's about time," Bobbett shouted as he turned his back to her.

They reminded Suzanne of two arguing children. She fled upstairs to her old bedroom to avoid having to listen to them. She sat down on the bed thinking about where to continue her search. The Pegasus had to be here somewhere on the premises. Surely her father wouldn't have lied about that.

Now that she thought about it, he hadn't actually said the horse was at Nanadoo's house. He just said the phones were inside the stuffed animal. But it had always been here. Her godmother admitted to being forgetful, but Suzanne knew in her heart she wouldn't have thrown the treasured toy away.

Nanadoo knew how to gather and keep precious memories, saving them for the times when you needed to have something good to hold onto. Times when you sprinkled your happy thoughts out before you like tiny gems too valuable to put a price on them.

Suzanne stirred and moved her hand on the bedspread. She felt her fingers touch something sharp. Her hand jerked back in surprise while she stared at the tip of something sticking out from beneath one of the small throw pillows on the bed. She snatched the pillow away and barely stopped herself from letting out a cry of alarm when she saw the single black feather.

She stared at the offensive symbol. How did it get there? It had to come after Nanadoo and the colonel left. Suzanne didn't like the idea of someone being in the house when they were away. On the other hand, it'd be even worse if that someone came while they were here.

Should she tell David? She hadn't told Thad. She wished she had. But she hated the idea of giving into the Montanes theatrical way of adding more stress to an already stressful situation. She wondered if Thad's agency knew about the connection between the feathers and the Montanes. Probably. They seemed to have an endless supply of information.

She sat concentrating so hard on the feather that her heart jumped when David called to her, scattering her thoughts like tufts of downy dandelions shedding their globular heads of seeds.

"Did you find anything?"

"No," she called back quickly, not wanting him to come up here.

"You may as well come down."

"Okay."

She wrapped the feather in some tissues and shoved it in her pocket. She would put it in her purse later until she decided what to do with it. She hurried down the stairs.

"Are you sure you didn't find anything?" David asked, watching her closely.

"Nothing."

"I see. Well, you took long enough. I thought you might be taking a little nap."

"Actually, that sounds tempting. I didn't sleep very well last night," she said staring at Bobbett.

201

He looked over at her mother sitting on the sofa filing her nails.

"Now that I can understand."

"Funny, but I never heard you complaining about your lack of sleep when we were in Cabo, Davy darling," she said in a sarcastic voice.

"Works both ways, Bobbie darling," he mocked in return.

Suzanne touched his sleeve drawing his attention to her again hoping to head off a full blown argument between them.

"Did you say we'll be leaving soon?"

"Yes. The cab will be here in fifteen minutes. I've been thinking we didn't find the Pegasus where your godmother thought it might be because your father probably hid it somewhere else around here."

"I'm sure you're right. I hope he hasn't forgotten where he put it considering all the delirium he's suffered from being so ill."

"Let's not go there. This is the first really good lead we've had."

"I know. I'll call my godmother and tell her what's happened."

Nesta answered on the first ring. "I've been waiting to hear from you. Did you find the horse?"

"No."

"Oh, I'm sorry. Do you want us to come home and help you look?"

"No, you stay where you are. David wants us to go back to the clinic now and talk to Dad again. I think he may have moved the Pegasus when he was here."

"Perhaps. Are you all right? You sound down. You're not missing that ugly bird James, are you?"

"Heavens, no. By the way, I didn't know you thought he was an ugly bird."

"Dumpling, I bet he could stab pickles out of a jar with that nose of his. It's a wonder he didn't poke you in the eyes when he kissed you."

Suzanne managed a brief laugh. "You make me feel good."

"But not good enough right now. It sounds like a few rose petals have fallen," Nesta said referring to their old code. "Should I come for you?"

"No. I'll be fine. I'm just frustrated."

"Also a little depressed I'm thinking. Are you upset because Thad left? I don't understand why his agency assigned this David to take over when Thad already invested so much time in looking after you."

Suzanne forced away the pain of her godmother's words.

"He asked to leave."

"He did? I find that difficult to believe after seeing the way he looked at you."

"I'm not sure what that look conveyed to you, but it couldn't have had anything to do with affection if that's what you're thinking. He told me himself he didn't want to be around me anymore."

"Did he now? Well, hmm. Something's amiss here."

"I don't think so. Thad made his feelings quite clear." Suzanne heard the sound of tears in her voice and knew she had to hang up before she ended up blubbering.

"I have to go now. Our taxi is on its way."

"All right. Good luck finding the Pegasus. Be sure to let me know what happens."

"I will. I love you."

"I love you too, darling."

Bobbett stood up.

"Ugh, what mush. I'm going to the bathroom to freshen up before we leave."

"Don't take too long. The cab will be here soon. Remember we've got another helicopter to catch," David called to her retreating back.

"Don't worry. I can't wait to get off this rock and be around people other than you two sour pusses."

He waited until she closed the door before turning to Suzanne.

"Has she always been like this?"

"Pretty much."

"Had I known, I may have asked to be assigned to you instead of letting Novak be the lucky one."

"I doubt if he feels he was all that lucky."

"I don't know what happened between you two to make him ask to be reassigned to another case."

Rosy color brightened her face.

"I tricked him and ran off on my own."

David whistled.

"Well, that explains a lot. Once you have that happen in our business with disastrous results, you aren't going to want to go through it again."

"What do you mean by 'disastrous results'?"

"I thought you knew. But since you don't, it's not my place to go into detail."

Suzanne grabbed his arm when he started to walk away. "David, please tell me what you meant."

"I'd rather not."

Thad rubbed a hand over his eyes and down his beard roughened face. He'd just come off a job involving long hours without any rest. The phone call woke him from some much needed sleep.

"Novak."

"Thank goodness you still have the same number. I wasn't sure if I'd be able to get a hold of you."

He leaned up on one elbow. "Mrs. Harold. This is a surprise. Is something wrong?"

"Yes. I'm calling you about Suzanne. She's in trouble."

His insides tightened before he made himself relax.

"I'm beginning to think that's her middle name."

"I suppose it does seem that way because you've only known her since all this business with her father began. She has never been troublesome before. She's in a bad way."

The hairs on his arms stood out.

"What's happened? Is she all right?"

"I wouldn't be calling you if she was all right. I want you to go back to her."

"I'm sure you're aware that I'm no longer on the case. Suzanne has a perfectly good man watching over her. I can give you his number if you're worried about something."

"That something happens to be you."

"I beg your pardon."

"When I said Suzanne was in trouble, I meant trouble of the heart. If ever two people needed each other it's you and my goddaughter. I can't understand why you left when she just found you."

"Who said I was lost?"

"Doing fine on your own, are you?"

"I'm . . . okay. I'm really not sure why you're calling me."

"I'm calling because Suzanne loves you, and I believe you left because you're in love with her, too."

Thad's heart gave a single hard bump against his chest before he pushed himself up to lean back against the headboard.

"Why would I leave if I love her?"

"Your reasons are you own. Tell me, wouldn't you like to have someone share your bed at night and wake up in the morning seeing them smile knowing you were the one who made them happy?"

"What sane man wouldn't? But I'm no good for your goddaughter."

"Why don't you let her be the judge of that? Unless I'm wrong and you don't love her."

His breath tumbled out of him on a tired sigh.

"I do love her, but that love puts her in danger. She needs someone who can be more objective to look after her."

"I admire such noble thoughts, but are you trying to convince me, or yourself?"

"I . . ." Thad swallowed. "Maybe when this is all over I'll give her a call."

"Suzanne's already been hurt enough by the people she loves. Are you going to smear her face in her own feelings like so many others have?"

"No, but I . . ."

205

Nesta interrupted him again. "I know when I see two people who belong together. Don't be like me, young man. I wasted a lot of years with the wrong men until I met the colonel. We're old and we don't have a lot of time left, but we're determined to enjoy every minute of what we do have. You and Suzanne are young enough to have plenty of years together if you're willing to take them. Are you going to throw that opportunity away?"

"The timing hasn't exactly been encouraging to make any long range plans."

"I realize that, but it looks as though this situation with Wendell will be coming to an end soon. When it does that means you and Suzanne can go back to just being two people in love."

Thad sat up straighter.

"What did you mean about the situation coming to an end soon?"

"I thought you knew."

"I've been out of the office quite a bit lately. What's happened?"

"Her father woke up enough to say he'd hidden the phones in a stuffed toy Pegasus I've kept from Suzanne's childhood. They didn't find it at my place, so the fellow with her now decided they needed to return and question Wendell again. You can see her if you go to the clinic."

"Love may not be enough for Suzanne considering the things I said when I walked out on her."

"Love is a darn good start, and I'm telling you my girl really does love you."

"I may not be the best person to protect her," he said in one last feeble attempt to dissuade Nesta.

"You are the only one who can. Don't fail her, dear boy," Nesta implored and hung up.

Thad set the phone aside and kicked back the sheet to swing his legs over the side of the bed while he thought of Nesta's comments. Love may be a good start, but a good start didn't guarantee a good ending. Countless lovers over the centuries had discovered that to their cost.

He realized what he'd felt for any other woman was nothing more than infatuation once his feelings for Suzanne began to develop and grow. Thad supposed he couldn't be blamed for confusing the two. He wouldn't be the first guy to have testosterone mess with his brain.

Who knew there could be so many layers to how you loved a person and how deep each level went until you couldn't draw a breath without thinking of that special someone? He hadn't forgotten Suzanne's tears when he left her. The memory continued to cut into him, gouging deeper grooves more and more with each passing day. Now, according to her godmother, Suzanne still loved him.

But that could just mean she'd drawn the short straw.

Twenty-one

Bobbett stumbled as she climbed out of the helicopter.

"Ugh. This eggbeater is messing up my hair."

David took her by the arm and grabbed Suzanne's hand before hurrying them to a charcoal gray sedan. He opened the doors and gestured for them to get in.

"Where's the limo?" Bobbett asked.

"You're not Cinderella going to the ball. This is all I could get on such short notice. Come on, we're due at the clinic."

"Did they tell you how my dad is doing?" Suzanne said while climbing into the back.

"About the same. I'm hoping once he hears your voice again he'll give us something more."

"And I hope you two get what you're after, so I can go back to enjoying myself," Bobbett grumbled.

Suzanne was more upset about her father's health than the Pegasus. Maybe he'd been confused about putting the phones inside the toy. She couldn't help being concerned about his chances of recovery. She also had the latest black feather to think about.

Bobbett wasn't the only one who wanted her life back. Suzanne not only wanted things to be normal again, but she wanted to share her life with Thad. The only problem with that idea was he didn't want to share his life with her. She stared out the car window with those depressing thoughts heavy on her mind and heart.

Thad went over various strategies on his way to the clinic thinking of how to tell Suzanne he was sorry that he left. His hands squeezed the steering wheel wishing to God he hadn't said he didn't want to be with her. He'd lied thinking it would make her angry enough to be glad he was going. He knew if Suzanne rejected his attempt to reconcile with her, it'd be his own fault. He'd actually thought not being around Suzanne would help him to get over her, which turned out to be an exercise in futility. The only thing he'd accomplished for himself by being away was to make him want to be with her more than ever.

Now he'd been given a second chance to take care of Suzanne. Perhaps her godmother was right, and he should start thinking about a career change. But he couldn't afford to ponder the future until he made sure he didn't repeat the mistakes he'd made in the past. He once thought love was all a person needed to ensure a happy life, but he'd been wrong.

And that knowledge had come at a costly price.

David stared at the doctor standing in front of the door to Wendell's room blocking the way.

"What do you mean I can't go in there? You didn't have a problem with it before. I'm supposed to be keeping an eye on both the women," he protested, pointing to Bobbett and Suzanne.

"I understand your job is to protect them. They'll be safe here. Mr. Conway has had too much excitement. I'm limiting the number of visitors. Ms. Conway has priority because she's his daughter."

"I'm glad you didn't include me. I certainly don't want to be in there," Bobbett shuddered.

"What about Muriel? She's not family. Why does she get to be with him?" David challenged.

"I'm allowing her to stay because her presence seems to be a comfort to Mr. Conway."

"We came back because I need to question my dad again," Suzanne explained. "All right?"

The doctor nodded.

"Yes, but don't try to force him. He'll talk when he's ready."

"I understand. May I see him now?"

He opened the door and stepped back. Suzanne started to go inside, but David squeezed her arm.

"You have to tell me as soon as your father gives you any information we can use."

"I know, David. Now please let go of me," she said and waited for him to step away.

She closed the door shutting out David's taut expression. Her father's eyes were closed. Muriel sat dozing in a chair by the bed, but stirred when Suzanne cleared her throat. Muriel struggled to her feet, pressing one hand to her back and the other on the chair.

"How is my dad doing?"

"He's been talking more and his thoughts seem clearer, but he hasn't mentioned the phones again. Maybe if you tell him you didn't find the toy horse, he'll add something else."

"That's why I came back, but I hate to wake him."

"He dozes off a lot, but he's not thrashing around like before, and his fever's down. Just take hold of his hand and let him know you're here. He's been asking about you. He wants to be sure you're okay."

"Has he . . ." She let her breath out slowly. "Has he talked about what happened at the motel?"

"I told him all about it. He said he had a feeling something was fishy with your friends. That's why he insisted we escape the way we did."

"Thank heavens he had enough sense to suspect them. I certainly didn't."

"Your father is a very wise man."

Suzanne would not have described her father in that way not so very long ago, but now she realized there was a lot she didn't know about him. She'd been so busy focusing on his negative traits that she never bothered to notice he had a lot of good in him. Her fingers gave his hand a gentle squeeze.

"Dad, it's Suzanne. I had to come back. I don't have the Pegasus. Can you tell me where you hid it?"

He continued to lie quietly for the next several seconds making Suzanne believe he hadn't heard her until she saw his eyelids flicker and open. She smiled at him and leaned down to kiss him on one cheek.

"Someone's given you a nice shave."

"The phones?" he rasped.

"I couldn't find my Pegasus in Nanadoo's house," she repeated.

"Not the house. I . . . "

He coughed. Muriel picked up a glass of water sitting nearby and adjusted the straw to his mouth while Suzanne lifted his head. He took a few sips before waving the glass away. He cleared his throat.

"Golf cart."

"Are you saying you hid the Pegasus in the colonel's golf cart?"

"Yes."

"I never thought of looking there. What a good idea you had. Don't worry. I'll see that we get the toy and the phones. You concentrate on getting out of this bed, so we can celebrate."

Muriel clasped her hands together in a gesture of prayer. "At last. Will you go get them now?"

Wendell's eyes closed again. Suzanne didn't want to leave him just yet. She knew David was outside the door and probably pacing the hallway. But she had a strong urge to sit with her father a while longer.

She didn't mind having Muriel be here. Somewhere during all this running back and forth she'd begun to think of her as a younger sister. The two women sat quietly each holding one of Wendell's hands.

"Do you have any siblings, Muriel?"

"No. I grew up lonely. I couldn't have playdates for obvious reasons. I do have one cousin, Franco, but we've never been close. He's a few years older and has inherited my uncle's meanness."

"I had a lonely childhood, too. We could pretend to be sisters. You know, bonded by my dad's love."

"I'd like that very much."

They reached for each other's free hands and clasped their fingers together.

"I hope you won't mind if we don't cut our wrists and share our blood."

Muriel shivered.

"God, no. I've seen enough blood to last me for the rest of my life. I think we should exchange a little gift. It doesn't have to be much, but it should be something very special to us."

"That's a much better idea than mine. I'm sorry about the wrist thing. Bad joke on my part."

Suzanne looked at her purse sitting on the floor by her chair. She gently tugged her hand free and bent down to unclip a tiny plastic unicorn her father had given to her years ago.

"My dad gave this to me. It's what started me collecting them when I was a child."

Muriel let go of Wendell's hand to accept the gift.

"Are you sure? Maybe you'd rather not let go of something from him."

"You said something special. Keep it, please."

"Thank you. I have something for you, but it isn't from my father because I don't want to keep anything from him."

Her mouth clenched for a moment, but softened again when she reached into a pocket of her jeans, pulled out a penny, and handed it to Suzanne.

"Your dad gave this to me the first time I met him. I was curious about him and went to his office. We introduced ourselves. He saw me look at the penny sitting on his desk. He handed it to me and said a lot of people didn't bother to keep pennies because they think one cent isn't significant enough to bother with. But he told me what people didn't realize is it was the beginning of a dollar and a dollar was the beginning of five dollars and so on. He explained that if you kept saving you never knew how much money you might accumulate from a single penny."

Suzanne closed her fingers over the coin.

"Thank you, Muriel. I never would have thought of a penny in those terms. You were right about my dad being a wise man."

"It wasn't so much what he said about the penny that became important to me. Rather, it's special because it came from your father."

David sat brooding in the cafeteria while Bobbett stood at the counter choosing a salad. He expected Suzanne to leave her father's bedside by now. His fingers drummed on the table. How much longer would he have to wait before he got his hands on those phones? He'd about run out of patience and he knew he wasn't the only one when his cell phone signaled a message making his body go ridged when he identified the caller. He rose quickly from his chair and motioned to a security guard entering the room.

"Keep an eye on Mrs. Conway for me, will you? I need a smoke."

"I'm on my break. You've got fifteen minutes."

"I'll be back in ten. Thanks," he called over his shoulder and hurried from the room.

Suzanne stood up and stretched. "Looks like Dad won't be waking up again for a while. Do you mind if I go outside for some fresh air? Or would you rather go first?"

"I've been out a couple times already. You should know you won't be allowed to be on your own."

"I know. David is probably having a fit by now and will insist on being the one to go with me."

Suzanne felt happy when she discovered David and her mother had gone to the cafeteria. She told the guard she was headed there for coffee. She walked away and slipped outside instead, anxious to be on her own only to have her privacy spoiled when she heard a man's voice coming from around the corner.

It sounded like he was talking on a phone. She soon realized it was David. Suzanne knew she was being a snoop, but she couldn't help wondering if he might be talking to someone in his office. Maybe it could be Thad. How pathetic to be relegated to listening in on someone's conversation hoping to hear any news about him. She decided to go back inside when something David said made her stop.

"Yes, Mr. Montane. I'm disappointed, too."

Her heart gave a sudden lurch. Why would he be talking to one of the Montanes? The realization went through her like an electric shock. She had to stay and find out what was going on. She stood there straining to hear his every word while her pulse began to pound like a two-year-old banging on a toy drum.

"This is just a little setback. Suzanne Conway is with her father right now asking him where he put the stuffed toy I told you about earlier. I'll be taking her back to her godmother's as soon as she tells me. Yes sir, I'll take care of her father for you. I know you'd rather do it yourself. What's that you say? You want me to make it as painful as possible. I'll do my best. Don't you worry, I won't fail. Those phones are as good as yours. I'll be in touch."

Suzanne almost tripped in her haste to get away. She ducked into a janitor's closet, panting heavily from the exertion and shock. She flattened herself against the door, shaken to her core. But she knew she wasn't the only one who was scared. She'd heard the way David's voice sounded. No doubt the Montanes weren't happy with his latest delay and when the Montanes weren't happy, no one was safe.

David hadn't been able to completely mask his fear and sometimes people who were afraid did fearful things. Unfortunately, in this instance that fear was going to result in her father being killed.

How long had David been a mole for the Montane brothers? Had he been the one who left the black feather at Nanadoo's? It boggled her mind just thinking about how many people they had doing their twisted bidding. Her father warned her about Thad and even David, suspecting them of not being honest. His instincts were certainly right about David. Suzanne knew she had to warn the staff that her father was in danger from a man who was supposed to be one of the good guys. And her father's life probably wasn't the only one in jeopardy. She and Muriel would no doubt be next on David's hit list.

Unless she could stop him.

David checked the time again wondering if he should go back and see if Suzanne had gotten anything more out of her father. He knew she better come through with something useful pretty damn quick or he'd never be able to get his hands on all that money the Montanes were willing to shell out. Not to mention what they'd do to him if he failed. He wiped away the burst of sweat that beaded his upper lip.

He'd have to use Bobbett to go in Conway's room and talk to her daughter. He also had to figure out a way to take care of the old man without anyone being wise to him. He started back to the cafeteria just as his phone rang and saw the caller was the security guard at the front gate. He'd bought the man's willingness to help by paying him every time he gave out any useful information.

"What's up?"

"Novak's on his way. I couldn't call you sooner because I had to check in a couple other people."

"What the hell is he doing back?" David grumbled.

"I told him I was surprised to see him since I'd heard he was off the case. He said he wanted to come and see how Wendell Conway is doing."

"I'm not buying that. I know Novak. He's got more on his mind than a friendly visit. He could be here to question Conway himself. I may be leaving sooner than I wanted to if he's going to be hanging around."

David shoved the phone into his pocket. Thad could turn out to be another complication he didn't need on top of everything else right now. He pushed the door open to the cafeteria. Quick strides took him over to Bobbett's table. She looked at him before going back to her eating.

"I want you to find out if Suzanne's made any progress with her father. I also need to know if there's anyone else in the room with him besides her and Muriel."

"You'll have to wait until I'm done eating."

His eyes flashed with impatience.

"Must I remind you that you were the one who wanted to get her life back? The sooner I find out where those phones are, the sooner you can get out of here. Work on your daughter. Get her to stop babying her father. How tough can it be to get him to say a few more words? He's already given us part of the equation, now we just need a little bit more to solve the problem."

"Don't plan on any miracles. My daughter and I aren't exactly on chummy terms in case that's escaped you. The gap between us is too big to change things."

"I've noticed. But I'm counting on you to close that gap enough to get the information I need. Do this for me my beautiful Bobby, and I'm going to make it worth your while. I've been promised a huge bonus if I can get those phones."

She put her fork down and gave him a speculative look.

"How much money are we talking here?"

"Enough to treat you like a queen."

"Now you're talking." Bobbett wiped her mouth on her napkin, tossed it onto the table, and stood up.

"It looks like I'm about to become my daughter's new best friend."

"I'm more interested in you becoming her confidant."

Twenty-two

"How's he doing?" Thad asked the security guard sitting outside Wendell's room.

"Coming around and showing good improvement according to what I hear."

"That's great news. I think I'll go in and pay my respects."

"You're supposed to check with the doctor, but I won't say anything. By the way, is this a personal courtesy call or are you on the case again?"

"Both. I asked to be reassigned."

"Welcome back."

"Thanks."

Muriel gave Thad a dubious look when he entered the room and introduced himself. "I thought Suzanne said you were gone."

"I was, but now I'm back. Where is she?"

"She went outside to get some fresh air. Is she expecting you?"

"No. I thought I'd surprise her."

"I'm sure you will. I just hope it'll be in a good way."

"So do I." He looked at Wendell. "I understand you're making good progress."

"Getting there."

"I'm glad. Mrs. Harold called and told me you left the phones at her house. I realize you haven't always trusted me, but I want you to know I'm willing to do pretty much anything to gain that trust."

Wendell eyed Thad for several seconds with wavering suspicion before exhaling a tired sigh.

"I hope to God you mean it because I don't have much choice right now except to take you at your word."

Muriel entered the conversation, knowing how difficult it was for Wendell to talk too long.

"Suzanne and her mother went with David to her godmother's to find the phones. Wendell hid them inside a stuffed toy horse there, but he forgot to tell them he put the toy in Mr. Harold's golf cart, instead of the house."

"Mrs. Harold told me about the Pegasus, but obviously she isn't aware of its location. Does Suzanne know about this latest development?"

"Yes, but she must not have told David yet. Otherwise, I'm sure he'd be pushing her to leave right now. He's very anxious to get back to the island."

All eyes turned to the door when Bobbett chose that moment to enter the room. She stopped when she saw Thad. Good looking, well-built men always caught her attention, especially if they were younger than her. She puffed out her chest, wet her lips, and gave him her most flirtatious smile.

"Well, who do we have here?" she cooed walking over to him with a provocative sway to her hips.

Muriel made the introductions.

"Mrs. Conway, this is Thad Novak. He used to be the man looking after Suzanne before David came here."

"Oh! I'm so glad to finally meet you and have this opportunity to thank you for watching over my little girl." She glanced around the room.

"Where is she, by the way?"

"Getting some fresh air," Muriel said.

"Why don't you and I get better acquainted Mr. Novak, while we're waiting for Suzanne? Or may I call you Thad? It's such a strong, masculine name and I can see it suits you very well. You must call me Bobby like all my special friends do."

Wendell let out a soft snort from his bed while Thad shifted his attention back to Muriel.

"When do you expect Suzanne to return?"

Muriel glanced at her watch and frowned.

"Actually, I expected her to be back by now."

This latest development meant more running away. But Suzanne knew she had to get back to Nanadoo's without David. Everything her father did to keep the phones safe would be for nothing if David got his hands on them. Were there other moles inside the clinic working for the Montane family?

She had no way of finding out right now, which meant she'd have to be very careful who she talked to.

She squatted behind a bush outside the clinic keeping her eyes on a laundry van. The bags of soiled laundry would be her hiding place if she could get inside. She eased herself closer to the back doors the driver left standing open. She waited until he was inside the clinic before she ran, climbed up, and dove into the stacks of cloth bags. She burrowed deep, wrinkling her nose at the disagreeable odors.

The driver came out of the building a few minutes later and tossed in a couple more bags. Suzanne heard him slam the doors shut. She felt the van move, drive a short distance, and stop at the gate. She prayed the guard wouldn't insist on doing a search. Her fingers unclenched from a fabric bag when the vehicle started moving again leaving her safely nestled among the dirty linens.

Suzanne settled back and began to concentrate on how she could get to the phones before David.

She doubted he would waste much time staying at the clinic when he couldn't find her. She had to alert Muriel to get extra protection for her dad. If only she had her phone, but she hadn't wanted to go back for her purse and take the chance of running into David or anyone else who may be helping him.

Her fingers gripped one of the laundry bags again remembering how David had talked about killing her father. He was more of a monster than the Montanes. At least they didn't pretend to be good. Suzanne forced her thoughts back to the phones. David would probably take a helicopter to get back to the island. That option of even taking a ferry wasn't available to her until she could get hold of some money.

The best way to beat him to the colonel's golf cart would be to have someone who was already on the island go and get the phones. It would have to be someone used to looking after

219

themselves in difficult situations. The only person Suzanne could think to call was Dewey.

She just hoped he was still on the island. Suzanne wasn't sure if he'd be willing to help her. But she knew Dewey had no love for the Montane brothers, so that could work in her favor. She needed to get in touch with him. Her fingers toyed with the string of a nearby bag, as she sat there thinking. Maybe she could somehow get the driver's cell. If she was lucky enough to be successful with that, then she'd have to hope Dewey could be trusted to either bring her the phones, or turn them over to the police himself.

Suzanne bit her lip. There were so many holes in her plan it made her think of Swiss cheese. If only Thad was here. His absence felt like a missing limb that throbbed with phantom pain. Suzanne listened to the sound of the tires. His name began to repeat itself over and over inside her head to the rhythm of the tires on the road.

Thad. Thad. Thad.

Thad rallied every available person to search the buildings and grounds for Suzanne when it became obvious too much time had gone by without her returning. No one had a way to get hold of her because she'd left her phone in her purse sitting in her father's room. Muriel offered to dump the contents out in the hopes they might be able to find a clue to Suzanne's disappearance.

When Muriel opened the tissues and found the black feather she dropped it as though she'd touched a hot coal. She didn't have to explain the significance to either Thad or Wendell. Both men knew what it meant and in that moment the fear for Suzanne's safety escalated to new, terrifying heights, especially when Wendell told Thad she'd received other feathers.

Thad walked out into the hallway when he heard David shouting at the security guards.

"How the hell could Suzanne just disappear? What kind of show are you people running here?"

"Cut them some slack," Thad said. "She has a talent for vanishing, and I speak from experience."

"I know, but Jesus!"

Thad looked at the guard from the front gate.

"What other vehicles left here besides passenger cars."

"The laundry van. The driver has clearance, so I didn't do a search."

"Are you thinking she could have left in that van?" David asked Thad.

"That'd be my guess, unless she climbed into someone's trunk. But knowing her, I have a feeling she's been up to her old tricks and fled the clinic with the dirty laundry."

"She might be going back to the island to get the phones." David frowned. "I can't figure out why she thought she had to go alone. I think it'd be best if you stayed here in case she returns. I'll go to the island, meet her at her godmother's place, and return with her and the phones."

Thad didn't answer right away. He was too busy mulling over his own concerns. He agreed with David that Suzanne may be trying to get the phones by herself. But why? It didn't make sense. Her father swore he hadn't advised her to go alone. He knew as well as Thad there was always the chance that one of the Montane's so-called associates could still be watching the house there. He didn't need the black feather to remind him they were always waiting in the background. If Suzanne was discovered to be on her own God knows what they would do to her knowing she didn't have anyone protecting her.

Indecision warred inside Thad. Should he go directly to the island himself and save the woman he loved from a possible death sentence? Or should he go to the laundry first and try to catch her before she left for her godmother's? David's voice interrupted his thoughts.

"Novak? Did you hear what I said? I'll leave right now for the island. You've already had to chase after Suzanne enough. You don't need this aggravation. Let me go. What do you say?"

The Black Feather
Olivia Claire High

"I'll have to think about that. Right now I'm going to call the laundry to inform them that their driver could unknowingly be carrying a hitchhiker."

David glowered at Thad.

"You know, I really don't have to ask for your permission, since you were assigned to another case."

"Well, I'm back now and for the record, Suzanne is more than just another case to me."

The van finally stopped. Suzanne heard the driver come to the back and open the doors. She peeked out from her hiding place and waited until he walked away carrying some of the bags before she climbed over the rest and scrambled out of the van. She sucked in some much needed clean air.

She hurried to the van's cab muttering under her breath, "Please let his phone be in the front seat."

The urge to give a whoop of happiness almost burst out of her when her wish was granted. Suzanne opened the door, grabbed the phone, and ran around the side of the building to hide. She began tapping in Dewey's number, thankful that she actually remembered it. Now she had to hope her luck would hold and he'd answer her summons.

"I'm out cleaning up after someone as usual. Leave a message."

Never had a voicemail sounded so unwanted. She ended the call without leaving a message. Maybe it was just as well for Dewey that he couldn't help her. Suzanne didn't know what would await him if he went to her godmother's. She didn't want to be responsible for sending him into danger and have that on her conscience along with all the other guilt she was juggling.

Man and violence. A volatile combination. The need to wound. To dominate the weak. To draw blood. She'd become a part of unleashing more of that violence even knowing she was trying to do something good. What choice did she have but to follow this dangerous path to its uncertain end? She knew the ugly images would still be burned in her brain even when this nightmare of a journey ended.

She started to call Muriel when the sound of the van driver's angry shout caused her to peek around the corner. She saw him standing by the vehicle. He did not look happy.

"Did one of you borrow my phone?" he yelled toward the open doorway of the building. No one answered. "Hey! Where's my phone?"

Suzanne stepped out into the open.

"I have it."

He whirled around to face her.

"I'm not stealing it. I left mine back at the clinic and I needed to make an urgent phone call."

"Who the heck are you?"

"My name is Suzanne Conway. My father is a patient at the clinic. I had to get away from a man back there who wants to kill my dad and come after me. I hid in your van to escape. I needed to call someone. I'd like to use your phone again if that's okay. It's an emergency," she added.

His gaze shifted to look over her shoulder. "Do you think the guy followed you here?"

"No. He doesn't know I left in your van. Please, may I use your phone for my call?"

"Yeah, sure."

"Thank you."

Muriel answered.

"Suzanne! Everyone is looking for you. Where are you? Are you okay?"

Suzanne interrupted the stream of questions.

"I'm fine. Is David Hamilton still at the clinic?"

"Yes and he's very upset with you. I also think you should know . . ."

Suzanne sliced through the words before Muriel could say that Thad had returned.

"Muriel, please listen to me, David is . . ."

"He's outside the door talking to the guard. I'll let you explain to him why you ran off."

Was the guard an accomplice? Suzanne almost dropped the phone in her haste to cut the connection.

David would be leaving the clinic once Muriel told him she'd called. He'd probably figure out she left in the van. That meant he could be on his way to the laundry at any moment. She had to get out of here. Suzanne handed the driver his phone.

He peered closely at her.

"I bet you're probably still shook up from that guy you mentioned. I'm done with my shift. I can take you wherever you need to go. I just have to check out."

"Thank you. That's very nice of you, but I . . ."

They both turned when a man came to the doorway. "Are you by any chance Suzanne Conway? Because if you are, there's some guy on the phone saying you need to stay here and he'll come for you."

David! Her heart skipped a couple beats. "Please tell him you never saw me."

The driver nodded to the other man.

"Yeah. Some creep is chasing her." He turned back to Suzanne. "Let me go inside and get my things and then I'll take you wherever you want to go. Maybe the police?"

Suzanne thanked him and watched as the two men hustled back into the building. She didn't waste any time running to the van and climbing into the driver's seat. The keys dangled in the ignition like a lifeline. She started the engine and drove away heading for the closest pier where she could get the Catalina Express. She didn't know the exact schedule, but with twenty-five daily departures there had to be one to suit her needs.

But none of that would matter if she couldn't come up with her fare. She didn't have her wallet and the only thing in her pockets was some lint. She looked down and saw the driver's wallet lying on the front seat and hoped there would be enough cash to take care of her money problem. She hated to take advantage of the man, especially since he'd been so sweet to her. She'd have to add hijacking a person's vehicle and taking their money without permission to her sins. Suzanne hoped she would be forgiven.

She parked on a side street and jogged to the area where she could wait until it was time to board.

She sat gnawing her thumbnail while her eyes never stopped inspecting the surroundings watching for any sign of trouble. She kept her back to a wall and made sure she positioned herself near an exit should she have to make a run for it.

Thad had taught her that.

She couldn't call his agency, not only because she didn't know the phone number, but no thanks to his secretiveness, she didn't even know the name of the place. Once again, she wished that Thad could be here with her. Not only because she missed him, but also because she felt nervous to be going for the phones on her own. She could even be too late.

David may have already called someone to go to Nanadoo's. But now that she thought about it, those phones were his personal top priority. He'd want to go to the island himself. She prayed her father wouldn't tell him where the horse was hidden because not telling would be the only thing keeping her dad alive.

She hadn't asked for this Machiavellian life, but because she'd been thrust into this world of deceit Suzanne knew she had to stay one step ahead of David and everyone else who wanted the phones for their own ill use. Hopefully one step would be enough.

If not . . . no one could say she hadn't tried.

Twenty-three

Suzanne stood on the ferry, a lone shape hiding in the shadows, surrounded by the sea. She stared into the soft gray distance, body tense, keeping her senses alert trying to prepare herself for whatever may come. She lingered there for several minutes until she decided to use the facilities. Luckily, the restroom was empty.

She splashed cold water on her face and stared in the mirror, wondering at the stranger who stared back. She felt numb. Suzanne had a feeling she could dive into icy water and not be cold. Or walk through fire and not feel the heat of the flames. But she did feel fear when she wanted to be brave and despair when she needed hope. She didn't want to die, but she could be giving death a helping hand by going to Nanadoo's unprotected.

If only she could call the clinic and tell someone about the viper in their midst. But if David did have others helping him her phone call could warn him that she knew of his duplicity. Suzanne closed her eyes remembering his vow to kill her dad. All it would take was for Muriel to ask the doctor's permission to invite David into the room and then leave thinking he would guard her father.

Suzanne opened her eyes. She was so tired. She felt as though she didn't have any defenses left. All she wanted to do was sleep, but she had to keep fighting to save her father and get his precious phones to the police. Cowering in this restroom wasn't going to do anyone any good. She yanked open the door, stepped into the hallway, and ran into a wall of hard muscle.

"This smacks of déjà vu, don't you think," a masculine voice rumbled close to her ear.

"You!" she gasped letting out a soft shriek at the sight of Thad standing there.

226

Suzanne struggled to sort out all the conflicting emotions crashing through her. She couldn't forget how Thad had turned his back on her despite bringing her to her knees, begging. Humiliation was somehow so much worse coming from someone you had just bared your soul to. Pride, that pathetic shield for self-preservation made her chin tilt up.

"What are you doing here?"

"You mean, rather than tripping little old ladies, as they cross the street? I wanted to see you."

"That's not the impression I got at our last meeting."

His throat moved as he swallowed.

"Turns out I was wrong."

"Really? You stomped all over my feelings and now you expect me to welcome you back with open arms."

She shook her head.

"A kiss or two would also be nice."

She started to walk away, but Thad stepped in front of her.

"Go away. I don't want you here."

"You may not want me, but you need me," he said gently.

"Since when has that made a difference? You knew what you were doing before, but you still left. I can't deal with you ripping holes in me."

"That should give you some idea how I felt every time you ran off on your own."

"I didn't do it to deliberately hurt you. I went because I had good intentions of trying to be helpful."

"Which wasn't much comfort to me when I didn't know whether or not I'd ever see you alive again."

"Well, we wouldn't want to have a blotch on your record if I did turn up dead, would we?"

Suzanne heard him suck in his breath. She wanted to hurt him because he'd wounded her. But she regretted her words as soon as she saw the haunted look in his eyes. This was a contest neither of them could win as long as she thought she had to keep score. Her resistance began to fall away making her burst into tears. Her crying galvanized Thad into action. He pulled her to him engulfing her in a fierce embrace. Suzanne stiffened for a few seconds before allowing herself to lean on him.

"Don't cry. Please. I made you cry before and I never want to do it again."

"I'm tired and . . . and I'm scared," she stuttered between sobs. "I feel like I've been running through a labyrinth without a compass, a map, or any signs to show me the right way to go."

"I know, sweetheart, I know. But it's going to be okay now. I'm here. I'll be your compass."

Suzanne moved back.

"I hate all this crying I seem to be doing lately. It makes me feel like a wuss."

She hiccupped and wiped the heels of her hands down her cheeks.

"I thought you'd be David."

"I don't blame you for preferring him after the way I treated you. I said regrettable things that I can't take back. But I'm hoping you'll forgive me. David asked to come, but I told him you were my responsibility."

"Is that all I am to you, a responsibility?" she asked, momentarily distracted from David's treachery.

"I didn't mean that how it sounded. You were right when you thought you were more than just another case to me. I tried to tell myself otherwise, but it didn't work. I want to be with you and not just because it's my job. That's why I'm here. David's at the clinic keeping an eye on your dad and Muriel."

"No! You've left the wolf to guard the sheep," she cried, digging her fingers hard into his arm.

"Ease up a bit, honey. I think you're about to draw blood. Now what is this about a wolf?"

Suzanne immediately removed her hand and ran it through her hair in a short, jerky motion.

"I'm talking about David. He's working for the Montanes."

"What!"

The word erupted out of Thad like a mini explosion.

"Who told you such a thing?"

228

"I overheard him talking to one of them on his phone back at the clinic. That's why I left without telling anyone. I'm sure David doesn't know that I'm onto him. I can only hope my father didn't let him know he put my stuffed Pegasus in the colonel's golf cart. The phones are in the toy. That's why I have to get to Nanadoo's as soon as possible. But I'm so afraid for my dad."

Thad held her by the arms when she began to shake.

"You need to sit down."

"Wait. I haven't finished. The Montanes want David to kill my father, and he agreed to do it."

"God!" Thad led her to a chair before whipping the phone out of his pocket.

Suzanne listened while he called the clinic and his agency. She sat on the edge of the chair watching him until he ended the call.

"Are my dad and Muriel okay? Did he tell David where the phones are?"

"Your dad and Muriel are safe and he didn't tell David about the phones."

"Thank goodness. What are the security people going to do about keeping David away from Dad?"

"They won't have to. He left the clinic right after I did and your mother went with him."

Suzanne raised her brows.

"She did? I thought they were on the outs when I left. He must have done or said something to make her like him again. I'm pretty sure she doesn't know about David's involvement with the Montanes."

"It's better that she doesn't. I don't think he'll hurt her as long as he thinks she's in the dark."

"What if he wanted her with him in case he needed her as a hostage?"

"Let's hope it doesn't come to that. The one good thing we can focus on is that he's away from the clinic. But your dad and Muriel are being secretly moved to another room as an extra precaution."

"You know David will be after the phones and he's going to get to the island way before we do. A helicopter is a lot faster than a laundry van."

Thad nodded.

"I had a feeling that's how you got away."

"Could you call the company and tell them where I parked it?" Suzanne named the street. "Also, that I put the keys in the glove compartment along with the driver's wallet. I put an IOU in there to let him know I would pay him back."

"Pay him back for what, stealing his van?" Thad joked.

"I merely borrowed it along with money for the ferry."

"Your ingenuity never ceases to amaze me. I'll take care of it and leave him a generous tip."

"Thanks. He was nice. I wished I had you taking care of things, despite what I said earlier."

"I hope that's not the only reason you missed me," he said, sounding endearingly unsure of himself.

"I'd be showing you how much I missed you if we had a room."

Thad hauled her into his arms and kissed her. "We've got to do something about that soon, but . . ."

"But the phones come first. I know. I called Dewey, but he didn't answer and I didn't try again. I decided I didn't want him getting hurt because of me. I think the Montanes already did something terrible to him or someone he knows."

Thad gave her a grim look.

"I don't know why, but they tortured and killed his brother."

Suzanne paled.

"Those monsters! Dad said his phones would help Dewey. He must have some evidence connecting them to that death. But I wasn't even sure if Dewey would have helped me."

"It's difficult to know who you can trust in a situation like this."

"I keep finding that out much to my cost," she said and shivered.

"You're cold." Thad took off his jacket and put it over her shoulders. "I'll get us some coffee."

She pulled the coat more fully around her absorbing the warmth and inhaling the lingering scent of his body. Her eyes lit up when he came back carrying coffee and a couple of donuts.

"Not a very nutritious meal, but the sugar will give you some energy."

Suzanne took the coffee and donut from him. A little moan of pleasure slipped through her lips after the first bite.

"This really hits the spot. I didn't think I'd be able to eat the way my stomach's been bouncing around."

"I can imagine. You've been through a lot the last few hours, not to mention your stress from before."

She grimaced.

"I'm storing memories I'd rather not have. Is that what you meant about the déjà vu?"

"No. This ferry reminded me of how we first met aboard a sailing vessel."

"I didn't think I'd ever say this, but I'd like to be able to finish that cruise some day."

"So would I, especially if we can go together."

"I'd like that even better."

They finished their impromptu meal in silence. Thad handed her an extra napkin.

"I'm curious about something."

Suzanne wiped the paper napkin over her mouth. "What?"

"Were you ever going to tell me about the black feathers? Muriel found one in your purse. Your dad said you told them there were others."

She winced.

"I got the first one aboard ship. I thought it was some kind of stunt. But I had a bad feeling when I found the second one in my bedroom."

"You had one in your house?" Thad's lips tightened. "Damn it, Suzanne. Why didn't you tell me?"

"I didn't want to worry you. I really didn't understand what they were all about until I asked my dad. I found the third one at Nanadoo's when I went with David and my mom to look for the phones. I bet he put it there to scare me into finding my Pegasus now that I know what he's up to."

"You're killing me here. I promised your godmother I'd look after you, but you don't make it easy."

Surprise flickered in her eyes.

"Nanadoo? When did you talk to her?"

"Don't be nosy."

"Oh, I get it now. You came back because she asked you to."

"I came back because I couldn't stay away," he corrected. "I also promised myself I'd take care of you, and this time I intend to no matter what I have to do. But you've got to tell me everything even if you think it's nothing important. Okay?"

"Yes. I've discovered I'm not very good at chasing after criminals on my own. I'm too chicken."

"Like hell. You're one of the bravest women I know."

"Thank you for not saying I'm also one of the most foolish and reckless you've ever met."

"We'll call it error in judgment and let it go at that."

Thad took their paper cups and napkins to the trash. He stood back for a moment studying Suzanne. She didn't have to tell him she was tired. One look at the gray shadows darkening the delicate skin beneath her eyes and the slump of her shoulders told him her body was about ready to give out.

He knew he loved her. He just hadn't realized how deep that love went until he'd been away from her. Thad had a feeling he wouldn't have been able to hold out much longer before he went crawling back to Suzanne. Her godmother had merely jumpstarted his return.

He'd made it a point over the years not to need anyone. He'd had other women in his life, but only for periods of brief companionship and physical release. Suzanne made him feel a vulnerability he wouldn't have thought possible. It overwhelmed, even unnerved him. But a great deal of pleasure was also mixed up in all these unfamiliar emotions.

Thad walked back and settled himself on a seat next to Suzanne. He tugged her gently over to him, so her head could rest on his shoulder while he gently stroked her hair.

"I love you, Thad. I know you don't want me to, but I can't help myself. Would you be willing to give us a chance together?"

Her admission, so openly given caused a constriction to rise up and tighten his throat making it difficult for him to immediately answer her. He chose his words carefully.

"Loving me may not be the best thing for you. But I want you to know that your love means everything to me, Suzanne."

She looked at him.

"Let's make a deal right now that neither of us will run out on each other again."

"I wish I could agree without reservation, but you know as well as I do sometimes there are certain circumstances, and you don't have any choice. What happened with you is a perfect example of that."

"I still feel like I'm letting people down by the decisions I've made."

"No. You keep letting yourself down while building everyone else up. You've spent your life trying to please others so much that you don't realize one of your greatest qualities is loyalty. I wouldn't have left you had I put that in the right perspective, instead of being so hung up on the trust issue."

"Trust is important. But I saw how selfish my parents were, and I didn't want to be like them. I guess I need to learn how to take a little more and give a little less. I also need to learn to ask you for help."

"Should I get that in writing?"

"Beast!" she chuckled before a yawn escaped her. "How are you going to handle David?"

Thad pulled her head back down to his shoulder.

"Go to sleep now. I'll think of something."

"I'm sure you will," she murmured before letting her eyes close.

Thad touched her cheek just enough to wake her. "We're almost to the island, honey."

Suzanne moaned, sat up, and knuckled the sleep out of her eyes. She sent him a sleepy smile that melted his heart. How the hell did he ever think he'd be able to get by without having her in his life? He must have suffered from temporary insanity.

"I'd better use the restroom. Do you think we have time for another cup of coffee?" she asked, standing up and stretching.

"A quick one. I'll get it."

"Thanks."

Suzanne hurried to the restroom. Thad returned by the time she used the facilities, washed her face, and combed her hair. He handed her a cup. She let the steam curl up and fill her head with its rich aroma before taking a tentative sip. He drank a few swallows before setting his cup aside.

"We don't have a lot of time before we dock, so let me tell you how we're going to do this."

He reached into a pocket and handed her a cell phone. She clutched it to her chest.

"Boy, am I ever glad to have this."

"I thought you would be. Here's the plan. We're going to start by renting two golf carts."

"Why two?"

"You'll follow me to your godmother's, but stop a short distance from the house. I don't want David to know you came with me. Leave your cart and walk the rest of the way. Give me a little time to keep them away from where Liam parks his cart. Just make sure they won't be able to see you."

She nodded.

"Got it."

"I want you to go immediately to where the helicopters are as soon as you have the phones. I've already made arrangements for you to be flown to Long Beach. Someone will meet you there."

"Shouldn't I let you know as soon as I get the phones?"

"I'd rather you wait until you're ready to board. I want you off the island before I start back."

"How will you get David to leave?"

"I'm going to tell him it's Muriel when you call. I'll say your father was mistaken about the phones being at the condo and now she's sure they're at the clinic. I'll explain that she doesn't want to look for them until David and I return."

"He's going to be furious for what he'll think is another wasted trip to Nanadoo's."

"Getting the phones should appease him enough to go back to the clinic with me. That way I can have him arrested once we're there and also get your mother away without any harm coming to her."

"Thank you. My mom makes me angry most of the time, but she's still my mother."

"Don't thank me yet. We've docked."

He took her by the hand.

"Are you ready to do this?"

"As ready as I'll ever be. I just hope I don't blow up when I see David again."

Thad made sure Suzanne was safely buckled inside her golf cart before climbing into his own. He gave her an encouraging smile. Nerves and the possibility they could end up running into more trouble made her hands squeeze the steering wheel way too hard.

"I want you to know how much I appreciate everything you've done to help me in case anything goes wrong," she said.

"You do everything the way we talked about and it'll all be fine. Those phones will be in the hands of the authorities tonight, and then I'm going to take you out to a steak dinner with champagne and candlelight. You just keep reminding yourself of that. All right?"

Suzanne nodded, took a deep, bracing breath, and started the cart. "By the way, I like my steak cooked medium rare."

David stared out the front windows of the condo. "Damn it! Where is your daughter?"

Bobbett yawned, and ran fingers through her hair.

"On a slow boat to China, apparently. I don't know why you insisted we get here so early."

"I wanted to be here when she arrives. It's not my fault her father wouldn't tell you or me where he stashed the toy. She'll probably want to turn the phones over to the police right away. I won't get the bonus if I can't personally take them to my agency. I don't want any slip-ups."

"I don't see how there can be. She shows you where those idiotic phones are, you give them to your boss, get the money, and we take off. I'd like to go to Hawaii instead of Mexico this time. You know, stay at one of those five star resorts where celebrities go. How does that sound?"

David turned from the window. "Yeah, Hawaii. Sure. But remember, no phones. No . . ."

"Money. I know. You've drilled that into my head enough times. Are you sure you won't have to share it with Thad Novak?"

"Not if I get the phones first. That's another reason I needed to get here early. I don't want your daughter thinking she has to give one of them to Novak for old time's sake."

"I thought he'd be here when we arrived, since he left ahead of us."

"Yeah, but your daughter left before all of us. Thad had to track her down at that laundry and then try to find out what ferry she took, or however she planned to come here."

"Maybe she decided to swim."

"Very funny. I could use a cup of coffee. Why don't you go to the kitchen and make some?"

"Do I look like a kitchen maid?"

He blew out an exasperated breath.

"For God's sake. Can't you ever do anything for anyone else?"

"I came here with you, didn't I? Don't forget that I expect you to keep your promise to reward me."

David pressed his upper arm against the gun in its shoulder holster hidden beneath his jacket. The smile he gave Bobbett didn't reach his eyes.

"Oh don't worry, I have a special reward in mind for you."

Thad made sure Suzanne stopped a few houses away before he pulled up in front of her godmother's condo. He walked the short distance to the front door and schooled his face into a surprised expression when David flung it open.

"What are you doing here, Hamilton? You're supposed to be back at the clinic keeping an eye on the Conways," he said, deliberately infusing some anger into his voice before pushing his way into the house.

"I know, but Wendell Conway is being well looked after. Mrs. Conway got so worried about Suzanne she begged me to bring her here. Didn't you?" he asked turning toward Bobbett.

"What? Oh yes. I've been worried sick. Isn't Suzanne with you?"

"I thought she'd be here. Are you saying you haven't seen her?"

David glared at Thad.

"We thought she was with you. Didn't you check the laundry? You said she probably got away in their van."

"I did, but she wasn't there. The driver told me he parked his van and went inside. It was missing when he came back out a few minutes later. I went directly to the dock from there and booked passage on a ferry, but I didn't see her. She must have been on another ferry that left from a different port."

"Now what are we supposed to do? Does that mean you aren't going to get that reward money?" Bobbett asked David.

Thad sent her a puzzled look

"What reward money?"

David gave her a warning glare before turning back to Thad. "Suzanne must have taken a later ferry."

"Or she may have hired a private boat. It looks like we'll have to wait her out." Thad looked toward the kitchen. "Any coffee going?"

"No, but Bobbett was just about to make a pot."

She started to sputter a refusal when Thad shrugged.

"I'll do it. You two may as well come and keep me company."

"It ticks me off that we have to sit around here until Suzanne decides to make an appearance," David complained.

237

"I don't see that we have any other choice."

"If she ever bothers to show up," Bobbett sniffed. "You never know what that girl is going to do. I swear she spent most of her childhood always running off."

Thad stopped and gave her a cold stare.

"Maybe she wouldn't have had to run anywhere if she'd had a reason to stay."

Twenty-four

Suzanne steered her golf cart off the road and parked behind a towering hedge of oleander bushes after waving to Thad, as he drove on ahead. She wanted to make sure she'd be well hidden in the event David should happen to come this way. She looked at her watch wondering how much time to give Thad before she started for Nanadoo's house.

"You can't park there."

Suzanne's head immediately jerked toward the sound of the voice. An elderly woman stood in the doorway of a nearby condo pointing at the golf cart.

"I'll only be here a little while. I just have to get something from a house down the street and I'll be on my way."

"Then park down there. This is private property."

"I understand that, ma'am, but I'd like your permission to leave my cart for a short time."

"You're blocking the driveway."

Suzanne saw that the rear end of the cart was parked a couple of inches onto the area where the woman pointed. "Not enough to be a problem."

"I want you to leave right now," the woman insisted, leaving the confines of her doorway.

One moment she was heading up the slight incline toward Suzanne and the next second she was falling, crying out as her body sprawled over a loose patch of gravel. Suzanne ran forward and got down flinching as her knees pressed into the tiny pebbles. She knelt next to the moaning woman.

"Where are you hurt?"

"I've twisted my ankle," she said, rubbing the afflicted area. "I must get back to my house."

She tried to stand, but cried out in pain as soon as she put weight on her foot. Suzanne pushed herself up and reached out to the woman.

"Can you put your arm around my neck? We may be able to get you inside if we work together."

It took several long, agonizing minutes before Suzanne managed to get the woman settled in a chair with an ottoman to support the wounded ankle.

"Is anyone else here?" Suzanne asked, looking around.

"My husband is, but he's bedridden with terminal cancer. I take care of him. I'll call my neighbor later and let her know about my fall. She's in town shopping right now."

Suzanne knew it was imperative that she get to Nanadoo's as soon as possible, but she couldn't justify leaving the woman without doing something to help. The poor soul wouldn't be in this state if she hadn't come outside to tell Suzanne to move the golf cart.

"You'll need some ice on that foot right away. Will you allow me to do that for you?"

"All right. The kitchen's behind me. There should be plenty of ice in the icemaker. I have a bottle of aspirin in the cupboard to the right of the sink. Would you mind bringing me a couple?"

Suzanne nodded and eased the afflicted foot out of the sandal while the woman dug her fingers into the chair's fabric. The skin surrounding the ankle was already swelling and stretching tight with a network of fragile blue veins visible beneath the aged flesh.

"I'll be right back."

Suzanne rushed into the kitchen and spotted the refrigerator before looking around for something to put the ice cubes in. She grabbed a couple of dish towels hanging on the handle to the oven door, layered them one on top of the other, and yanked open the freezer side of the fridge where she scooped up a couple of handfuls of ice. She dumped the cubes onto the towels and tied the ends together for a makeshift icepack.

She tossed a few extra cubes of ice into a glass, filled it with water, and shook out a couple aspirins from the bottle. She glanced at the wall clock before hurrying back into the living room. The phones waited this long to be found and it looked like they'd have to wait a little while longer. Hopefully Thad would be able to keep David occupied until she could get to the colonel's golf cart and complete her part of their mission.

Bobbett lifted her cup in a toast to Thad.

"You make delicious coffee." She smiled at him over the rim of her cup. "I have a feeling you know your way around the bedroom, oops, I mean kitchen. I'd love to have you share your menu with me."

David glared at her and slammed his empty mug down onto the table.

"Suzanne should have been here by now."

His words echoed the same worry spinning inside Thad's head. He expected her call long before this. He had to think of a way to get David and Bobbett away from the condo, so he could check Liam's golf cart himself. He didn't like the idea of letting them out of his sight, but finding out what happened to Suzanne had to be his main concern at the moment. Nerves could have made her forget to let him know she had the phones. That'd be okay with him as long as she was on her way off the island.

"Why don't you two go down to the dock and check the ferries? I'll stay here in case Suzanne shows up. I might even question some of the neighbors."

David's eyes shifted between Thad and Bobbett. "How about you two go and I'll stay here?"

Thad knew he couldn't deal with David the way the man deserved. It wouldn't be too smart to antagonize the antagonist until the phones, Suzanne, and her mother were all safely out of his reach.

"We're back to our original clients if you'll recall. You take care of Mrs. Conway while I take care of her daughter. Call me as soon as you find out anything and I'll do the same. We're going to have to assume Suzanne decided to go someplace else if she doesn't show up here pretty damn soon."

"Why would she do that if the phones are here?"

"Maybe they aren't. Her father could be confused about that, considering how ill he's been."

"I always thought the man was confused even when he was supposed to be healthy," Bobbett said.

David shook his head at her.

"You're unbelievable."

"Why thank you, darling."

"Come on," he snapped in disgust.

Thad waited for them to drive out of sight before he ran out of the house to Liam's cart. Concern for Suzanne made him call the helicopter port as he went only to be told she hadn't shown up. He shoved the phone back into his pocket and practically hurled himself around the corner to where the cart sat parked.

He yanked up the lid to the little storage area behind the driver's seat, tossed aside a towel, and drew in a sharp breath at the sight of the stuffed Pegasus before lifting it in his hands. Thad pulled at the rough stitching. The material tore away to reveal two phones nestled among the stuffing. Relief at finding them was brief knowing that this meant Suzanne hadn't been here herself.

His hands squeezed the toy for a moment. Where could she be? She'd been right behind him. How was it possible for her to get into trouble in such a short period of time? She must have run into some kind of difficulty to keep her from coming here as she intended.

Thad started to reach for the phones when the hairs on the back of his neck stood on end. His body pivoted, ready to defend himself when something hard smashed into the side of his head sending a shower of lights bursting behind his eyes.

The toy horse slid from his hands, as his body slumped to the ground.

The insistent pounding inside his head brought Thad to full awareness. The phones! He'd had them in his hands before pain exploded in his skull. Someone obviously was lurking by the golf cart lying in wait. Whoever did this had to be someone strong enough to drag him to where he now lay on his side, bound and gagged. Thad tested his body for range of movement. The inventory wasn't encouraging with his hands tied behind his back, ankles bound together and tape over his mouth and eyes.

He knew by his position that he was lying on a hillside. He inhaled and smelled earth and plants, reminding him of the night he and Suzanne had crawled around the backyard of her childhood home.

He listened for sounds hoping to get some idea about his location. A bee buzzed near his head momentarily investigating his hair for any sign of a scent before abandoning him for more promising fare. A dog barked in the distance, as it competed with the sound of a lawnmower's relentless droning. He had no idea how long he'd been out, but the sun's warmth meant it was still around midday.

A sudden breeze carried a brief whiff of the sea. Thad decided there was a good possibility he'd been left on the hill behind the Harold's condo. He could only hope he hadn't been carried someplace further away. Should he try to wiggle upward going by instinct and the angle of his body hoping to end up somewhere near their house? Or would he be risking another assault from his attacker?

But reason told him getting away would be their priority. Whoever had done this to him was most likely long gone and on their way to handing those phones over to the Montanes. Bitterness filled him at the thought of the notorious brothers evading retribution once again. The resentment he felt wasn't so much for himself, as it was for so many others who had suffered from their cruelty over the years.

There wasn't anything he could do until he got out of his present situation, which meant it was time to start moving. Thad hoped he wouldn't end up going way out of his way considering he was without a clue as to how far he was from the house, or even if he was still near the condo.

He began to move and felt an instant burst of nausea as pain squeezed his head like an ancient instrument of torture. This was going to be a lot harder than he thought. But every journey had to begin with the first step. Or in his case, the first twisting of his body.

Thad forced air in through his nostrils and steeled himself to endure what he knew was probably going to turn out to be a very unpleasant trip. He began to inch forward. Sweat bathed his body and dampened his shirt within seconds. Rocks, clods of dirt, and heavy plants scraped against his skin making him wince, while fear for Suzanne made him push onward.

The woman rewarded Suzanne for her help by allowing her to keep the golf cart parked on her property. Suzanne jogged the rest of the way to her godmother's condo. She spotted Thad's cart parked in front, but no others. Was David already gone? She snuck along the side of the house going directly to the colonel's cart, but stopped when she spotted her ruined Pegasus on the ground. Suzanne bent and picked up the torn toy. She knew even before she pulled the material apart that the phones weren't inside.

Disappointment turned to shock and she almost dropped the toy when she saw the black feather tucked inside. Had David done this one last theatrical gesture to thumb his nose at them all? She looked around. Were her mother and Thad safe? The thought of any possible violence she might find in the house made a mockery of the peaceful outdoor setting.

Her godmother's flowerbeds bloomed with color while birds trilled and bees buzzed nearby. But Suzanne knew in the midst of all this beauty something ugly had happened here. The feather was proof of that. She looked down at the damaged Pegasus still clutched in her hands. This had once been a symbol of beauty for her, too. She set the toy back onto the cart.

She had to find Thad to let him know why she'd been delayed and to assure herself that he was all right. Menacing thoughts taunted her with visions of things she didn't want to think about, as she walked slowly toward the patio. She peeked around the corner of the sliding glass doors, looked inside, and saw that the living room was empty of people.

Momentary relief flowed through her as soon as she realized everything was as it should be. She couldn't detect any signs of struggle, no evidence of blood, and best of all there were not any bodies lying on the floor. Dare she go inside and investigate the rest of the house?

Something that sounded like a muffled groan made her spin around and stare behind her. She didn't notice anything unusual, but the sense that someone was there made her duck behind a huge flowerpot. She squatted there watching and listening until she caught the unmistakable sound of labored breathing.

She reached out a shaky hand, snatched up a pair of small pruning shears lying on the edge of the pot, and cautiously worked her way toward the edge of the patio. Suzanne heard what she thought might be something being dragged over the ground. A body? She shivered and clutched the shears tighter, ready to use them as a weapon to defend herself if necessary. Rustling movements off to the right made her look in that direction. She squinted into the sunlight and nearly shrieked at the sight of Thad laboriously inching his way up the hill.

"Oh God, oh God, oh God!"

She flung the shears aside and ran over to him.

"Are you all right? What happened? Who did this to you?"

She fired questions at him while her hands poked and prodded his body. His garbled grunts made her realize he couldn't answer her because of the tape covering his mouth. All the anxiety she felt simply took over, and she tore the offending tape away without a thought to how it would feel.

Thad breathed out a gasp of pain.

"Ouch! Jesus! Take it easy. Are my lips still attached to my face?"

"Oh Thad, I'm so sorry. I didn't mean to hurt you. Let me get the tape away from your eyes. I'll be more careful," she assured him.

"I'd rather do it myself to be sure my eyeballs still stay in their sockets, if you don't mind. Can you find something to free my hands and ankles?"

Suzanne looked frantically around and spotted the shears. She scurried over to pick them up and hurried back to Thad. "I have some garden shears that should do the trick."

245

"Okay, but go easy, honey. I'm trusting you to be careful. I don't have a lot of feeling left and I wouldn't want to lose any digits that might come in handy later."

She had to admire his sense of humor knowing how uncomfortable he must be. Suzanne knelt there, carefully snipping, feeling the first rush of relief fill her as the tape fell away and Thad began to slowly work his muscles free. She saw him grit his teeth against the discomfort of the blood beginning to flow back into his limbs. She sat back on her heels and waited until he began to ease the tape away from his eyes himself. They both winced when several strands of his hair came away. He was covered in dirt and grimy with sweat, but thankfully she didn't see any sign of blood.

"Did David do this to you?"

"I doubt it. I sent him along with your mother to the docks to look for you, so I could go for the phones. I knew something had to be wrong when you didn't call me. I went to Liam's golf cart the minute they left."

"So you have the phones. Thank the lord."

Thad shook his head.

"Save your prayers. I had them for a few seconds, but that was before someone hit me from behind. The next thing I became aware of was being in the state you just found me. Only I happened to be further down the hill before you got here. I take it you don't have the phones, either."

"No. Can you walk? I think it might be a good idea to get you in the house. I'm sure you'd like some water and a shower."

"Water in any form sounds pretty good right now," he agreed, and dragged himself to his feet.

They'd just walked inside when the front door flung open carrying with it enough anger to fill the room. David and Bobbett were so busy verbally swiping at each other they didn't seem to realize they weren't the only two people in the house.

"I swear to God that is the last time I'm going on another wild-goose chase with you!" she yelled.

"Fine by me! Turns out your daughter is about as reliable as you are," he shouted in return.

"Don't you dare compare me to her. She probably got herself lost somewhere. I'm not that stupid."

Suzanne stepped forward.

"Nice to see you, too, Mother."

Bobbett yelped, and staggered back a couple of steps.

David looked at Suzanne and scowled.

"It's about time you showed up." He frowned at Thad. "Why are your clothes so dirty?"

"I had company right after you left. Caught me from behind. Bound me up and tossed me down the hill like yesterday's garbage. Suzanne arrived a little bit ago and helped me get free."

David turned to her.

"I'm assuming you're here because your father told you where to find the phones. Do you have them?"

"No. They were in the colonel's golf cart. Whoever clobbered Thad must have taken them."

"In the golf cart? Is that so? Why should I believe you?"

She blinked.

"Excuse me?"

"You heard me. How do I know you're not lying?"

She saw the subtle movement of his hand to where she knew he kept his sidearm. But knowing David was playing his dual role made Suzanne throw caution aside. She walked over to where he stood and glared up at him, her eyes sparkling with fury.

"You can believe me because I wouldn't lie about something that could make the difference between life and death."

She poked him in the chest with her finger.

"Can you say the same thing about yourself?"

Twenty-five

Suzanne might have gone on chastising David if Thad hadn't coughed and cleared his throat loud enough to make her realize she needed to shut up.

"I could use a glass of water, Suzanne."

Tension in the room had everyone's eyes flicking back and forth between each other. Suzanne's teeth clamped down on her bottom lip while she watched to see how David was going to react to her outburst. He finally appeared to understand his error in challenging her and lowered his hand to his side. She knew what this effort at controlling himself must have cost him considering his predicament.

"Hey, take it easy. We're all a little on edge here. No need to get on the defensive. I was just asking. You were supposed to tell me about the phones after you talked to your dad, remember?"

"I know, but I thought it would be better to leave you at the clinic to protect my mother and Muriel."

Did she say, 'protect'? Suzanne almost choked on the word knowing what he really planned to do to them.

"If I'd known Thad was coming back I would have had you come here with me."

Amazing how the lies just kept flowing like streams of water over smooth rocks. So much for claiming she didn't lie, but she reminded herself she lied to protect, unlike David who lied to do harm.

"Okay, I get that, but I'd like to know what kept you so long in coming here. You left the clinic way before any of us did."

"I'll tell you, but first I want to get Thad some water and then he needs to go clean up."

"I'll take the water, but I'd be interested in hearing where you've been all this time before I shower."

She nodded and walked quickly to the kitchen, filled the biggest glass she could find with water, and brought it back to him. He drained it immediately and shook his head when she offered to get more.

Suzanne knew she couldn't stall any longer with everyone watching and waiting for her explanation.

She went over the part for David's benefit about her leaving the clinic in the laundry van, spending the night at the pier, and taking the early morning ferry to the island.

"That still doesn't explain why you weren't in this house when your mother and I got here."

Suzanne gave him an impatient look.

"I'm getting to that. I was only a few houses away driving a golf cart when I happened to look over just as an elderly woman fell coming out of her house. I stopped to help her. She had a badly sprained ankle and needed assistance getting back inside. Once I got her to a chair she told me her husband was bedridden with cancer. I could see that the ankle was swelling and causing her pain. I stayed to make an icepack and see that she was settled before I came here."

"And discovered the phones had been taken."

"Yes."

"You should have come here first," David insisted. "If you had, the phones might have still been in the golf cart. Now we have nothing, damn it!"

"The woman couldn't get up on her own, David. I couldn't very well leave her like that."

"You could have gone back to her after you had the phones."

"She did what she thought was best at the time," Thad said.

"That's easy for you to say."

"That's right," Bobbett said, pouting at Suzanne. "Davy was going to take me to Hawaii when he got his bonus money. Now you've probably blown it for us because you decided to play nursemaid to some old woman you don't even know."

Thad frowned at her.

"You mentioned something about that money before. Am I missing something?"

"No. She's a little confused,"

David hastened to answer.

Bobbett rounded on him.

"What do you mean by that? Are you, or are you not going to take me to Hawaii, David Hamilton?"

"While you two are discussing that, why don't you go take your shower, Thad?" Suzanne suggested.

"I'll follow you and you can give me your clothes, so I can run them through the washer and dryer."

He nodded, and they started upstairs with the sound of Bobbett accusing David of being a welsher ringing in their ears. Suzanne slumped against the closed door as soon as she entered the bedroom.

"Jeez, it's a wonder those two haven't killed each other the way they keep going at it."

Thad's mouth curved into a ghost of a smile.

"Not exactly a match made in heaven."

"I thought David was actually going to draw his weapon there for a moment."

"I think he was tempted. He's scared now because he knows the Montanes will be running out of patience, and when they do they'll come after him. He can't afford to reveal his true intentions until he still thinks he has a chance to get the phones."

Thad began to strip off his soiled clothes.

"The phones, the phones," Suzanne muttered. "I'm getting to the point where I'm going to start putting my hands over my ears like Quasimodo did when he heard the bells, the bells."

"You kind of worried me when you started to go off on David."

"That was really dumb. He just makes me so mad I feel like wringing his neck, especially when . . ."

Suzanne stopped in midsentence as the last article of Thad's clothing dropped to the floor. All thoughts of phones and anything else flew right out of her head at the sight of him standing there naked.

"A woman who looks at a man like you're doing is asking to be kissed."

"Be my guest."

"I'm filthy."

Suzanne raised on her toes and put her hands on his shoulders. "I don't care."

Thad pulled her to him and dipped his head to her mouth. She reminded herself to be careful knowing his lips were probably still tender from the tape. They kissed, drawing strength and warmth, enjoying the pleasure of these precious few moments alone. She moved back with reluctance and by the state of his body, Suzanne knew Thad was ready for more than just a few kisses.

"Come and shower with me."

Raised voices drifted upstairs followed by the sound of breaking glass.

"That's a lovely suggestion and there's nothing I'd like more, but I think I'd better get back downstairs before those two do some serious damage to Nanadoo's things."

Thad gave her a playful slap on her backside when she bent to scoop his dirty clothes off the floor.

"Come back if you don't have to take too long playing referee."

"I just might do that," she said and left the room wondering how much longer she was going to have to tolerate the two combatants awaiting her.

"What do you suggest we do now?" David demanded to know, as soon as Thad joined them again.

Bobbett's mouth gaped open at the sight of him clad only in a bath towel. Suzanne couldn't very well blame her mom remembering how her own tongue had practically flopped out of her mouth the first time she saw him like that. Thad leaned his hip against the back of the couch and crossed his arms over his bare chest.

"Suzanne, who else besides the Harolds and yourself might have a key here?"

"I'm not sure. Maybe the neighbors. My godmother kept a spare on the patio, but I moved it."

"Do you think it's possible anyone might know where the key was before you took it?"

"I don't know. I'd have to ask Nanadoo if she mentioned it to any of her friends."

"How about delivery people? Would they have permission to leave something inside the door if your godmother and the colonel knew they wouldn't be home?"

"That's ridiculous. No one gives access to their house key to delivery people," David argued.

"They might if they trusted them perhaps after having them come here on a regular basis over a long period of time. And speaking of the key – how is it that you were able to get in here?"

David's eyes moved toward Suzanne.

"Don't get all ticked off, but I took it out of your purse when we were here before and had a copy made. I thought it'd be a good idea to have it in case you weren't around. Turns out I was right when you didn't show up. What's the big deal about the key anyway?"

"The big deal, as you call it, is the fact that there are no signs of forced entry. Yet someone is coming and going in this house when no one is supposed to be home, which leads me to believe they've been in the area all along watching the place. Suzanne, I'd like you to question the neighbors and find out if they've noticed anyone hanging about."

"Okay." She started to walk away, but stopped and slapped a hand against her forehead. "I forgot to tell you with so much going on. I found another black feather inside my toy horse before I saw you."

They both turned to David when he hissed out a noisy breath. Bobbett wrinkled her nose.

"What's going on with the black feathers? Are there birds molting all over the place or something?"

"Have you seen a black feather yourself, Mrs. Conway?"Thad asked in a polite voice.

She answered, despite David's warning glare.

"We found one on the driver's seat in our rental car in Cabo and another one in our hotel room. Why do you ask?"

He looked at David.

"I take it you know what the black feather means and who sent it?"

"Yeah, but I thought it best not to say anything and upset Bobbie." He looked at Suzanne. "You never told me you've seen them, too."

"Would someone please tell me what you're talking about?"

"It's the Montanes way of saying they're watching us, Mother."

"You already know that, so why are you all acting so weird?"

David whirled to face her.

"Because it means something bad is going to happen when they leave a feather. We've got to get those phones."

"That's what we're trying to do," Thad reminded him.

"Not by sitting here, we're not."

Suzanne looked at Thad.

"I've been thinking what you said about Nanadoo possibly giving a key to a longtime delivery person. The only one I can think of is the water guy. They've been having bottled water delivered to the house for years."

"Then we need to find out more about him."

"You take care of that, Novak while I go with Suzanne to question the neighbors."

"No offense, but I think I'll have better luck on my own. The people here know me. They may feel a little intimidated by you."

"She has a valid point," Thad remarked. "You do seem a little agitated."

"Hell yes I'm agitated, and so should you two be."

David faced Suzanne. "I'm going to feel a lot less agitated if you find out something useful and bother to tell me."

She heard his veiled warning and had to stop herself before the words she really wanted to say popped out of her mouth. Once again, the insult of having to stand there facing a man she knew to be a traitor implying that she might be one too, poked at her like a sharp barb.

The gall that he could demand she help him when he was secretly planning to give the phones away made her fingers itch to slap him. Indignation warred inside her fighting a battle with her anger making her answer him in a cold, clipped voice.

"I'll give you all the information you deserve," she said and stormed out of the house.

Suzanne stopped on the porch and took a couple deep breaths trying to calm down. She couldn't very well go to the neighbors looking like she was going to attack them. David deserved to be the recipient of bodily harm right now. She didn't care what the Montanes did to him. He hadn't earned the right to any leniency for being so money hungry and especially for being a would-be murderer.

Of course, now that the phones were gone, whoever took them may have already delivered them to the Montane brothers and David would be out the money anyway. Questioning the neighbors could be a waste of time, but Suzanne wanted to do everything she could before she faced her father again.

She started down the steps slowly inhaling more breaths and felt in better control by the time she arrived at Mrs. Neal's condo. She rang the doorbell three times before the woman answered.

"Hello, Mrs. Neal. Remember me, Suzanne Conway, Nesta's goddaughter?"

"Why yes. How nice to see you, but I'm sorry to say you've missed them. They're on vacation."

Yes, I know. I was wondering if you . . ."

"Why don't you come in, dear? I have cookies in the oven, and I wouldn't want them to burn."

She walked away leaving Suzanne to close the door and follow her to the kitchen. Suzanne watched her shove her hand into a mitt before opening the oven door to take out a baking sheet.

She frowned at the cookies. "I guess they need to stay in a bit longer. I forgot to set the timer."

Suzanne looked and saw that the cookies hadn't baked at all. A quick peek at the stove told her the timer wasn't the only thing Mildred had forgotten to set. No heat came from the oven. She glanced at the recipe card on the counter and turned the dial to the correct temperature while Mildred's back was turned.

"Why don't you wait a bit longer? The oven may not have preheated enough?"

"You're probably right. I think there must be something wrong with it. I swear, sometimes things bake just fine and other times I can't get it to work at all. Would you like a cup of tea?"

"No thank you. I can't stay long. I came to ask you if you happened to notice anyone hanging around my godmother's house while they've been away."

"Not that I know of, but I don't see very well. Luckily, Bart has excellent eyesight. He's been helping me keep an eye on the place. I thought that was him when you came to the door. He must have forgotten his key. I'm baking these cookies for him."

"I don't believe I know who this Bart is, Mrs. Neal."

"Really? I'm sure you must have met him. He is Liam's grandson, after all."

Alarm bells began to go off inside Suzanne's head. She knew for a fact that Liam didn't have any grandson by the name of Bart because Liam had neither children nor grandchildren. She struggled to keep the uneasiness from showing in her expression.

"Oh yes, um, Bart. I haven't seen him in a long time. Has he been staying with you long?"

"Well, let me see now. I think it was right after Liam and Nesta left. Yes, that's right. He knocked on my door when no one answered at their house. The poor boy looked so upset. He came all the way from the east coast to surprise them. I invited him to stay here until they get back. It's been so nice having him for company. He's kept a very good eye on his grandpa's house."

Suzanne almost groaned thinking how this vulnerable woman had let a stranger into her home. She had to try and find out what he was up to.

"I'm sure he has. Does he ever go inside?"

"Well of course, dear. How else could he make sure everything is okay? I still had a key from when Nesta went on vacation before. Good thing, too because she left in such a hurry this time."

Suzanne had a feeling her godmother had deliberately not given a key to her neighbor and had simply forgotten about leaving one in the past.

"I haven't seen Bart in a long time. Could you refresh my memory on what he looks like?"

"He's a nice looking young man with lots of curly blond hair. Built kind of slender for a man. He doesn't say much. I think it's because he's so sad."

"You mean because of not getting here in time to see Liam and Nesta?" Suzanne asked, continuing her gentle probing, wanting to gather every bit of information she could.

"No, although I know he is disappointed about that. I think he's suffering from a broken heart."

"Oh? What makes you think that?"

"One day he spilled hot coffee on his shirt and had to take it off immediately. He has a tattoo right above his heart of a butterfly crying tears and the name TINA printed there. I asked him about it. All he would say was that he'd lost her."

"Maybe she was a girlfriend who broke up with him."

"I have a feeling it was more than that. I saw tears in his eyes before he left the room." She leaned closer to Suzanne and whispered, as though Bart might be in the room listening. "I think the young woman died and he's still mourning her."

Suzanne nodded in sympathy.

"That sounds very sad. How long has Bart been gone?"

Mildred squinted at the wall clock. "I can't remember when he left, but it seems like it's been an awfully long time. We were having breakfast when he saw a golf cart pull up next door. He told me not to leave the house while he checked to be sure everything was all right. I finished eating and when I peeked out the window there were two carts parked there."

Suzanne realized the first golf cart must be David's and the second one would be Thad's. She pulled her mind back to Mildred as the woman continued with her explanation.

"I got busy doing things and didn't pay much attention to the time when Bart came back."

"He came back? I thought you said he hadn't returned."

"I meant he hasn't returned to stay. He came earlier, but just for a bit. I asked him about the golf carts. He said they belonged to people doing some work on the house that Liam ordered before he left."

"Did he happen to have anything with him?"

"Why yes. He carried a towel with something inside."

Suzanne had a sinking feeling that something was her father's phones. "Could you see what it was?"

"No. I asked and he said it was a broken part for whatever the people were working on in the house and he offered to go to town to get a replacement. He ran into his bedroom and came out a few minutes later carrying his backpack. He told me I should stay in my house. I decided to surprise him and bake the cookies before he got back."

"That's very nice of you. Well, thank you for the visit. I have to go back to my godmother's."

Mildred scrunched her face into a thoughtful frown.

"I don't think that'll do you much good. Did I tell you Nesta's away right now?"

"Yes. Be sure you stay in the house, as Bart told you to and lock your doors. Oh, and don't forget to set the timer for those cookies, Mrs. Neal," Suzanne reminded her, as they walked to the front door.

"I'll send Bart over with some for you when he returns."

"That would be nice. Thank you."

Suzanne didn't have the heart to tell the old woman that her houseguest most likely would never be coming back. He'd accomplished his mission. The mysterious Bart probably had the phones and what he planned to do with them was anyone's guess. The one good thing was now the scheming David wouldn't be fulfilling his promise to the Montanes.

Suzanne hurried next door, anxious to tell Thad the latest news.

And suggest that it might be a good time to rein in David's leash.

Twenty-Six

David met Suzanne at the front door. "Did you find out anything? Come on, come on. Give!"

She had to grit her teeth to stop herself from telling him what she'd really like to give him was a big fat lip.

"I talked to Mrs. Neal. She said a man named Bart has been helping her keep an eye on the house. He told her he was Liam's grandson, but that's not possible because Liam never had any kids, adopted or otherwise. She said this Bart came over here when he saw the golf carts, but left right after that."

David's reaction reminded her of an overgrown child throwing a tantrum. He stomped his foot, stuck out his bottom lip, and glared at her.

"She must know more. Go back and talk to her again."

"She told me everything."

"How can you be so sure? The old woman has dementia, is half blind, and hard of hearing. She could be imagining the guy."

"I don't think so. She gave me too many details to be making him up."

David faced Thad.

"You better call the agency and see what they can find out about this Bart."

"I thought you'd rather do it. You also may as well tell them we missed out on getting the phones."

Bobbett jumped up from her chair.

"I'm sick to death hearing about those phones. That's all any of you can think about. I'm going to the bathroom and when I come out I'm leaving."

Her eyes rested on David. "I'm going on my own. It's obvious you're never going to get any extra money."

They watched as she spun on her heel and slammed the door to the bathroom.

259

"I think you've upset my mother again,"

"Who the hell cares? Having her around doesn't exactly make my day."

"Perhaps you'll feel better after you call the agency." Thad suggested.

David grumbled before pulling his phone out of a pocket. Suzanne motioned Thad to join her in the kitchen. He lifted a questioning brow at her.

"Something else on your mind?"

"There's more to Mrs. Neal's story. I didn't want to give David too much information."

She told Thad about the tattoo. He listened, leaning against a counter pressing his hands on the edge.

"I realize Mrs. Neal isn't the best source of information, but I really think this guy does exist."

"You're right, but his real name is Eric. The tattoo gave him away. He was Tina's boyfriend."

"Okay, and who might this Tina be?"

Thad straightened away from the sink.

"My client's late daughter."

"The one the Montanes kidnapped?"

He nodded.

"My God. He must be trying to avenge her."

"Sounds like it."

"Mrs. Neal said he wasn't a very big man. How could he manage to move you down the hill?"

"I don't think it was Eric. I got a quick glimpse before I lost consciousness. The person who hit me was closer to my height and build."

"Maybe this Eric had someone helping him," Suzanne suggested.

"Possibly. Or, he was watching and saw what happened. He could have grabbed the phones while my attacker was busy putting me out of commission. Eric may have left the feather instead of David to make me think it was one of the people working for the Montanes."

"Or the guy who jumped you could have left it. I'm wondering if he might be our pseudo waterman. Dad said he was big."

"Maybe."

"I hope this Bart, I mean Eric, is taking the phones to the police if he really does have them."

"Yeah. Can you keep David distracted while I call my office and tell them about Eric?"

"I'll try, but please make it quick. He's acting more and more like he's about to snap."

Suzanne hurried back into the living room just as David ended his call.

He frowned at her.

"They don't seem to be very anxious to help me. I got the feeling I'm being given the brush off."

"Oh? Why would the people you work for want to give you the brush off?"

"Because Novak's their golden boy. It's no secret he gets all the high profile cases, and the rest of us get whatever's left over."

"It seems to me some of those high profile cases are pretty dangerous. Maybe you should be glad you don't get assigned to them."

David made an indignant snort.

"That's what he'd like you to believe. He rakes in the big money while I scramble for loose change. Even when he messes up, he gets to come back, no questions asked."

Suzanne watched him closely. He obviously didn't like Thad and had kept his feelings under control, but now he seemed to be slowly losing that control. The more she observed him the more his behavior reminded her of sand pouring through an hourglass with every bit of who he had pretended to be shifting down to the man he really was.

Thad came into the living room, and David renewed his complaints about his phone call to their office.

"I'm supposed to be working on this case, but they act like I'm intruding for God's sake."

"I'm sure you're mistaken."

261

"I don't think so. I'm not getting the cooperation I deserve." David rounded on Suzanne. "Just like you've been doing. I'm sick of you treating me like some flunky, too."

"I haven't done that; and because I haven't, I'm not going to stand here listening to your insult." She started to step away from him feeling certain he was a man heading into the eye of a self-inflicted storm.

David grabbed her by the arm.

"Don't you dare walk away from me."

She yelped in pain as his fingers dug into soft flesh.

"I suggest you remove your hand while you still have the capacity to use it."

Thad's voice sounded calm, belying the flash of fury in his eyes. His body language gave clear warning that he would be defending Suzanne if his demand should be ignored. But the last grain of David's control slid away. He angled his body away from Thad, tore the gun from his shoulder holster, and pressed the weapon to Suzanne's temple with one hand while his other hand clutched her throat.

"What the hell is the matter with you?" Thad stepped forward, but David brandished the gun, waving him away.

"Don't come a step closer, or I swear to God I'll finish her."

Thad stopped and held his hands out in front of him in a gesture of appeasement.

"Okay, okay, just take it easy. Let's talk."

David's eyes raked over Thad while his mouth curled into a sneer.

"What is there to talk about? I'm sick of walking in your shadow. We may be working for the same outfit, but you get all the glory, the money, and the best women. I can't believe you didn't get fired after what happened to Matthew Cameron's sister. We all knew you had a thing for her. You took what you wanted from Ann Marie and then left her to die."

Thad's eyes drilled into David like twin rods of steel.

"You were misinformed."

"I doubt that, but of course everyone believed you. Personally, I think you were negligent. How much longer did

262

you think I would stand back and accept the crumbs you left behind?"

"You've been paid very well for your work."

David's resentment rose, blended with hatred mixed into a bitter brew in a cauldron ready to boil over.

"Not well enough. I finally had a chance to get some real money and go out on my own, but you and your girlfriend here ruined it for me."

"How so?"

"You took the phones. I know you did," he snarled and squeezed Suzanne's neck making her gag.

"I do not have the phones. If I did, believe me, I would be handing them over to you right now. I'm the one you want. Let Suzanne go."

"You're through telling me what to do, and it suits me to keep her right where she is."

"What good is it going to do you to use Suzanne like this?"

"I know her father took a good size chunk of money when he ran out on the Montanes. I may not have a chance to get the phones, but I bet I can still get her old man to give me that money to save his precious daughter."

"Let . . . let me go to my dad. I'll tell him to give you the money," she sputtered, clawing at his hand in an attempt to release the pressure on her throat.

David's laughter scraped through the air sounding as irritating as fingernails being dragged down a chalkboard. "You're not going anywhere, and neither is your mother."

Thad caught a movement out of the corner of his eye and saw Bobbett opening the bathroom door. He gave a subtle motion with his hand at his side indicating that she shouldn't come out and much to his relief she stepped back into the bathroom quietly closing the door again.

"Tell me what you want me to do," Thad said keeping David's attention focused on him

"I want you to go back to the clinic and talk to her father. I'm keeping both women here with me. I'll let her mother go once I get the money."

Thad's hands fisted at his sides.

"And Suzanne?"

"She goes with me as insurance until I'm sure I'm safely out of the country."

Every instinct made Thad want to rush the man and pound him until he heard bones crack. The heat of anger burned his throat and had his pulse hammering through his veins like streams of lava. The terror on Suzanne's face tortured him knowing he had to stand there and watch, helpless to take away that fear.

David reminded him of a beast who had escaped from his cage while Thad felt like an animal suddenly finding himself trapped inside one. The two men glared at each other, fighting for what they wanted. One for greed and the other for his woman. Thad's brain worked frantically trying to think of a way to help Suzanne without getting her killed or seriously injured.

If only he could divert David's attention away from Suzanne for just a moment it might be enough to free her. He knew a moment would be all he'd have, and even then it would be risky. Any sudden disturbance could bring disaster with David being half crazed.

Thad silently cursed himself for letting things get to this point with David. But what good were regrets knowing his error in judgment might cost the life of someone so dear to him? Was it arrogance that had him believing he could string David along? Suzanne trusted him to take care of her, not deliver her into the hands of this desperate maniac holding her fate by the fragile thread of whatever control he had left. Thad could only hope that thin line of sanity would hold long enough to spare Suzanne.

Hope came in a most unexpected way just when Thad decided to try one more appeal to get Suzanne freed. He remained standing very still while he watched Bobbett creep up behind David and raise the heavy looking figurine she carried. The sound of metal hitting flesh and bone along with the grunt of pain was music to his ears.

David pitched forward sending Suzanne scrambling out of his reach.

Thad rushed to catch her while kicking David's gun away. He helped her to the sofa where she sat coughing.

She stared wide-eyed at her mother.

"Mom, you . . . you saved me," Suzanne wheezed.

Bobbett rolled her eyes. "No need to get so emotional. He made me mad, that's all."

"Nice work, Mrs. Conway," Thad said, as he knelt to check on David. "How did you manage it?"

"I climbed out of the bathroom window without making a mess I might add. But I did break a fingernail I see. I'll have to see my manicurist when I get home," she said frowning at her hands.

"I'd be happy to pay for that," Thad offered. "What did you do after you left the bathroom?"

"I used the outside stairs and went up to the guest bedroom. I knew the sliding glass door was unlocked because I opened it myself earlier to air out the place."

She pointed to David.

"Is he dead?"

"No, but he's going to have one hell of a headache when he wakes up. Probably needs stitches."

"Serves him right. Now, will one of you tell me why he was holding his gun to Suzanne's head?"

"Suzanne recently found out that he's working for the Montanes. The reward money he talked about was going to come from them once he got the phones. He planned to leave the country without you."

"Why that snake! I should have given up on him a long time ago. He was starting to bore me anyway. I hope you lock him away for a very long time in a very small cell."

"My sentiments exactly," Suzanne groaned, rubbing the red marks on her throat.

Thad made the arrangements to have David secured and taken into custody before he escorted Suzanne and Bobbett safely off the island. It'd been a long, very eventful day, and it wasn't over for him. Once he had the two women settled in the house his client had provided, Thad needed to see if he could find out what happened to Eric.

No one had heard from him as far as Thad knew. Did he, or did he not have the phones? Would he turn them over to the authorities if they were in his possession? Were they safe? Was he? Eric had either been very lucky or very clever to elude capture by the Montane brothers this long. Would his luck hold, or had he fallen into their treacherous clutches? God help him if it was the latter.

Suzanne walked with him to the door while her mother was busy inspecting the house.

"I assume you're leaving to try and find Eric."

Thad nodded. "I am."

"When do you think you'll be back?"

"I have no idea, but better not wait up for me."

"Mom is going to think she's a prisoner in a gilded cage. Are you sure you can't stay around and help me keep her entertained?"

"I would think you'd appreciate the time alone with her. The woman saved your life, Suzanne."

"I'm still trying to get over the surprise of that. I've spent my life thinking my parents didn't give a fig about me, and now I find out they do care. It's kind of strange, but in a nice way."

"Give a fig?" he repeated with a lopsided grin.

She smiled in return.

"Another one of Nanadoo's sayings. I wish you didn't have to go. I don't want anything to happen to you. You're the first guy I've met who can cook a real meal."

"I seduced you with my cooking? I thought it was supposed to be the other way around."

"I'll cook dinner if you'll stay and afterwards we can share that big tub in the master suite."

"Thanks, but it'll have to wait. And for the record, I don't want anything to happen to me, either."

"Are you going to where Eric lives?"

"No, I had his apartment checked and he hasn't shown up. Muriel mentioned a restaurant he used to meet with her and

Tina late at night. He still goes there. He's friends with a waitress working that shift. Apparently she's always had a crush on Eric. I want to see if he's been in touch with her."

"She may not want to tell you if she's trying to protect him."

"I'd still like to talk to her."

"It seems kind of sad to think of him going back to their old hangout."

"Sometimes people hold onto the past because they're afraid to face the future after losing someone they loved."

Suzanne touched his arm.

"Are you talking about Eric, or yourself?"

"Why would you think I meant myself?"

"I thought you might be referring to Ann Marie Cameron. What was she to you, Thad?"

The muscles in his arm tightened beneath her hand before he pulled away.

"I guess it was dumb of me to think you'd let that go. If a person throws enough mud some of it is bound to stick."

"I'm sorry. I just . . ."

"Wondered if I was responsible for her death?" he cut her short, his voice clipped and unfriendly.

"No! I can't imagine you ever deliberately leaving someone to die. I shouldn't have brought it up."

"Then why did you?"

"I'm not sure." Suzanne shoved her hands behind her, hiding her fidgeting fingers.

"I don't have time to explain things right now."

"You don't have to explain anything to me. Please forget I asked."

"As if I could. Just so you know, I get tired of having to justify myself to satisfy morbid curiosity."

He turned away and walked out of the house. Thad thought Suzanne might come after him and felt grateful when she didn't. His throat tightened when painful memories grabbed at him like cold, hard fingers squeezing to cut off his breath.

Thad dragged in a mouthful of the bracing evening air. No matter how hard he'd tried to forget the past some scars went so deep it seemed as though they would never heal. But now wasn't the time to reopen old wounds while he was trying to prevent new ones from occurring. He shook off the anger, got into his truck and drove away, concentrating on what he had to do.

Thad knew from talking to his client earlier that the man had kept in touch with Eric, sharing their grief over Tina's death. But that hadn't been all he'd shared with his late daughter's boyfriend. The older man, blinded by his mourning had poured out details giving the younger man enough knowledge to send him to Catalina Island and the Harold's condo.

Only time would tell if it turned out to be a mistake, or a blessing. It'd be pretty amazing if Eric ended up outdoing everyone by being the one to topple the Montanes. Thad drummed his fingers on the steering wheel. A lot of people were involved in this case, some more intimately connected than others. But the common denominator that joined them all was the evidence Wendell Conway had collected.

The Montanes needed the phones to stay out of prison and keep their criminal activities going. Muriel wanted them to avenge her dead lover, as did Eric. His client thought they would bring him closure in his daughter's death. And he couldn't forget the Martins who wanted the phones for the money they hoped to get to cover Aaron's gambling losses.

What about himself? Why was he so anxious to get his hands on the phones? To bring the Montane brothers down? Definitely. But Thad knew he needed to prove that he could do this job right. He thought of Suzanne. He didn't want to have another young woman he cared about coming to a tragic end.

His best hadn't been good enough before. He'd been exonerated, but that didn't mean he'd forgotten what had happened. Sometimes a man needed more than vindication to free him from the past. Sometimes he needed to prove to himself that he still had what it took to protect his own.

Twenty-seven

Thad entered the brightly lit restaurant as a large man was exiting. They bumped into each other; and for a moment Thad felt an odd sense of awareness, before the man hurried away. Thad shook off the feeling and walked inside to the combined odor of fried foods and strong coffee filling the air.

Opened 24/7, the surroundings showed the deterioration of too many customers and not enough time to thoroughly clean up after so much wear and tear. He assumed they would be pretty crowded during regular dining hours since he knew what a popular chain diner it was with their reasonable prices. But it was late now and only three other customers occupied the premises.

He saw an elderly man at a nearby table with his head dipped low over his plate, as he ate his ham and eggs. Thad felt his own stomach rumble with hunger. A man and woman sat in a booth further away ignoring the mugs in front of them, apparently opting instead to concentrate on their conversation.

A young waitress dressed in black jeans and black tee shirt sauntered toward him. Her dark hair with its blond streaks wobbled atop her head in an untidy bun. She greeted him with a practiced smile.

"One?" Thad nodded.

"Table or booth?" she asked while pulling out a menu from a rake near the register.

"Booth."

"This way."

Thad followed her slender swaying hips past several booths lined up along a wall of windows. She continued across the dark carpet, spotted here and there with stains varying in size and color. He noticed some of the red vinyl seats were split and peeling in places reminding him of slashes against a bloody

269

background. He shifted his eyes away. That certainly wasn't something he wanted to be thinking about when he was about to order a meal. The girl stopped at the last booth in the row, thankfully with its seats still intact.

Thad slid behind the table; and she placed the menu in front of him.

"I'll give you a few minutes to decide."

He handed her back the menu without opening it.

"I already know what I want."

She lifted a questioning brow.

"Ham, and eggs over; hash browns, wheat toast, black coffee, and a glass of water. I'll take the drinks now, please."

"Well, that didn't take long. Are you always so sure of yourself?"

He caught the hint of flirtation in her voice and decided to cultivate her interest in the hopes of getting information. Muriel said the waitress who had the crush on Eric was named Billie. Thad intended to explore the possibility that this might be the same woman.

"Depends on the situation. I'm new here. Just got in from a little town in Iowa. So far I've been sneered at, flipped off, and darned near rear ended; and that's just coming across town from my motel."

"You're in the big city now. You're probably going to find things are done a lot differently here."

"I can see that. I have to tell you I sure do appreciate your friendly face."

Her tired eyes brightened at his compliment.

"I'll put in your order and bring those drinks right away," she said, scooping the menu off the table.

"Thanks. My name's Jim Lucas and you are . . .?"

"I'm Billie Paget."

Thad didn't let the relief he felt show on his face.

"It's a pleasure to meet you – you're my first new friend. Have you worked here long?"

"A little over three years. I'll be right back."

Thad watched her hurry away thinking how hungry some people were for a simple compliment. But he would say what he had to if it helped him find Eric. He pulled out his phone and called his office giving them Billie's full name, the restaurant's name, and location.

"Get me everything you can on her, including directions to her home, as soon as possible."

He slid the phone away, just as she came back with his coffee and water.

Thad smiled at her. "Thank you."

"You're welcome. Your food won't take long. We're not exactly rushed right now as you can see."

"It is quiet."

"That's one of the reasons I like this shift. I'd rather not be too busy after working at my day job, plus going to college."

Thad decided that explained why she looked so tired. "You have two jobs and you go to school? That's commendable. What's your major?"

"I haven't declared one yet. I can only take a couple classes at a time and I just started last year. I'm thinking of going for accounting. I work in my brother-in-law's pawn shop during the day waiting on customers and doing his books. I like doing the books."

"You mustn't have much time for fun being so busy. How does that sit with the man in your life?"

"No man. No problem."

"A pretty girl like you. I find that hard to believe."

Pink color tinted her cheeks. "Well, there is a guy and I'd sure take the time to have that fun if he wanted to join me."

Going with what Muriel had told him, Thad hoped Billie meant Eric.

"Does the guy not want you because he has someone else?" he infused sympathy into his tone encouraging her to share more details.

"He did, but she died, and he can't get over her death. So far he just wants us to be friends."

Bingo! Once again he kept his expression bland to hide the excitement he felt at her confession.

"I'm sorry for your friend's loss. I'm sure his grief will ease given enough time."

271

"I don't know. It's been several months already. I keep trying to be there for him, but so far he only calls me when he's feeling lonely."

"Well, that's a start. Has he called you lately?"

"It's been a while. The last time I heard from him he said he had to go out of town and didn't know how long he'd be gone. I was hoping he'd call from wherever he went, but he hasn't."

"You could always call him."

She shook her head.

"He doesn't like me to."

The cook called to Billie that Thad's order was ready. She hurried away. Thad took a sip of his coffee and let his eyes travel around the place. The elderly man finished his meal and was walking to the register with the bill in his hand. Billie arrived with Thad's food and set it in front of him.

"Enjoy. I have to take care of the guy at the register. I'll be right back to see if your food's okay."

"No rush."

Thad cut into the thick slice of ham and followed that bite with a couple mouthfuls of egg and potatoes. He watched the old man pay Billie and shuffle through the double doors leading out of the restaurant. Thad couldn't help comparing him to the younger, stronger looking guy he'd collided with when he arrived.

He started to take another bite of food and froze. His fork dropped causing it to make a clattering sound on the plate. Now he knew why he'd had that odd sensation brushing against the big man. This wasn't their first encounter.

"Son of a . . ." Thad cut off the softly spoken curse, reached into his wallet, tossed some folding money onto the table, and waved to Billie, as he hurried toward the exit.

"Hey! Is everything okay? I have fresh coffee," she held up the pot she carried.

"I have to leave. Money's on the table. Thanks."

He hurried outside and scanned the parking lot. The guy was probably gone. Then again, maybe not. The flash of a small flame lit up the cab of a dark colored pickup truck as someone lit a cigarette. Thad walked to his own vehicle, slid inside, and shoved his key in the ignition.

He knew in his gut this was the man responsible for knocking him unconscious and rolling him down the hill on Catalina Island. If he was right that meant this could very well be the man who put the black feather in Liam's golf cart. Thad had to admit he wouldn't mind having a chance to get even if this really was the guy who attacked him from behind.

He doubted it was a coincidence that the man happened to be here at the restaurant where Billie worked. The Montanes were thorough and probably knew of her friendship with Eric and Tina. They may not suspect that he had the phones. Yet. Thad knew he had to find Eric before they figured it out.

His office called with the information he needed about Billie. He no sooner ended that call when his phone signaled another one. He answered it right away when he saw it was from his client.

"Novak."

"The boy did it! He came through."

Thad didn't miss the excitement in the man's voice. "Sir?"

"Eric, the young man who was going with my daughter. You were right about him."

"He has the phones?"

"Better than that. He turned them into the police. I'm at the station with him now."

Thad squeezed his hand on the steering wheel for a moment. "That's wonderful news. Congratulations. I'm very happy for you, but a little embarrassed I didn't do my job better."

"You did plenty. The main thing is that the phones are finally in the hands of the authorities. I'll leave it up to you to let Conway and Muriel know."

"I'll do that."

Thad realized the man he'd been watching was pulling out of the parking lot. Curious to know just where the guy was headed, he started his own vehicle while continuing to listen to his client.

"Will you come to the station? They'll want to hear about your part in this."

"As soon as I can. I have something I need to take care of first. Congratulations again, sir."

Thad ended the call and began to tail the truck, keeping well enough back to elude the man's attention. He picked up his phone and made his promised calls. He didn't expect anyone to answer because of the late hour, but he wouldn't feel right delaying the good news about the phones.

He left messages on Muriel's and Suzanne's phones all the while keeping track of the truck's progress in front of him. Getting even with the man who'd tied him up like a rump roast was another little chore he was looking forward to. It didn't take long to see, now that he had directions to Billie's apartment, that the guy was heading that way.

Thad immediately took a shortcut knowing he needed to beat him there. He arrived in time to set himself up as a surprise reception committee and smiled in the darkness, anticipating the coming confrontation.

Thad had a couple of aching ribs and a black eye when he walked into the police station, but that was a small price to pay for the feeling of satisfaction. Eric gave him a wary look.

"I'm sorry I didn't help you on the island, but I wasn't sure who I could trust. Besides that, the guy who hit you was a lot bigger than I am. I doubt if I could have stopped him."

"Don't worry about it. What made you so suspicious about the man?"

"I was at the next door neighbor's and . . ." Eric stopped. "Oh gosh, I forgot about Mrs. Neal. I couldn't have done what I did without her letting me stay at her place. I owe her an explanation for running out on her."

"I'm pretty sure the Harolds would be willing to help you with that."

"That'd be good. Anyway, I've been keeping my eye on the guy. He was posing as a water deliveryman and hanging around your friends' house. I heard he drugged them."

"So it was him? No one was sure. We can be thankful that's all he did."

Eric nodded.

"For sure. I had a feeling he might be working for the Montanes. I knew I was right when I saw him put a black feather in Mr. Harold's golf cart. I grabbed the phones while he was lugging you down the hill. I apologize again for not helping you. I should have called someone and told them what happened, but I was so nervous I forgot."

"You got the phones here and that's what matters. You should be commended for doing a great job."

"I don't need any praise."

Eric's eyes misted with tears.

"I . . . I did it for Tina."

The last stars were fading away signaling the end of night, when Thad finally left the station. Early morning traffic was already picking up, as was activity around the building. He walked to his vehicle just as his phone signaled a message. Suzanne, wanting to know when he would be coming home. Home. Now there was a word that hadn't fit into his vocabulary for a long, long time. Thad said it out loud and liked the sound of it. He also liked the idea of seeing her again even more. Did this mean she'd forgiven him for his display of temper?

Time to find out.

Suzanne came out of the kitchen, as Thad was letting himself into the house.

"What happened to your eye?" she asked, peering closely at his face.

"I had a little run in with an old acquaintance."

"What did you do, greet each other by bumping heads together?"

"Something like that."

She exhaled a sigh.

"Are you going to share, or do I have to play Twenty Questions with you?"

"He was another one of the Montanes hirelings, better known as our fake-water-bottle guy."

275

"Ah. Well, I'm not surprised. I assume he's now in custody."

Thad nodded.

"Tucked up in a cell like a baby at bedtime; I didn't expect to see you up so early."

"I couldn't sleep."

He looked over her shoulder.

"I take it your mother is still in bed."

"Nothing interferes with my mother's beauty sleep."

"How are things going between you two? Have you had any good girl talks?"

"Mom doesn't do girl talks."

"I thought surely after that episode on the island things may have changed."

"Not happening. I'm thankful she got David away from me, naturally. At least I'll always have that to remember, even if she did do it because she was angry with him more than out of concern for me. I got your message about the phones," she said, changing the subject. "That's wonderful news. How is Eric?"

"He's good."

Thad sniffed the air.

"I smell coffee. Do you mind if we talk while I have a cup – or maybe even two?"

She shrugged.

"All right."

Thad followed her into the kitchen. She poured him a cup of the steaming brew, and they sat down at the table.

"Eric is one brave young man," Suzanne said, when Thad finished telling her what happened.

"Yes he is."

"I'm so ready for this to finally be coming to an end."

"Actually, getting those phones to the police will start a whole new beginning. It's going to take a lot of man hours to investigate the information your father collected. The Montane lawyers will be fighting this every step of the way."

Her fingers gripped the edge of the table.

"You don't think they'll get them off, do you?"

276

"No, but it'll take months to sift through everything. The authorities are going to have their hands full making sure the Montane brothers are kept where they can't slip away."

Thad's phone rang, and he checked the screen.

"It's Muriel."

Suzanne stood up.

"Go ahead and take it. I've already talked to her and my dad. I'm going to shower. Then I'll check on the Queen Bee."

"Thanks for the coffee."

"No big deal. It was already made."

Thad frowned at her.

"Are you okay?"

"Sure. Why wouldn't I be?"

"I'm thinking you may be upset with me after the way I left things between us."

"I guess I am overly sensitive. But the thing is Thad, I keep forgetting that you like to play by your own rules, and most of the time I end up fouling out of the game."

He watched her leave and thought of following when his phone chimed reminding him of his call.

Suzanne headed for her bedroom. Thad was probably right when he said this was only the beginning. Once again, she thought of what so many people had gone through to get those phones with the damning evidence. But most of all she thought of her father and how brave he'd been in daring to defy the odds against him to gather the incriminating data.

Her dad was a hero, and come to think of it, her mother was in her own way. It certainly felt good to finally feel like she had parents she could be proud of for a change. What about Thad? He'd put himself in harm's way to keep her safe. Didn't that make him a hero? But what about the woman, Ann Marie? Was Thad responsible for her death, as David claimed? That wouldn't make him much of a hero in anyone's book if it was true.

Suzanne supposed she was guilty of being morbidly curious, as Thad had accused her. But who wouldn't be in her position? Would Thad ever tell her the full story? Part of her wished he would, but another part of her wanted to let it go, especially after witnessing Thad's angry reaction to her query.

The man still had the ability to confuse her no matter how many times she thought she'd figured him out. She pinched the bridge of her nose between her thumb and forefinger wondering why it was so difficult to find love without always having so many complications thrown at her.

She remembered how he'd told her he longed for her touch. He'd said it to her, but perhaps he was really thinking about the Cameron woman at the time. Suzanne lowered her hand and stood quietly, thinking. Maybe he couldn't get the girl out of his mind because they were lovers. And maybe that was because he was still in love with her. Was that why he couldn't bring himself to talk about his feelings?

Another, more disturbing thought wedged its way into her conflicting theories. Perhaps Thad couldn't forget the woman because he was haunted by something else. Maybe he didn't like sharing what his life had been like with her for another reason. Could that reason be because he really had been responsible in some way for her death? If that was true, then just how much was Thad actually involved?

Had Ann Marie Cameron lost her life because Thad left her?

Or had she died because he'd stayed?

Twenty-eight

Suzanne showered, wrapped a large towel around herself, and walked into the bedroom. She stopped when she saw Thad sprawled across the bed on his back breathing deeply. She couldn't help thinking that he looked dangerous even in his sleep. She saw that he'd removed his shoes and unbuttoned his shirt exposing his bruised ribs.

She should have known he'd keep any other injuries from her. The man was a master at evasion, including talking about past lovers. Thad may never tell her about Ann Marie. Could she live with that? She didn't know. It wasn't fair that he had a whole file of data about her thanks to his agency, while she had to pry out of him what little she knew; and who's to say that was real?

She went to the closet, took out a blanket, and spread it over him. His eyes immediately snapped open, and he bolted up, wincing as he jarred his sore ribs. She'd forgotten how easily he could be awakened.

"What are you doing?"

"Covering you with a blanket. Go back to sleep. Everything's fine."

Thad mumbled his thanks and closed his eyes. She tiptoed around gathering her clothes before letting herself quietly out of the room. Bobbett joined her just as Suzanne finished pulling on her jeans.

"What are you doing dressing in the living room?"

"Thad's asleep in the bedroom. I didn't want to wake him."

"What'd you do, tire him out with some early morning sex?"

Suzanne's fingers clenched on the hem of her tee shirt, as she jerked the garment in place.

"Not even close. What would you like for breakfast?"

"Just black coffee and a piece of dry toast. My stomach doesn't do well if I eat too much so early."

"I thought you'd sleep longer."

"So did I, but I kept having nightmares about people waving guns and chasing me."

Suzanne nodded.

"Welcome to my dreams."

"Well who needs that? Did Thad find the kid he was talking about?"

"Yes; and not only that, but Eric was able to get the phones to the police. They're rounding up the Montane brothers and their henchmen as we speak."

"About time. Much more of this and I'd go crazy. I hope this means I'll be able to go back to normal living again. I've decided I'm tired of being gone; I want to spend more time in my condo and catching up with my social life. Am I going to have to have someone dogging my every move?"

"I wouldn't think so."

"Good. You can arrange for my transportation after you fix my breakfast. I've got a million phone calls to make myself. I hope I can get an appointment with my beauty salon. My hair and nails are a mess, and I'm in desperate need of a massage, not to mention a session with my personal trainer."

Suzanne's nostrils flared.

"Is that all you can think about? A lot of people put their lives on hold and in danger to get those phones to the right people. Doesn't that mean anything to you?"

"You celebrate in your way, and I will in mine. But to answer your question, yes I know about the sacrifices that were made. That was their choice."

"People don't always have choices, Mother. Sometimes we have to do things we don't want to do."

"I can't do anything about that. There's nothing wrong with looking after oneself. People do, you know. I just don't hide the fact. If you want to keep laying your head on the chopping block that's your business, but don't try to make me feel guilty because I'm not there holding your hand."

Her mother's indifferent attitude made something inside Suzanne snap.

"No, you'd be the one holding the axe."

Bobbett lifted her brows.

"That's not a very nice thing to say about your mother."

"What else would you expect? You've never been a mother to me. You've always been too busy doing some kind of personal body maintenance or trying to snag your next man. Don't you ever worry about having men respect you?"

"If I wanted respect from them I would have become a nun. And now that we're on the subject, look where all that respect has gotten you when it comes to men. You drive them away, while I prefer to reel them in."

She nodded toward the kitchen.

"So, how about my breakfast?"

"There's coffee in the pot and bread in the breadbox. I'm sure you can handle that while I make the arrangements for someone to take you home."

Suzanne whirled around and fled the room. How could she have possibly thought of her mother as a hero? The woman was far too self-centered to ever truly care about anyone except herself. The sooner Bobbett left the better off they'd both be. She made the call for her mother's transportation and returned to the kitchen a few minutes later.

"Your ride will be here in an hour. Don't keep them waiting," she said in a frosty tone.

"What are you so crabby about?"

Suzanne's hands clenched at her sides.

"You just don't get it, do you? Having a manicure is more important to you than seeing that innocent people get justice. A lot of people suffered at the hands of the Montane brothers."

"Oh climb off your soapbox. How many more times are you going to give me the same old lecture?"

"Oh don't worry, I'm done."

Suzanne had to leave the room because her mother's continued callous behavior was making her sick to her stomach. She walked outside onto the patio hoping the fresh morning air would help to clear away the anger that had her bound up in its grip.

Bobbett tapped on the sliding glass door a little under an hour later.

"My limo's here."

"Fine. Have a nice ride home."

"It sounds like you still have that chip on your shoulder. You should learn to lighten up more."

"Seriously, Mother?"

Suzanne let out a weary sigh.

"Oh come on, I'll walk with you outside."

Later, when she was asked to describe what happened in the next few seconds Suzanne could barely recall the details because it had all gone so fast. She opened the front door and the man standing there pulled out a gun from beneath his suit jacket. Bobbett instantly pushed Suzanne away and ended up taking the bullet herself.

Suzanne remembered screaming as her mother fell, and then hearing the sound of another gun being fired. She spun around to see Thad standing there holding his weapon, before she fell to her knees to cradle her mother in her arms.

"Mom!" she yelled in a strangled voice.

"Oh my God. Why did you do that?"

"I guess I do get it after all," Bobbett moaned, before her body went limp.

Suzanne paced the floor in the hospital hallway waiting for news of how Bobbett's surgery was going. Her mother saved her life. Again. Now she might die without giving her daughter a chance to thank her. Thad came up behind her.

"I brought you some coffee."

"Thank you, but I don't think I could swallow right now."

"Try. It might help. I'm guessing your throat is feeling pretty raw right now from crying."

She took the cup from him.

"I know I've been a big baby."

"I didn't say that. You have a right to be upset. It's not every day a person witnesses what you saw."

"I'm so ashamed. I'd just given Mom a lecture on her selfishness and how little she cares about other people. Then she goes and does something like this. I'll never be able to forgive myself."

Suzanne allowed him to guide her to a row of black plastic chairs. They sat. She took a tentative sip. The liquid slid down her throat, soothing and warm. She drank a bit more trying to chase away the chill that seemed to be engulfing her body.

She set the Styrofoam cup aside.

"I can't get it out of my head the things I said to Mom."

"You wanted proof that she loves you, and you got it."

"Not like this. The whole façade she'd perfected over the years just crumbled away; and for a moment I didn't recognize my own mother."

"I'll admit it's pretty drastic, but sometimes people need a real jolt before they realize their true feelings. Your mother is strong, and she has a good surgeon working on her. Think positive."

"I'll try. Thanks for taking out that guy who shot Mom. Do you know who he was?"

"Another one of Montane's goons, posing as the limo driver. His orders to take care of you came before the police had the phones."

"But how did he get through the security?"

"He had all the right credentials and checked out fine. The Montane brothers have always been very good at getting people to take care of things when they want a job done."

"Yes. They seem to be quite good at being very bad. Will there be others?"

"I doubt it, but we've increased the security at the house in case anyone else tries to slip through."

"That's a comfort."

She rubbed her hands over her face before gripping them together in her lap.

"I don't think I can take much more of the Montanes. I'm sick of them haunting my every waking moment, not to mention when I'm trying to sleep, too."

Thad reached over and held her hand. They sat quietly for the next several minutes until he pointed.

"I believe that's your mother's doctor coming."

Suzanne immediately stood up to meet him.

"How is my mother? Is she going to be all right?"

"She came through the surgery fine. She's in a recovery room right now. A nurse will let you know when you can see her. But don't expect too much response right away."

"I understand. Just seeing her will make me feel better."

Suzanne spent the next few minutes talking with the doctor, asking questions, and listening intently to his explanations while Thad sat quietly in the background.

Thad stood on the patio at the house several days later. He felt too restless to stay indoors. It'd become Suzanne's routine to spend the day at the hospital with her mother. He glanced at his watch and knew she would probably be returning like she did every night around this time.

Not that it would make any difference to him.

She'd been so wrapped up with her mother's condition he barely had more than a few fleeting words with her. He did not begrudge her this sudden devotion with her parent. It was long overdue for both of them. But he had a feeling it wasn't just the situation with Bobbett that had put a kink in his relationship with Suzanne.

Something else was bothering her to the point that she'd become increasingly skittish around him. Thad had a feeling he knew what that something was; and the only way to clear the air between them would be to talk about something he'd rather not discuss.

He heard Suzanne drive up a few minutes later and go into the house. She usually took her meals at the hospital with her mother and only came home to shower and sleep. Thad didn't expect tonight to be any different. He turned in surprise when the glass door to the patio slid open, and she stepped outside.

"How'd it go today?"

She sucked in a rush of air.

"You startled me. I didn't know you were out here."

He moved out of the shadows.

"How's Bobbett?"

"Good. She, um, is getting stronger every day. The doctor says she can do her convalescing at my house if things continue the way they're going. I'm making arrangements for a home health care nurse to check in on her."

"That's good."

"Thank you for arranging it so I could stay here while she's in the hospital."

"It seemed like the logical thing to do since you're so much closer. I'm glad you and your mother are getting along so well."

"So am I. I'm just sorry it had to come about because of her being shot, but she's a changed person."

"Staring at your own possible death has a tendency to do that."

Suzanne looped a lock of hair behind her ear.

"Are you speaking from experience?"

"It sometimes happens in my line of work."

"Of course. Well, I guess I'll turn in now."

"You needn't be afraid of me, you know," Thad said, keeping his voice low and even.

Suzanne froze.

"What . . . what are you talking about? I'm not afraid of you."

"No? You think I don't hear you lock your bedroom door at night? Look at you now, ready to run back inside as though you think I'm about to pounce on you."

"I don't think any such thing. I'm just tired."

"Are you sure that's all it is? I guess I can't blame you the way I acted before I went looking for Eric. I know I was pretty rough on you. We never did get to clear that up."

"Forget it."

"You know that's not what either of us wants."

Thad paused for a moment.

"Ask me, Suzanne."

She shot him a surprised look.

"Ask you what?"

He studied her noting how rigid she held herself and how her hand gripped the handle to the door.

"I didn't leave that girl to die."

"What girl?"

Thad lifted a brow.

"Oh, you mean the one David mentioned? I forgot all about her."

"Have you now?" he softly challenged.

"Okay, maybe I have thought about her a little. But you said you were cleared of everything, so that's the end of it."

"We both know it's not going to be the end until I tell you what happened in my own words."

"You don't have to explain."

"I do if you you're still interested in us having any kind of a future together."

Suzanne stared at him for several seconds.

"All right. Tell me if it'll make you feel any better."

"I'd like to think I'll make you feel better as well. Why don't you have a seat?"

"I'd rather stand," she said, crossing her arms over her chest.

Thad rubbed a hand around the back of his neck. He gave every appearance of a man summoning painful memories from deep inside himself. His silence caused Suzanne to clear her throat.

"Why don't we do this another time? I really am tired."

She turned to go, but stopped when Thad began to speak.

"Ann Marie Cameron was one of the most beautiful young women I'd ever seen. She also had a vulnerable look that drew me to her. At first I thought her brother was too hard on her, but he was paying me to be her bodyguard and not ask questions. She said he was a control freak and rarely let her

286

have any fun. It would have helped if he'd told me she was mentally unstable."

"Mentally unstable? In what way?"

"Mood swings from bubbly happy to downright mean and nasty. One minute she was buying me gifts and crawling naked in my bed; and the next thing I knew she was. . ."

"So you slept with her." Suzanne lowered her arms to her sides. "I didn't need to know that."

"I said she crawled into my bed, but I didn't let her stay. She thought her offer of sex would get me to disobey her brother's orders. When I refused she ended up swinging a baseball bat at me."

Suzanne's eyes widened.

"Did her brother know?"

"Yes. She ran with a rough crowd. Got into drugs, drinking, and sleeping around. She was constantly running off getting into trouble of some kind. That's why he hired me."

Suzanne winced when she thought of all the times she'd run out on him.

"I had my hands full. She got out of the house one night while I was having a break. Her brother was supposed to be watching her. He let his guard down when he thought she was asleep."

"It sounds like he needed to hire more than one bodyguard."

"It would have helped. She slipped away and went to one of her friend's where a big party was going on. She was wasted by the time I finally tracked her down. I tried to talk her into leaving peacefully, but she went berserk. She started kicking me and screaming. A guy pulled a knife. Ann Marie jumped in while I fought the guy off. She got nicked and had some blood on her, but it looked worse than it was. She was never in danger of dying, despite what David told you."

"Someone should have still called the police."

"Someone did. Ann Marie told the cops I was the one who attacked her and her friend when he tried to save her from me. She later told her brother I was going to leave her there to die. He didn't believe her, and I was cleared of all blame once the facts came out. Her brother finally realized he couldn't keep her at home any longer and put her in a mental health facility to live. I know he did it because he loved Ann Marie. But love wasn't enough in this case."

"What happened?" Suzanne asked, fully engrossed in his story now.

"She blamed me for being kicked out of her, I quote, 'happy home' because I got her in trouble with the cops. I thought that was the end of it until her brother called me several weeks later and said Ann Marie was doing a lot better. She wanted to apologize to me and asked that I go see her."

"Did you go?"

Thad nodded.

"Yes. I had lunch with her. She seemed upbeat, telling me she was taking painting classes and how she'd paint me a picture. We visited until it was time for me to go. I stood up to leave, and she grabbed my hand and blurted out that she loved me. She insisted she was well enough to know her true feelings and hoped I'd want to marry her some day."

"Awkward."

"To say the least. I told her I loved her as a friend, but that was all. She said she thought as much, but could I blame a girl for trying? She thanked me for coming and said she looked forward to my next visit."

"That should have made you feel better."

"It might have if things had turned out differently. A member of the staff found her dead the next morning. She hung herself during the night."

Suzanne caught her breath.

"Oh Thad. I'm so sorry. Hopefully she's found some peace at last."

"That's what her brother said, but I can't help wondering if I'd loved her the way she wanted she might still be alive." He shoved his hands in his pockets. "Now you know what happened to Ann Marie."

"You mustn't blame yourself. You aren't responsible for that girl's death. She was obviously still not well."

Suzanne rubbed her forehead.

288

"I created some wild ideas about you and Ann Marie, but what else did you expect when you got so angry because I asked about her? You left me with empty spaces, and my imagination filled in the gaps."

"I had a feeling it was something like that. Have I cleared things up in your mind now?"

She nodded.

"Forgive me?"

"There's nothing to forgive. But I wish you had come to me when your colorful imagination painted the wrong picture."

"I guess all this that's happened to me lately has messed with my mind more than I realized."

"That, and the fact that you've spent years dealing with your parents' screwing with your head."

"Probably, but I think things are going to be better now. Thanks for explaining about Ann Marie."

"I wanted to do it before I leave here."

Suzanne frowned at him.

"You're leaving? Why?"

"I've been reassigned. I want you to know I asked to stay here, but I'm needed elsewhere."

"That's a nice contrast to how you left me before. I appreciate knowing the difference. When will I get to see you?"

"I'm not sure. I'm being sent to New Orleans," he said taking his hands out of his pockets.

"So far? Shoot! How long will you be gone?"

"I don't know. It'll depend on how long the client thinks he needs me."

Suzanne plopped down into a nearby chair.

"How are we still going to be a couple?"

"We should be able to stay in touch, thanks to the wonderful world of technology."

"Yeah, in touch without touching," she grumbled. "When do you have to leave?"

"Tomorrow."

She practically leaped out of the chair. "So soon? How long have you known about this?"

"A couple of days. I tried to tell you before, but you haven't been too talkative lately."

"I've been stupid. Come on."

She grabbed him by the hand and tugged him toward the door.

"Where are we going?"

"To my bedroom to make up for lost time."

"I thought you were tired," Thad said, trying unsuccessfully to hide his grin.

"Looks like I just got my second wind."

Twenty-nine

Whether separated by miles, mixed emotions, or misunderstandings, their lovemaking always held a sense of desperation when they came together again. Their first coupling was fast and frantic, both too anxious for the physical contact to waste time with extended foreplay. But making love the second time in the early dawn had a sweeter, more leisurely rhythm that left them both feeling happily satisfied.

The phone rang shattering the quiet. Suzanne answered when she saw it was her father.

"Dad, how are you doing? How is Muriel?"

She listened for the next few minutes before saying goodbye and snuggling back in Thad's arms.

"So, how are things?"

"They're both fine and very happy to be out of the clinic. He says he's loving their secret paradise."

"I thought you said there wasn't any romance between them."

"There isn't. Muriel still thinks of my dad as a father figure. She wants him to be her baby's adopted grandpa. He says she has wonderful friends there who'd do anything to keep her away from her father and uncle. Dad already has his eye on a widow, and apparently she has her eye on him. Thank goodness she's closer to his own age. He sounded very happy. I'm glad he finally seems to be settling down."

Thad nodded.

"Makes it nice for you, too. Have you heard from the Martins, or shouldn't I ask?"

"They've been calling me, begging forgiveness. I told them I need more time."

"Understandable. By the way, Linc called. He and Maya said hello. They're on another assignment."

"They must enjoy their work."

291

She sighed.

"I wish you didn't have to go. It's going to be tough trying to keep a relationship going with your kind of work. But I'm willing to take what time I can get. Would you consider moving in with me after my mom is well enough to go back to her own place?"

"That depends."

Suzanne raised her head to look at him.

"On what?"

"I've been offered a teaching/coaching job in a junior college down here."

Excitement at such an opportunity made her push herself into a sitting position.

"That's wonderful. I remember you telling me you did teach now and then. But I didn't know you were fully qualified with a teaching credential.

"I pursued getting one in between jobs because I knew I didn't want to continue in my present line of work for the rest of my life, especially after I discovered I enjoyed teaching."

"So, does that mean you intend to take the college position instead of going to New Orleans?"

"There's something I need to know before I decide. I don't want us to just live together, Suzanne."

"But I thought . . ." She stopped and stared at him. "I'm not sure I know what you do want."

Thad leveled his gaze on her.

"Yes you do."

Suzanne walked into her classroom at the start of the new school year and stood at the front of the room smiling at her students. "Good morning. Welcome to my class. My name is Mrs. Novak. I'm looking forward to working with you. I have a feeling this is going to be a wonderful year for us all."

And it was . . . in every way possible.

Other Select Books Published by Fireside Publications

Available at: www.firesidepubs.com or
Amazon.com; Kindle; Nook

The Crystal Angel	Olivia Claire High
The Rose Cottage	Olivia Claire High
Dreams: Shadows of the Night	Olivia Claire High
A Stranger's Eyes	Olivia Claire High
The Wolf Deception	Olivia Claire High
Kari's Destiny: No More Tomorrows	Olivia Claire High

Essays: On Living with Alzheimer's Disease:	
The First Twelve Months	Lois Wilmoth-Bennett
The Furax Connection	Stephen L. Kanne
The Find	James J. Valko
Above Honor: Rachel's Story	Donald Himelstein
Beyond Forever	Taylor Shaye
The Cleansing	Dr. Ben F. Eller
The Death of Learning	Dr. Ben F. Eller
18 Days in September	Allen N. Hunt, Ph.D
Independence Day Plague	Carla Lee Suson
Odds & Ends ~Bits & Pieces	Joye O'Keefe
The Serpent Sea	Linda Lehmann Masek
Where Danger Lurks	Judith Groudine Finkel
Texas Justice	Judith Groudine Finkel
Ice Rose	Alison Neuman
Searching for Normal: A Memoir	Alison Neuman
Raven April	Nelson Trout
Amanda's Voice	Eileen Bennett
Silver Strands	Eileen Bennett